DINNER IN THE LABYRINTH

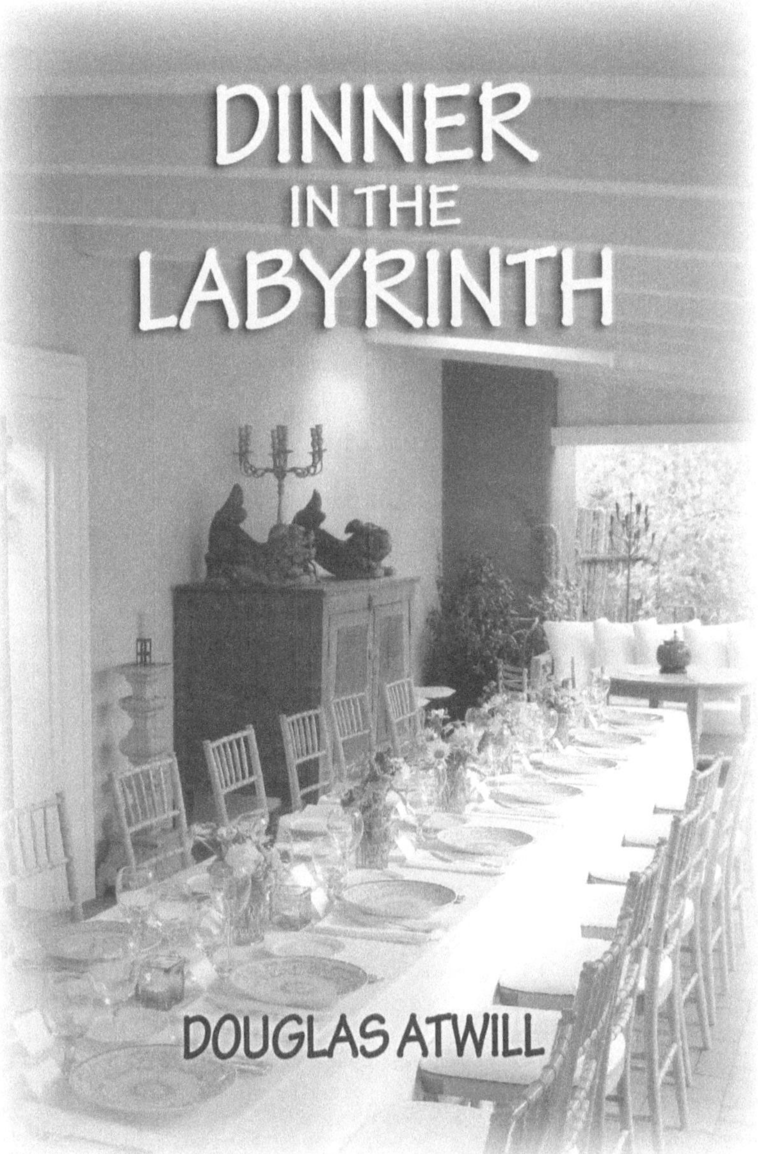

DINNER IN THE LABYRINTH

DOUGLAS ATWILL

SANTA FE

Sunstone books may be purchased for educational, business, or sales promotional use.
For information please write: Special Markets Department, Sunstone Press,
P.O. Box 2321, Santa Fe, New Mexico 87504-2321.

Body typeface › Poliphilus MT Pro
Printed on acid-free paper
∞
eBook 978-1-61139-447-4

Library of Congress Cataloging-in-Publication Data

Names: Atwill, Douglas, author.
Title: Dinner in the labyrinth : a novel / by Douglas Atwill.
Description: Santa Fe : Sunstone Press, [2016]
Identifiers: LCCN 2015044709 (print) | LCCN 2015047158 (ebook) | ISBN 9781632931061 (softcover : acid-free paper) | ISBN 9781611394474 ()
Subjects: LCSH: Biographers--Fiction. | Triangles (Interpersonal relations)--Fiction.
Classification: LCC PS3601.T85 D56 2016 (print) | LCC PS3601.T85 (ebook) | DDC 813/.6--dc23
LC record available at http://lccn.loc.gov/2015044709

SUNSTONE PRESS IS COMMITTED TO MINIMIZING OUR ENVIRONMENTAL IMPACT ON THE PLANET.
THE PAPER USED IN THIS BOOK IS FROM RESPONSIBLY MANAGED FORESTS. OUR PRINTER HAS RECEIVED CHAIN OF CUSTODY (COC) CERTIFICATION FROM: THE FOREST STEWARDSHIP COUNCIL™ (FSC®), PROGRAMME FOR THE ENDORSEMENT OF FOREST CERTIFICATION™ (PEFC™), AND THE SUSTAINABLE FORESTRY INITIATIVE® (SFI®).
THE FSC® COUNCIL IS A NON-PROFIT ORGANIZATION, PROMOTING THE ENVIRONMENTALLY APPROPRIATE, SOCIALLY BENEFICIAL AND ECONOMICALLY VIABLE MANAGEMENT OF THE WORLD'S FORESTS. FSC® CERTIFICATION IS RECOGNIZED INTERNATIONALLY AS A RIGOROUS ENVIRONMENTAL AND SOCIAL STANDARD FOR RESPONSIBLE FOREST MANAGEMENT.

WWW.SUNSTONEPRESS.COM
SUNSTONE PRESS / POST OFFICE BOX 2321 / SANTA FE, NM 87504-2321 /USA
(505) 988-4418 / ORDERS ONLY (800) 243-5644 / FAX (505) 988-1025

1

Al Fresco

24 July 2011, 10:00 AM

It is Celia's birthday today, a major one, and I am organizing the last-minute preparations for tonight's dinner party, caterers arriving by late afternoon to start the chopping, slicing and braising. Despite Celia's accomplishments in the art world, she has little patience with crowded gatherings or ceremonies, and it took some expert inveigling on my part for her even to think about such a party. I tried to limit the number of guests, but we ended up with forty friends and family invited for cocktails and a seated dinner, with the possibility of a few more unexpected guests. There is a prediction of a rainstorm in the evening, but this morning I plan to clear a place for the long table on the back verandah.

"Do you want me to do the flowers?" Juan Carlos asks, looking into my writing room from the doorway. He is Celia's aging cousin who lives nearby.

"Do you mind?"

"Not a bit. Paloma's garden is full and you know how I like arranging."

"It's a long table, so what about ten small bouquets?"

"Will do, Graham," he says with a courtly, mocking bow. Juan Carlos is the almost unpaid butler at our house since he prefers to be in the middle of our many activities rather than the quiet rhythms of his life with Paloma. He discreetly tends to the quotidian matters in our household, appearing and disappearing like a morning breeze. Without discussing it, we have fallen into an amicable master and servant relationship.

Celia is in her studio painting on one of her canvases, as she does every morning at this time. The pattern of our days is unchanged for many years: I go early to my writing studio and she walks over to her much larger painting studio, each of us doing what we love until it is time for a late lunch together.

We have actual children, twin girls who are now young women, but our true offspring are the books and paintings we create, a mere dozen or so for me and many hundreds for Celia. We are the archetypal artistic couple, Celia Prosper and Graham Obermann. Media writers want to interview and photograph us, asking to reveal the secrets to our long years of togetherness. These interruptions are few since both of us treasure our working hours, the ringing phone ignored and the front gates locked. People who do not know the whole story call our marriage one in a million and our life paradise on earth. Perhaps it is.

We live most of the year at El Molino, her family's twenty-acre compound in the foothills above Santa Fe, New Mexico, in one of the many houses and studios spread out among the apple orchards, fields and vineyard rows. El Molino was named for the gristmill that stood there in the last century, well before her grandfather and grand-uncles monopolized the state legislature, earning the many-branched family fortune. Her brothers and sisters, as well as other family members, have houses there now, and it is a sylvan place with the gurgle of running water from the irrigation ditches and often redolent with the aroma of newly mown hay or the bloom of the apple trees.

Celia just last night opened a solo exhibit of her new paintings at the Ludlow Gallery in downtown Santa Fe, open to the public for a week before being shipped overnight to the LaPlace Gallery in New York. Her wall-sized canvases seldom sell here, but over the years she has been loyal to the Ludlows since they were the first to celebrate her talent. Last night several paintings did sell, however, to crafty collectors who flew out for the event in private planes to short-circuit the avid buyers awaiting on the East Coast. Celia's shows sell out with regularity now, her shimmering canvases priced vastly more than a productive farm in the best black soil of the Midwest.

I have an immense pride in Celia, a success in the top-ranking world usually reserved for men. People say her paintings have a masculine strength, a comment that invariably angers her, but I can see the power of her large canvases. Her work has evolved over the years, now totally non-objective studies of ineffable aspects of nature. The current work resembles rainstorms to me, as if the viewer were in the middle of falling lines of raindrops, some of which have been blown off their course. Of course, I know better than to commit words to the description of her paintings. When asked outright by art reporters what they mean, she invariably replies—*Nothing at all.*

From the outset I planned to become a writer about art, describing the movements in art, lives of the artists themselves and aspects of their art that were unknown beforehand. If my books are different from those of my peers, it is my care in describing how the sensual life makes its mark on the artist's work. I was roundly criticized in the early years for being a mere "Boudoir Historian," opening the salacious parts of an artist's life only to sell books. The writing of biographies has caught up with the wisdom of looking at the whole person and how sexual proclivity affects what is produced. No serious writer would consider ignoring the lesbian aspects of Georgia O'Keeffe's canvases or how Matisse's lecherous eye inserted itself in his many scenes of reclining sultry models. Indeed, to not bring the artist's sexual inclinations into scrutiny today would bring down the wrath of editors, book reviewers and certainly readers.

Celia and I have attained fame in our separate endeavors, she reaching a much higher mountain than even exists in the foothills of my world of academic biographies. It is right that we honor Celia at this stage in her life: this dinner will mark an end to a cycle, a day of harvest. I see it as an occasion to stop and observe what has been reaped and to lift a glass in her praise. The guests will expect me to say in my toast that she is the love of my life, but that is not entirely true. I love another one of the Prospers as much, if not more.

I walk over to the verandah—what Santa Fe people call a portal—to see Juan Carlos arriving with his helpers to take away the small tables and chairs and wash off the paving bricks. We will place in their stead a single long dining table, actually six eight-foot-long tables placed end to end. I had asked the caterers early about the suitability of several round tables, but we decided that one long table held a grander sense of occasion. Twenty people will sit on each side in the warm summer evening with the clink of crystal glasses and the sound of silverware on plates, and a view across to Celia's lighted studio. This cricket-songed night asked for an elegant al fresco dinner with a white cloth, linen napkins and candlelight. Even if the weather takes a turn, the guests will be out of the rain, if not away from the gusts of wind.

Celia has never had any interest whatsoever in the fine points of our domicile, so the responsibility has been mine from the start. She could have lived and worked happily in a warehouse or a barn, so if we were to have a higher level of household comfort, it was always up to me to provide it. Things might have been the other way around, but they are not.

In fact, I have become the care-keeper for all the Prosper family: the difficult but sweet-on-the-surface matriarch Dolores, the brothers and sisters, and one generation down. These are our two daughters, a nephew and a recently discovered niece. A talented lot, most of them are gifted with the Prosper charm and good looks, but they have little sense of money, how to maintain property or how to plan for the future. I worry about what will happen to them and the nurturing fields of El Molino when their Uncle Graham is not here to orchestrate. How is it that I, an in-law to this family, have become the one they turn to in a complex crisis, the one who sits on the prow of their ship looking for rogue waves in the distance? I think back to my university years when we students sat upon the night steps, full of ourselves, drinking wine and talking about what it was that made a good life. A simple life made a good life, we all agreed. Perhaps I cannot plainly hear it, but I am sure there is mean-spirited laughter echoing down to this mortal from Mount Olympus.

2

Tanna Tuva

1960

Graham Obermann arrived in the university town for his graduate study without a place to stay. He felt sure that something would turn up once he was there. The student newspaper held a half-page of housing-for-rent advertisements, but only one that caught his eye:

> *Come by and see for yourself at*
> *nine a.m., an elegant apartment*
> *for men (only) in the old*
> *Bornstein Mansion,*
> *900 Eucalyptus Street.*

Leaving his luggage at the student center, he walked the few blocks over to the street, which was lined with century-old mansions on both sides, their side-yards full of the namesake eucalyptus trees and over-grown ornamental shrubs. These were old houses with turrets and wide porches, houses that had been converted to student apartments, the industrialist owners long dead and their heirs seeking income from the bygone grandeur, now falling into disrepair, the balustrades missing more than a few spindles. At the listed address, a woman in a house-robe and slippers was talking on the front steps to a young man holding the same newspaper. She waved for Graham to join them.

"Since you're the only two who've come by, I'll tell you both about it," she said, gesturing to the pair of wide doors behind her. "The apartment is actually the front downstairs of my grandfather Bornstein's house. Sitting room, front hall and library. The three finest rooms of the whole house. My brothers and I hired contractors to add the bathroom and kitchen and seal off where the staircase went to the second floor. The rent is two hundred a month with the same for an advance deposit."

"Month to month?" asked Graham.

"No, dear. For the whole school year only, September through May. There are six other apartments, but this is the best of the lot. I'm Pearl Bornstein and I live right there over the garage." The building she pointed to looked more suitable for horses and carriages than motorcars, the eaves and windows smothered with English ivy.

The other young man said, "I'll take it."

"But I'm here too," said Graham. "Shouldn't we flip for it?"

"It's a two bedroom," said the woman. "Perhaps you can share, if you've the hearts to get along."

"Let's look inside," said the other man. "My name is Karl Prosper, by the way."

All three of them walked up the steps and into the front hall. What was left of the staircase was opulent, oaken steps with ornate white handrails that curved out as they came down, but going up to end at the ceiling like a movie set. A single bathroom with two closets had been added to one side of the stairs and a kitchenette arrangement to the other. Heavy pocket doors with bronze hardware and mahogany panels could close off the rooms on either side, and the sitting room was to the left and the library to the right. The high, dark-wood ceilings were divided into coffered squares with beading and crown moldings.

"String quartets played here in the library, with canapés passed on silver trays. Before my time, of course," Miss Bornstein said, tightening the belt to her wrapper. "It still has good bones, don't you think?"

Graham could see that Karl was as delighted as he was with the Bornstein rooms. Perhaps sharing would make his graduate school money go further, and this other man looked presentable. Could their living together in this back-lot set of *The Magnificent Ambersons* make them happy?

"I'm game to share, if you are, Karl. I'm Graham Obermann, from Pasadena."

She did not need a rental agreement, Miss Bornstein said, because she had a good eye for honest faces. However, the rent was due exactly on the first of each month. She was very fussy about that because she and her brothers had fallen on hard times. Why else would she be living in the garage apartment? And no late parties, she added.

"I sleep as lightly as a white owl."

They each paid Miss Bornstein their share in cash, which she stuffed away in her pocket. The two men moved in together, Graham taking the library side and Karl the living room side. There was an assortment of Bornstein heyday furniture, awkward Victorian pieces with marble tops and lions feet, but each of their rooms had a large worktable, a green shaded student lamp, a comfortable-looking reading chair with a floor lamp and a twin bed. They spent the rest of the day unpacking, Karl from his car parked out front and Graham bringing over the suitcases he had left at the student center. Graham's books filled only a partial shelf in the middle of the dozens of other, empty bookshelves. It was good that neither man had many clothes because their closets were a scant three feet wide. They had time to talk as the sun was setting and shared a bottle of wine on the front steps outside.

"I'm doing art history," Graham said. "For a master's, maybe a doctorate."

"Me, too."

"Do you plan to teach?"

"No. My father is a painter. Wingrave Prosper. I'm not an artist myself, but I am sure that I can write fiction about painters. I've witnessed a lot of his shenanigans and those of his friends. They're all in the journals I've kept."

"I want to write about artists too, but not fiction. We studied Lytton Strachey's books in undergraduate school, and I knew right away that was what I wanted to do. Modern biographies like his that dig deep down and expose the hidden stories."

"Maybe you could start with Wingrave. He's been looking for a writer to tell his story."

"I don't know anything about your father. Let me look into his life."

"What about your own family? Can you write about them?"

"I'm not sure anybody would be interested in reading about them. My mother died when I was seven, and Father now lives with his sister, my Aunt Ella. They came over to the states from Switzerland in the thirties, getting as far as they could from the war, buying a house in Pasadena. Grandfather Obermann was a professional coin and stamp collector in Zurich. He all but cornered the market on some Russian stamps and we've been living on them since. Ella sends them by mail all over the world in glassine stamp packets."

"That sounds like an interesting book."

"Not to me. The Tanna Tuva stamps made a living for us, and every now and then Father and Ella part with an old coin, a golden Roman ducat or a Greek drachma."

"Graham, I'm glad that we're going to live together. I think we are going to be friends."

"Me, too."

"For time immemorial."

"I hope so."

This friendship grew more solid through the school year and the men decided to keep the staircase apartment for the next school year. Were there omens that they should have seen, signs that their time together was going to be many years rather than many months? They attracted a circle of friends from the graduate school, men and women who came to sit into the night on their grand staircase, drinking wine and beer, talking about art and beauty and truth, in hushed voices lest the White Owl awake and flex her claws. Graham enjoyed the end-of-the-empire quality to their rooms, as if earnest young nomads had taken up life in a crumbling Roman villa, grasping their education from the surrounding tumult.

As the summer recess approached, Graham told Karl that he had decided about the biography of Wingrave Prosper. His thesis advisor at the graduate school thought it would make an exemplary document. Would Karl ask his father about it over the summer?

"I'm sure he'll say yes. But maybe you shouldn't dig down too deep."

"That's what will make it good."

"There's plenty down there."

"Such as what?"

"Such as murder, incest, perversion—like all the fine old Santa Fe families."

3

Prize-winning Apples

24 July 2011, 11:00 AM

My writing studio suits me admirably. It was Celia's painting studio in the beginning year of our marriage, but the low roof proved too confining for her ideas. We found a contractor to build what she needed and when it was done, I moved my writing desk under that supposedly oppressive ceiling while the carpenters put the finishing touches on the bookshelves. From the casements next to my desk, I can watch Celia working at the easel in her high-windowed building, but she cannot see back through my smaller windows to me.

This writing room has been where I have put the finish on my books, many of them started abroad in hotel rooms and rented country cottages while I researched and outlined. I prefer to retrieve my facts first-hand from the people who remember, to have interviews with the neighbors and the village merchants who might bring up the odd item or the telling remembrance. Since the stories of the Post-Impressionists became my specialty, most of the sources lived in France and I worked on perfecting my French. Celia had learned to speak faultless French in her early school years in Switzerland, when languages came easily, and she corrected me as I learned. Friends in France say that I have an odd, almost British accent, wandering off without reason into the future conditional, but I can understand and be understood, so vital to my work there.

Planning Celia's party brings up an old image in my mind of another party years ago at El Molino, before our house and the studios were built. It was a summer party with a similar long table on the side portal of Wingrave's and Dolores's main house, a white cloth blowing in the breeze, young friends from Santa Fe over to celebrate an earlier birthday. There is not enough spare time right now to look for it, but I know I described it in the smallest detail in my journal. The entry would refresh my memories of a happy time in the deckle-edged past, when Karl sat to my right and Celia to my left.

Early on in life I stumbled upon the wisdom of keeping a daily journal, written the very next morning when the ideas, people and events were still fresh and pertinent, even if I was under the hazed hours of a hangover or the current year's influenza. I cannot claim that I had unusual foresight in the writing of a daily journal, since it was mostly a way to keep my writing arm up to par, as one does in golf or tennis. Once I found a source for the three-hundred-page, pigskin-bound books from a family shop operating even today in Boston, they kept coming out to me on a regular basis. The writing in the journal still remains as much a part of my morning as the cups of coffee.

Those early diaries were longer and more detailed than the ones I write today. The eager young writer was anxious not to omit the smallest detail, so he would have all the facts at his disposal awaiting the full interpretation that many more years of life might bring. The journals sit in matched rows on my bookshelves.

It amuses me now to see the handwriting of me at twenty-two years, regimented and spacious, many flourishes and double underlines, so unlike the hasty, crabbed words I leave on paper today. I treasured then the gold-nibbed fountain pen, coal black, of bulky diameter with a well-engineered screw top, so proud that I could afford to buy it. Rereading those pages today brings up the aroma of the opaque India ink, a sophisticated perfume for a young writer as he wrote of his aesthetic adventures of the day before. Often I thought it necessary to include sketches—ground-plans of the houses, maps of the locales with streams and trees included, compass directions and quick renderings of rooms and streets.

I drew line portraits of the people I talked about, heads that looked artfully into the page from the margins. How the page looked was important, as others might in later years read the pages and make judgments. I still include black-and-white marginal drawings in my journals, but only to instruct me how a painting was put together. My rough sketches only emphasize the brilliance of the original and remind me of the difficulty of making art. There is a sketch somewhere in my files of almost every painting I have ever seen, often with notes scribbled to the side.

There will be time after lunch to go over to my studio and find that journal. I know exactly where it is, on a high shelf in the left bookcase. There is an idea there that calls to me and I can remember most of it, but not the fine details. It is a notion I have that there exists an unhappy equilibrium in most large families, a sense of action and reaction. If several members, or even just one of them, becomes illustrious in the eyes of the world, accomplished and acclaimed, does it take away that same amount from the other members? Does every large family have its lost brothers and sisters, unable to cope in the same world in which their lustrous siblings have succeeded so well? If so, it is a horrid law of physics, taking away as much as granting. The more memorable and acclaimed a single member becomes—like Wingrave Prosper—the deeper into the chasm his progeny fall.

When I was first a young guest at the Prosper house, I tried to assess the brothers and sisters, how much above or below the waterline each might be. My Karl and my Celia had risen well above. Mikal and Roberto were well below; Artemis and Paloma were bobbing about at sea level. Wingrave accused me of taking away the prize-winning apples, a raider from the steppes, plundering the culmination of generations. He never tired of finding new metaphors for my crime at dinner parties. I was a kidnapping water bird taking away his chicks in my clutched talons. Or I was the outright thief, climbing through the night window for his unprotected crown jewels. Or I was an enemy of the French people, stealing the last two good loaves of family bread, leaving the others to starve. I will write all these thoughts in my journal tomorrow, before the birthday party fades away in the mind and the fallen bits of lettuce and dropped cocktail olives are being washed away from the portal floor.

4

The Young Lieutenant

1961

Karl and Graham returned to the staircase apartment for the fall semester, both of them happy to settle into a familiar setting. This was the year that Graham must make progress on the writing of his thesis, so in anticipation of Wingrave Prosper's approval, he started the research at the university library and other public sources. There were many citations: newspaper articles from across the nation, several dozen magazine articles, birth and marriage certificates on file, ledgers with property records and tax filings. By November, he had the strongest picture of the man that mere paper research can provide, but nothing of the real man. Karl invited him to visit his father over the Thanksgiving holiday and stay with the family at their Santa Fe home. Graham could then begin the questioning of the man himself.

The library papers were full of the years before and during the war, when Wingrave rose to national acclaim as a portrait painter of the rich and important. A professor in New York told the young Wingrave that he would always live a good life if he painted portraits—like Augustus John, Titian and Gainsborough. Rich people always wanted to admire their likenesses, even when harvests fail and governments fall. It proved to be true as Wingrave worked without hiatus through the Depression and World War II. He painted movie stars, politicians, industrialists, whole families from Mexico City on one canvas and anybody who could afford his five thousand dollar fee. Six heads on one canvas cost thirty thousand dollars. *Daily Variety* reported that Mercedes de Acosta paid for portraits of Greta Garbo and herself in sailor uniforms, and then again as aviators with leather headpieces and goggles. The two women remained sub-rosa a few weeks in Santa Fe, making the citizens crazy with hopes of a casual movie star viewing. *The New Mexican* newspaper with regularity reported who was spotted at La Fonda Hotel while Wingrave worked on their portraits.

Magazines prized his cover and full-page illustrations for their fiction in the early thirties, but by the end of the decade photographs had taken over the lucrative days for illustrators. In 1943 Wingrave enlisted in the Army and became an Army photographer. He took pictures throughout Europe and won several awards for his treatments of people affected by the war—widows, orphans and the wounded. His most famous photograph is included often in group exhibits, titled *The Young Lieutenant.* It pictured a boy of twelve or thirteen in uniform with an elaborate officer's cap, oversized German epaulettes and boots too high above the knees, all obviously borrowed or stolen when he was promoted in the desperate last hours of the war. At first, the boy looked to be leaning back against a wall to take the sun, but then with a closer look the viewer could see from the dark, round stain on the chest that he was dead. It became a powerful image for anti-war group posters and pacifist organizations throughout the world.

Wingrave returned from the war to Santa Fe and his studio in 1946 with a waiting list of commissions to be painted. Between portraits he drew book illustrations for leather-bound volumes of *Treasure Island*, *Arabian Knights* and the King Arthur tales. *Life* magazine published an article on the painter's family, with a double-page spread of them on their horses with a back-drop of the Sangre de Cristos. Graham, spending several minutes looking through the magnifying glass, thought Karl looked more handsome than the others even then.

He continued to ask Karl questions as they drove east to New Mexico.

"Did your father ever paint portraits of you?"

"Not portraits really, but set pieces from the bible, David and Goliath, and of me as crouching Indian boy with bow and arrow."

"What about your brothers and sisters?"

"Same way. Always in costume, in a setting. Paintings that he sold in galleries. He painted Celia dozens of times, even as a vestal in front of a circular temple with orange thunderclouds behind."

"Why her so often?

"She's the prettiest. Artemis didn't get the Prosper looks and Paloma was too young, too fidgety. Roberto, my oldest brother, after a while refused to sit for him, the two of them rarely on good terms. Father once painted Mikal and me together, as Cain and Abel, with a Holy Land background."

"You must have been Cain."

"Such judgment from an unbiased biographer."

"Watch the road."

They spent a night along the way and arrived in Santa Fe in the late morning. The first views of El Molino impressed Graham as they drove down its gravel drive lined with ancient weeping willows along a running stream. Brushing the top of the car, their leaves made golden curtains in the November sun, as if the autumn frosts had held off for their arrival. The oldest parts of the house at the drive's end were of pale sienna stone, the later wings of thick adobe with a stucco of a similar color. The house had a substantial, of-the-earth feeling, windows deeply set in the walls, vines here and there clambering up to the parapets. Adobe and river-rock buttresses held up the corners and the chimneys, as if the whole structure had risen by itself out of the ground. A separate chapel sat over by the willows, also covered with vines now turning red in the autumn chill.

"That used to be the mill pond," Karl said, pointing to a sunken lawn now encircled with thickets. "The mill wheel rotted away a century ago and the grinding room is now our kitchen."

The house was cool and dark inside, despite the morning sun. Shiny, dark brown logs held up the ceilings and the floors were crafted of polished brick or wide-planked oak. Graham could smell the ambient incense of a century of piñon fires with, even in the morning, several fireplaces alight against the chill. The house felt like a home that protected its inhabitants not only from the winter winds but also from the indescribable unknown. It could have been the Ithaca house that Ulysses spent so much time thinking about, a massive stump of the olive tree hidden away in a back bedroom.

Karl hugged the old woman who appeared out of a darkened side door and the two of them spoke in Spanish. She motioned away down a hallway and said that they would stay in Karl's old room, sharing the pair of spindle-headed twin beds with striped blankets for covers. These were the innocent-appearing beds of boyhood, secrets hidden away in their folded wool.

The one nearest the window was his, Karl said, and he opened the closet for their suitcases. On the wall behind them there were the crossed tennis rackets of a boy immersed in athletics, medals for a cross-country run and several plaque trophies for a member of a winning soccer team.

Graham wondered how this room had influenced his friend when he was a boy, imbuing him with a deep-rooted security that he never felt in his own Pasadena room. Did boyhood rooms make a mark that could be felt the whole life? Of course they must. He made a note to always ask to see the first bedroom, to look for signs there of happiness or unhappiness. He was not sure which he saw in Karl's room.

The seeds that would make the biographer were already sprouting. As Graham wondered how to proceed with the Wingrave Prosper project, Karl said that Graham should walk across to his father's studio but knock before going in.

"Aren't you coming with me?"

"You've got to sink or swim on your own."

"You're a cruel friend."

"It's like hunting the Minotaur in his cave, isn't it?

"A lot like that."

Karl pointed out to Graham the way across to the studio, the roof to be seen on the far side of the mill-pond lawn behind the willow thickets. It was not an old adobe building like the others, but a wooden structure resembling the familiar Greene and Greene cottages in Pasadena. Craftsman cottages were still a popular style in the early 1930s, when Graham figured that Wingrave must have commissioned it. The low-pitched roof had a deep overhang with dark brown shingles and large multi-paned windows. Japanese-like joinery gave an expert carpenter's finish to the protruding, well-oiled beams and joists.

"You're Graham, then?" Wingrave said from the open door.

"Yes, sir. Hello."

"Let's get over the 'sir' right away. Let me look at you. A fine Roman nose you don't see so often."

"My grandfather was Swiss."

"Good long head and hands. You're taller than most Swiss.

"I grew up in California."

"That explains it. Better nutrition. Don't fret, I like your looks. Sit down, son. I've already made the decision to follow Karl's suggestion, to let you write my biography."

"Thank you very much, Mr. Prosper."

"Let's get started."

Graham took out his notepad and sat where Wingrave indicated. After the first round of questions, he knew that Wingrave was going to be the fount of information he had hoped for. With bold strokes, the older man described his childhood in a New England doctor's family of privilege. The Prospers were Italian, Americanized from the old country name of Prospero, the first generations succeeding in the New World. Graham wondered if magic and spirits and spells came with such a name. Wingrave was sent to boarding school and Harvard for a year before he escaped to the Art Student's League on 57th Street. Dr. Prosper was a kind father, quick to give his approval to whatever Wingrave wanted, paying for a year in Europe after the Bachelor of Arts from the League in 1928.

"Did you study painting over there?" Graham asked.

"No, I mostly chased Karl's mother, Dolores, around from city to city. I first glimpsed her in Rome at an embassy party, where resident Americans came to meet one another. She took my heart the minute we were introduced."

"She was on a grand tour?"

"With her sisters and her Uncle Parchment, a stern chaperone. I proposed to Dolores later when I followed them to Venice and asked Parchment for permission, but he only laughed, insisted that the Garcia elders expected grander stuff than an untested young painter. I kept asking and asking as they moved about, and Parchment tried several times to leave secretly in the night for the next destination without me. He finally relented in London, saying he would keep a close eye on me, in spite of Dolores's apparent delight."

"Were you married in London, then?"

"Oh, no. A year later back here at El Molino. Once when we were alone, Parchment said he could never trust an artist, particularly me. He would see to it that the Garcia fortune would never be mine, so I'd better get cracking. So I did."

"Did your paintings sell right from the start?"

"Almost. Dolores didn't see too much of me those first years. I often wonder if Dolores would have been happier with a local man, a politician or a judge. Somebody who understood the Santa Fe ways."

"Six children would say differently."

"Perhaps. You seem older than Karl. As if you were just back from the wars."

"My father bragged to his Swiss friends that I was born with *Weltschmerz*, no need to send me back for schooling in the old country. I envy Karl's optimism and innocence, but it's not part of me."

"What do you think of his becoming a novelist?"

"I believe he will be a good one. He's let me read several of his stories about artists."

"Artists like me?"

"Somewhat. He wants to begin a novel about a famous portrait painter—a patriarch and how his fame affects the whole family. He says it is a universal tale of father and son."

"I should probably be on my guard."

Wingrave continued the interview for an hour more, telling stories about his sitters, the quirks of generals and admirals who came for the portraits. He confessed to a roving eye and encounters with the women who came to sit. It was the way of the art world, he said without guilt, but never did it endanger his family. When you sit looking at a great beauty, drawing the curves and puffy places, a hunger grows inside of you. A man must have his sexual sorties, particularly an artist, he said. Graham admired Wingrave's candor and his not appearing to hold back unsavory details.

"Did you have an encounter with Greta Garbo?"

"I tried, but her lesbian side kick wouldn't have it."

"Who else?" Graham asked, hoping he would continue along this line and confess to trysts with high-profile names.

"I best leave it there, for now."

"Can we talk some more tomorrow?"

"I'll have more names for you then."

By the interview's end Graham had twenty pages of notes, personal details that would give blood and breath to the dry boxes of reference cards back at the apartment. He knew that this was the way he wanted to write a biography, with the personally retrieved pieces of information, golden nuggets pulled up from a fast-moving stream. What a man wanted for dinner, how he dressed, what his neighbors thought, what sort of automobile driver he was, where he looked when he talked, and on and on. This would make the painter come forward from the pages, be alive to the readers, who though they would never have the chance to touch or see him, just might imagine the multi-colored dirt under the artist's fingernails or the obsessive arrangement of paint tubes in a perfect line on the painting table.

When Karl grew older, Graham thought, he would look just like his father. Not a bad thing, because Wingrave had kept his muscular, slim-waisted form, a handsome man aging well—good Italian bones. They had the same pale brown eyes, but Karl's let the onlooker see into the worry behind them. There was no similar worry in Wingrave's eyes.

Thanksgiving was a full feast with most of the Prosper family in attendance. The old-time family cook who had hugged Karl so sweetly brought platters and bowls from the kitchen, her fast footsteps making a clicking sound on the brick floor. Dolores seated Graham on her right with Karl on her left. Artemis, Mikal, Paloma, Juan Carlos—the cousin from next door—and Wingrave filled in the other spots. Dolores explained that Celia, the other sister, and Roberto, the brother, were not in town. Dolores placed a cool hand on Graham's hand as conversation went around the table.

"Karl says he likes you better than any of his other roommates," she said. "That says a lot, because he's been to a great many schools and has had many roommates."

"Not so many, Mother," Karl said.

"It seemed like dozens to us. Nobody was good enough for the likings of our middle boy."

"We were lucky to arrive at Miss Bornstein's at the same time," Graham said, hoping to stop this well-polished argument before it got too far.

"Graham, you have the soul of a peacemaker," Dolores said. "You're always welcome here," Dolores said. "Consider El Molino your home and us your friends."

Graham thought about that as the meal progressed—how long would he and Karl be friends? College roommates sometimes moved on to separate apartments in the city, never connecting again, or they could buy a summer house together, take trips around the world, become companions for a lifetime. He hoped that he and Karl would be forever friends. What a romantic, foolish young man he had become, Graham thought. Like his father might have said, be a man, son—stop daydreaming.

As if reading his thoughts, Paloma asked Graham, "Will you stay on with Karl after you both graduate?"

"I don't know, Paloma. I hope so."

"You both will write books, so it makes sense."

"It does make sense, but we'll see."

He looked across at Karl as he said that, but Karl's face was clouded with a flat look, neither negative nor positive. Secret agents must learn that look, giving nothing away so governmental agendas remain safe.

"What do you think, Karl?" Graham asked.

"I can't imagine a time when we aren't friends."

On the next day's interview, Wingrave asked if he could sketch Graham while they talked. He seated Graham next to the large north window, a right-facing profile. There must have been a Roman-nosed soldier or two in your Swiss family's village, the artist said as he started a series of pen-and-ink sketches.

Graham, wanting off the topic of his facial features, asked, "Do you think you have had to compromise your art in portraiture? To settle for less than you could have been?"

"Don't turn your head when you talk. Without a doubt. People don't want to see the real themselves. They want who they think they are. But such a painting can still be art, if you do it well. Look at Holbein. Henry VIII loved his work then, but today we see right into his pock-marked soul."

Graham thought about the reproductions of Wingrave's work he had studied in the library books—generals in ornate uniforms, admirals with a disturbed sea as a backdrop and women against dark backgrounds, dimly illuminated nearby furnishings with the glint of ormolu edges. There was often a sense of high drama in a Prosper portrait, odd colors glowing from the dark side. Green seemed a favorite color, as if a garden door had been left open, distilling foliage colors to wash the shady side of a face.

"Did Sargent inspire you? Many of your paintings have a similar black background, subjects small in a large room, women in white dresses that catch the raking horizontal light."

"I admire Sargent. My portraits start where his left off, painting the way he might have had he lived on. The difference is that his are nineteenth century paintings, mine are twentieth century."

"And what about the portraits of Madame Cezanne?"

"I also admire those."

"How are they different from your work?"

"People expect more spirit, less technique today, and they understand the difference."

"Do you think of your portraits as fine art? Paintings that will survive time?"

"Some of them. Some are very good art."

"Will you tell me which ones are art and which not?"

"No."

"Then tell me another thing. How you came by this Greene and Greene studio so far from the West Coast." Graham had recognized the iconic look from Southern California, several dozen of their houses in Pasadena alone.

"It just looks like the Greene brothers."

"Did you design it yourself?"

"Very close to it. I painted a portrait in Pasadena in the early thirties, a spoiled woman. I sketched the details of her Greene and Greene house each morning while I waited for her to get dressed. Then I painted her sister, also a spoiled woman, also with her own Greene and Greene house, who was also very late, and when I was done with them I had a sketchbook full of architectural secrets. I gave it to the designer brother at Rivera Construction and he came up with this in 1931."

Graham felt he had what he came for. He made a note to explore if the fake Greene and Greene studio was just the first of more fakery. At the doorway he noticed the framed print of *The Young Lieutenant* he had not seen before. He would also ask about that on the next trip. Wingrave told him to keep coming back, that it was good to be able to talk so openly with a young man. His sons closed up when they came around, as if they were afraid of him.

"Why would that be?" Graham asked.

"All sons are afraid of their fathers. It is in the scheme of things."

"Is Karl afraid of you?"

"Why don't you ask him?"

Graham knew he would not ask Karl that question just now. Graham had to be careful not to hurt his friend or make him jealous.

"Did you and Wingrave get along?" Karl asked, back in the bedroom. "Did he tell the family secrets?"

"All of them. You are under my power now."

"Father seems more comfortable with you than any of us. I know it's just for a book, but I've watched the body language over these days. You've clearly bonded with him."

"He likes my nose, Karl. Says it belongs on a Roman senator. Cicero or, perhaps, Cato."

"You don't have a Roman nose."

"He drew a dozen drawings of me in a toga."

"You dressed up for him?"

"No, Karl. Only from his imagination."

"I had forgotten how Father used that game on all his sitters, picking out a feature and complimenting it. Beautiful eyes, long neck, abundant hair. He said I had strong hands for a boy."

"I liked your hands, too, right from the start. For a boy, that is."

Karl would not be amused. Graham sensed a strand of jealousy in Karl's response to his time with Wingrave, as if Karl did not want him to become too close with the subject of his book. What odd currents ran through this Prosper family.

They drove straight through back to the university, a day-long ordeal. Graham saw that his delving into Prosper family matters would continue to make Karl uneasy—perhaps too much light in the dark corners. Graham expected that there would be more secrets, some he'd better not write about.

5

Hesitation Waltz

24 July 2011, 12:00 Noon

It is doubtful that I will get any writing or journal reading done today, the various tasks of Celia's party coming to the fore while the clock keeps moving on. Our life together continues as a reversal of ordinary roles, Celia the breadwinner and I the keeper of the hearth. Her time in the studio is too valuable, emotionally and financially, to pester her with life's small details. I know that there are those who take on new tasks with gusto, take on responsibility, and those who shun it. Definitely the former, I move into a void and make order. I am the one who sorts out things, makes the white space for us to play out our days together.

Only I can sort the silverware for the party—forty large forks, forty small forks for the salad course, and as many knives and spoons. The plates are from the hodgepodge stacks in the pantry: the Luneville demi-porcelain from Grandmother Obermann, the white porcelain plates with nearly rubbed-away gold rims that I found in Paris years ago and the Blue Circle Minton that Uncle Parchment gave us for a wedding present. Celia pointed out that her grand-uncle craftily bought the pattern already in the Garcia pantry lest it have to be melded back there should I prove unacceptable. I count them all out on the kitchen table—dinner, salad and dessert plates, forty of each. The caterers will provide everything else: the tablecloths, napkins, wine and water glasses, coffee cups and saucers, and salt-and-pepper shakers.

The sound of the Minton plates ringing together brings up the memory of another meal with Celia at El Molino, a family dinner on one of my trips here with Karl. Celia had been away at art school on my previous trips, so this was the first time we met. Dolores had seated me again on her right with Celia to my right, Karl across from us, the direct family and Juan Carlos in the various other seats. Glancing back and forth between them, I summoned the idea that Celia was a more beautiful version of Karl. Even today, when I look at her I often see Karl's face off to the side, the siblings merging into one, very complex persona. Her pale brown eyes, like her father's, did not reveal the inside thoughts like Karl's. Her features were the same, but slightly smaller than Karl's—as if someone had ordered two versions of the same being, one for the evening and one for the day.

Celia was definitely for wearing in the evening. She moved with a grace and refinement that in Karl was only beginning to take form. She laughed more often than he did. And, as I think about that first dinner, I realize I never think now of one without the other. Karl-Celia-Karl or Celia-Karl-Celia. How unexpected that this could have gone on this way for all these years.

"Shall you stay with us for a while, Graham?" Celia asked. Her years at school in Switzerland gave a foreign tone to her speaking, not an actual accent, but a clipped way of pronouncing words.

"Only for the weekend."

"Then let's walk up the canyon after dinner, get to know each other."

"I would like that."

"Karl, you can't come. I want him alone."

She took my hand as soon as we left the house. We walked out the front drive under the long strands of spring-leaved willows and onto the road that led up the canyon. We went under a frail wooden bridge that brought the irrigation water across, and up again to a piñon-covered peninsula of land looking out over the whole valley. There was a bench-like rock where we sat down to gaze at the valley. The acres of El Molino lay below us, verdant and productive.

"I want to have sex with you," she said.

"Me too."

"I know you and Karl are doing it and I want to be included."

"Can I come to your room tonight, after Karl is asleep?"

It was early morning before I walked quietly down the darkened hallway to her room. She smelled different from Karl, but there was an aura that was the same as his. Her body was softer and I knew many traps awaited me.

Her breasts were small, but I could feel in the dark that her nipples were large. I went slowly, exploring every inch. She was not the first in my experience with a woman, but the memory of the others has faded away. As I ventured further, I realized that her former men must have taken her quickly, almost raping her, because my slow advance won her over. It won us both over, in fact.

"I know you love Karl, but you must now love me, too."

"I do love Karl."

"In many ways, we are the same person. You are not being unfaithful to him, just loving another side of him."

"Who is the dark side, who the light?"

"It doesn't matter."

Karl knew about our tryst the next morning, but he was not upset by it. I had been anxious that he, unlike her, might not accept the romantic myth, like a passage from Charlotte Bronte, that they were but the one person. Even though the whole family and all our university friends had seen my obvious infatuation with Karl, we had not made love yet. It was surely on the horizon, like a cumulus cloud coming our way. He drove us back to the university without another mention of my night-time desertion, as if he were happy that the full story was beginning, that the overture was at last finished. I had no inkling then of how the two of them would monopolize the rest of my life—a hesitation waltz, dance with her, dance with him, smile for the cameras, do it all again.

Today she sits across from me at the round lunch table on the terrace outside of her studio. We usually have lunch together there, a basket of sandwiches, fruit in season, cookies and iced tea brought over in a hamper from the kitchen. I can tell her thoughts are back at the easel, that this lunch will be short.

"Everything going okay, for the party?" she asks.

"Nothing to worry about. Walter's people arrive around two and they'll do everything. I hope to get in a couple of hours of writing."

"Good. You're a lamb to do this for me."

"I know you'd rather that we did nothing for your birthday, but we'll have fun."

"Fun is an odd word."

I peel an orange with my fingers, a skill from growing up in California, where no boy becomes a man who cannot deftly peel an orange, and I split it into segments, placing half on her plate. I am the hunter-gatherer providing for his clan, pulling fish from the shallows and fruits from the high branches. Celia's brain is already back in front of her painting, solving higher problems than the perfect orange segments or this evening's impending dinner party.

6

Mountain Overnights

1962

Graham and Karl drove back to El Molino over the spring break, with several days for Graham and Wingrave to meet for their interviews. Graham's respect for the old painter had grown as he wrote out his story, but there were still shadows—time periods unaccounted for, anecdotes that did not fit in anywhere, painting techniques that Graham did not understand.

They got right to it in his studio. Wingrave explained his glazing techniques, how he painted the first image in shades of blue or raw sienna, then over-glazed that with clear colors, darker and darker, and after that the bright and light highlights. The critics noted Wingrave's brilliant use of patterned fabrics, striped linens and black-and-white weavings, in the tradition of Matisse. Graham wanted to explore that idea.

There was an Italianate period for Wingrave in the early thirties, responding to commissions from Hollywood, where fake Cinquecento landscapes behind the film stars looked across the haze to an imagined Assisi or Orvieto. And there were many paintings in the Art Deco period later on, when sitters wanted to be seen as if in a stateroom on the *Queen Mary*, posed on crocodile luggage, the ship's departure horns about to blow, a wisp of steam or a curl of confetti across the canvas.

Then, there was the matter of money—how much he had made over the years, how he had dealt with such a total, and how having a rich wife made the path easier for him. It was the second day of this round of interviews. Graham got to the business of the rich wife by asking him if it did, indeed, make his career easier.

"In some ways, yes. I did not have to worry about my own family being comfortable, taken care of. The Garcia fortune did that."

"Did it make the actual painting easier?"

"Yes, in that I could concentrate on techniques and refinements, not the ultimate sale. And I think it reinforced my position when we came to talking about the fees. With El Molino looming around us, everyone knew that I was not a starving artist. Almost nobody asked for a discount."

"How much have you made over the years?"

"Millions. I have no idea how many."

"What have you done with it?"

"You'll have to ask Dolores. She has the register, all the names, how much we got, where it was invested, where we spend it."

"So it was invested?"

"It must have been. I'll ask her to let you read the register."

Graham thought it odd that Wingrave knew so little about his own finances. He wondered if that was a feminine characteristic, household finances looked after by the spouse. Since everything else about Wingrave was so macho, so filled with testosterone, this could be an interesting path to pursue.

Graham mentioned this to Karl as they prepared for bed. "Do you think there are feminine qualities in your father?"

"You mean homosexual tendencies?"

"I suppose."

"I'll tell you about when I was a young boy. Father loved hiking up in the mountains, spending a night or two in a tent, cooking outdoors, listening to the sound of the streams. I always wanted to go."

Karl's story explained a lot to Graham. The path up to the high mountains started right at the El Molino gates, and at first Wingrave took along Roberto, the firstborn son. After a couple of years, Roberto did not want to go up with his father anymore, making many different excuses. Dolores took Roberto's side—*let the boy stay here, Wingrave, it's too cold up on the mountain.*

When Karl started turning into a man on his twelfth birthday, Wingrave began to show an interest in him, especially since Roberto used every method to avoid his father. At the time, Wingrave was painting Karl in his continuing Bible series—David with the head of Goliath, David with the sheep—and then included him on one of his mountain overnights. When a summer squall up there turned to snow, Karl remembered sharing a sleeping bag with his father, but he could not come up with any details. What he did remember was that it felt like sleeping next to Zeus, his father's electricity coursing through his own body, making him tingle.

"You mean you had sex with your father?" asked Graham.

"Not exactly. Not like Roberto."

"You mean Wingrave and Roberto were lovers for a while?"

"No. I think it was more abuse on Wingrave's part. Roberto never talked to me about it, but I knew he was hurt and ashamed."

"Did you go up to the mountains more than once?"

"Many times, two or three summers. I looked forward to when it snowed up there. I knew that I was loved."

"Did any of the girls go up there?"

"Only the boys."

"Did you ever talk to Wingrave about it afterwards?"

"No. I decided that he was pansexual or omnisexual or whatever you call it. Available for either gender—like you are. It seemed right at the time, the way things ought to be."

Graham wondered if he was in fact available for either gender. Was he pansexual? He decided to file that away, to not respond to Karl.

"Has it affected you like it did Roberto?" he asked instead.

"It was different for me. Just the mention now of a mountain overnight can give me an erection. Ganymede, Zeus and the cockerel all mixed up in my head."

The next day Graham asked Wingrave more about his bible scenes. Did he hire local models after the Prosper boys grew too old to sit? Yes, but he also hired a lot of local girls as well.

"Do you think your extracurricular sex life informed your paintings?"

"No question. I look at those old paintings and see sex everywhere. Obelisks and orifices in the background, suggestive shapes in all the bible scenes. That may be what people liked about my work, made it so popular."

"Did you consciously include those shapes?"

"I'm not sure."

Graham had been thinking about how to put the question so it would not anger Wingrave. "With all that beauty coming and going in your studio, did you find male models as attractive as you had the female models?"

Wingrave paused at this, looking for a few moments out of the window. "I dabbled, like most men at the time, but it was not for me."

"Can you tell me who they were?"

"Let's leave that alone, Graham."

"Then, I have another subject, Wingrave. The young lieutenant. Where were you when you photographed him?"

"Just outside of Berlin, a small town. I still think about him."

"Tell me about it."

"It was 1945. Our soldiers had just cleared the town ahead of me, marching on east. I walked over to an empty side street, and there he was. I thought about my sons, how he could have been one of them. Just after I took the picture, his old grandmother came after me. *Schlächter, schlächter*, she yelled. Butcher, butcher. It was sad."

"It is a famous anti-war photograph."

"Maybe more famous than any of my paintings. I wondered if I should have been a photographer instead."

"Why is that?"

"There is something unemotional about snapping a picture. You can photograph a person and move along. A painted portrait takes more time and brings the subject into your life."

As he said that, Wingrave went over to the framed photo and put his hand flat on the glass.

"Now I have a question for you, Graham."

"We're reversing the process?"

"Are you in love with Karl? Are the two of you having a relationship?"

"Does it show that much?"

"You would be happier loving Celia."

"I do love Celia, but I'm not sure I can help the same with Karl."

"You should up and run away. I see a trap for you here."

"I think it's too late, Wingrave."

"I hope you don't make both of them unhappy, just to please yourself."

Graham knew that he ought to pay attention to Wingrave. On the last trip to Pasadena his father said the Prospers had taken him over, that he never came to visit his own family anymore. The letters home were about nothing else except El Molino and the wonder of the Prospers. Graham suspected then that these were only the opening pages to a Prosper chronicle, many chapters to follow.

Wingrave's biography had come together. All the data Graham had collected on this trip would fill the open spaces in his manuscript back at the apartment. There were only the financial data from Dolores's register. But she would not let Graham see into that matter—not in the public interest, she said. There was nothing else to ask. Graham felt he had played all the notes on the keyboard, the intense high ones and the bass notes coming up from the inside. He was excited and anxious to be back at his desk.

After they drove back to the university, the two men resumed their daily patterns in the staircase apartment. Karl worked on his short stories about Cezanne and the pine trees he painted. Each story was a different episode that Karl imagined—the painter at his easel fighting the Mistral wind or renting a house near a grove of perfect specimens so he could paint them from a window or watching as a wildfire courses across before he has finished with a scene, destroying the trees. These were impressionist stories without the usual structure of beginning to end, thoughts more than actions, snapshots in a disjointed time and place. His thesis advisors were very supportive of his work, and they all but promised the stories would be accepted in lieu of his final thesis. This was the way of the new short story, the academics said, the structured old patterns fading away. This was also the start of Karl's deep involvement with fiction and how an imagined story can be an intense parallel to the real world.

He composed the stories longhand on unlined yellow legal pads with black India ink. Graham saw the pages as art in themselves, Karl's upright writing always without corrections, lines perfectly horizontal like medieval breviaries on lambskins. He often included small sketches in the margins, a branch of a tree or a passing cloud. Karl said that when he made mistakes, he rewrote the page until it was perfect. Only then did he move on to the rest of the story and he seldom went back to edit once a page was done.

Karl walked over to where Graham was typing. "I have an idea, bud. Let's take a month off and go to France, give our manuscripts a rest. I want to see the trees I'm writing about. What do you think?"

"I'm not sure I have the money."

"I just got a check from home. Uncle Parchment made a distribution."

"I'll have to pay you back later."

"No problem. I'll get the tickets for us to leave this weekend."

They flew to Paris and rented a car from a bureau in the Etoile. The garage-man opened the door and waved them forward right into the circular traffic around the arch, around and around and around, until Karl thought to push out to the right, against the in-pressing outer circle and off on the road to the south. Several days through the Loire, then down the Rhone to Avignon. By Thursday they were in Aix-en-Provence.

Graham's undergraduate French was better than Karl's, despite the resident French tutor hired for the early years at El Molino. They found a small hotel off the *Cours Mirabeau*, unpacked and, greedy for time, explored the old city. Karl had a small camera to capture the trees he thought might be Cezanne's, the parasol pines with their distinctive curved canopies and the expansive horsechestnuts. There were more specimens as they walked out from the center up into the low hills with red-roofed stucco houses. The farther they walked the more yellow ochre and sienna houses they saw, and Cezanne's paintings came alive on these country roads.

When they returned to the hotel, there was a message at the concierge desk: Karl's brother, Roberto, and wife Olivia, were in Frejus for a convention of Beechcraft Bonanza owners. Paloma had told them where Karl and Graham were in Aix-en-Provence and engineered from afar a lunch meeting for the four. *You have to get together—after all you're brothers.*

The couple flew their leased Bonanza over to the Aix airport for the re-union, their leather aviators' gear getting many stares from the other customers in the restaurant. Olivia was as loquacious as Roberto was quiet.

"What a headache I have. The French drink so much more than we do," she said.

"Are you having fun?" Karl asked.

"Loads. We've met the most interesting fliers, from all over. Several are coming next year to Santa Fe. I told them about flying over the ancient pueblo ruins just as the sun is going down, like Mother and I did when I was learning."

Olivia's mother was an early woman aviator—Karl made the mistake of calling her an aviatrix just once—and taught her daughter, and later Roberto, to fly like the barnstormers of the twenties.

"Olivia is maybe too friendly," Roberto said. "We get invited to at least one party every night, then we take the plane up all the next day. I need to go home to get some sleep before going back to the office."

"We've spent all of Roberto's vacation time from the bank," Olivia said. "I tried to get my father to give him more time off, but he is being difficult with his son-in-law."

"Olivia's father is old-school," Roberto said. "No extras for the future vice president."

"It's so tiresome being between them," she said.

"Who's looking after young Parchment?" Karl asked. Their son had the great misfortune of being named after his great-grand uncle Parchment, Roberto not having the original family suggestion of Wingrave II. The Parchment name survived from several generations back—great-great-grand-mother Emmeline Parchment, a New England heiress who married into the Garcia family. The Parchment whale-oil and ball-bearing monies came west with her and mingled easily with grist-mill profits of the Garcias. In payment for her largesse, Emmeline burdened her son and, later, her grandson with her maiden name, and it continued to vex generations beyond, like an undigested meal moving through a python.

"Parchment's staying with Paloma," Olivia said. "I think that he loves her more than me. Maybe we'll let her adopt him."

Karl noted that they went through three bottles of Bandol at lunch and double glasses of Pear William afterwards. Olivia talked about the French countess whose biplane crashed into the sea, she surviving to host a party that night. The ways of the French were settling upon Olivia and there might be a notable Bastille Day celebration back in Santa Fe next year. Karl wondered if alcohol was becoming a problem in his brother's household. The Bandol and Pear William could be a dangerous step up. Heads turned in the restaurant as the couple stood up to restore their flying gear and stride straight out to their taxi for the local airport.

Karl asked Graham, "Do I put on the dog like them?"

"I can't tell you how embarrassed I am sometimes."

"Bullshit."

7

Across the Sea

24 July 2011, 2:15 PM

If the long-dead Wingrave could have arisen from his cool bed in the camposanto and wandered up to the verandah, like the ghost in a Mozart opera, he would have a rewarding view of our dinner, seeing how everything turned out. In the beginning Wingrave was not happy with me for taking away the affections of two of his children, perhaps his favorite two out of the six. Wingrave once asked me, not entirely in jest, how many Prospers can the monster devour in one sitting? Must we sit still and watch him munching away? In time he came to see that Karl and Celia were the only happy ones of all his children. Lest it gave me too big a head, Wingrave said that I got the pick of his litter and they were easy to please. Perhaps he did not know his two favorites as well as he thought he did.

Paloma is coming by soon to write out the name cards in her cursive script. I need to decide about where everyone will sit. It will definitely not be with me seated at the end of the table, but instead, in the more continental style, where the host sits in the middle of the side with the hostess across from him. It will be good to see Celia right across from me. Karl to her left, I think, rather than next to me as I might prefer.

Dolores, the oldest woman, must be next to me on the right, and Jullian Closson, Celia's best friend from her school-days, should sit on her right. I have observed that they speak a language not known to others, laughing or turning solemn together as it burbles along, leaning towards each other in their secret bond. I draw out the table on a piece of paper, working out from the middle with the names—man, woman, man, man, woman. It is better not to seat a husband and wife too near each other, but close enough for a smile or a wink now and then over the table. There are some strong dislikes that I need to respect, keeping true enemies far apart. Crossing the plan out here, adding there, the forty guests fall into their places. If there are last-minute additions to our list, they can be seated at the end chairs of the table.

I think I hear the caterer's truck arriving, but it turns out to be a delivery from FedEx. *Rush, Do Not Delay, Urgent* it says on the outside. Why a publisher has to send overnight the manuscripts about long-dead painters eludes me, but I know that my next book is what is in the box. It will be the interlinear work from my editor, small red handwriting in the margins questioning my sources and recommending changes of grammar. Harry is the deliveryman, a grown man still looking like a teenager.

"Morning, Dr. Obermann. Another manuscript?"

"Thanks, Harry. I'll let you know when it's ready to go back."

"I'm still reading the book you gave me, a few pages each night."

"You'll be finished in plenty of time for this new one."

Harry reminds me of David Lawston, who had the same shock of blond hair when he lived next door in Pasadena. We went through the primary schools together, played at sexual games with each other in the storeroom off the garage and over at his house when it was without his mother's supervising eyes. We spent a summer vacation working at a seafood restaurant on Balboa Island, washing the plates and pots until midnight, sharing an upstairs room, avoiding the riptides in the Newport Beach surf until noon.

The exploration of the body beautiful continued, boys playing with the first rush of joy. It was a summer of freedom from the Swiss ways in Pasadena and I thought that all was possible with David. We could go through life together, living on dishwasher's wages at the edge of Bohemia, swimming in the sea by day. By September, I knew that David would start his years at Caltech and enter the adult world. He would go on to marry and have children, but I thought that I would not, maybe becoming a professor instead. Professors at that time all appeared to be celibate and monastic, living a life of high thoughts and timeless concepts. If I could not figure out my own sexuality, then I would live apart from it. Too bad that entering a monastery was only for the devout and good, not for those who wanted to hide.

David did marry—our mutual friend Marjorie from down the block. The wedding was held during my undergraduate years and I went back to

Pasadena to be the best man, staying with Father and Aunt Ella. The ceremony was to be in the same San Gabriel church where we went for my mother's funeral. Father, Ella and I came early, walking back to Mother's grave in the cemetery behind the church, the jacaranda trees again in bloom. Time seemed to have stopped there, her funeral only yesterday. How different all our lives would have been had she lived, I thought, but I did not know exactly how or why. That was the first fork in the road, I was sure, when change came after change. At the cemetery I tried to put my inchoate thoughts into words, but I was cut short by seeing my father's misty eyes. We walked back to the church as the last guests were finding their seats to an organ overture.

Marjorie knew about David's and my time at the seaside, our dalliances away from her. She told me after the ceremony that I was a good person to let David come back to her, to not take him off across the sea. When my thoughts return to them, I wonder what life would have been like across the sea with David. It would not be very happy on our scullery-maid wages, even with his blond body at my beck and call. David was surely happier with Marjorie, both of them studying at Caltech to become scientists.

Paloma arrives and I give her the list of guests. She has a square bottle of sepia ink and her favorite square-nibbed pen. I watch as she inscribes each of the cards with the cursive letters of the fifteenth century, loops, side ornaments, crisscrossed underscorings. The cards could have been for quite a different occasion, centuries earlier, at a table more fine with guests more lofty. I will put them aside for when the table is set.

"How is it all going?" she asks.

"Your sister wishes it would go away."

"She was never big on celebrations."

"Artemis wrote that she and the girls won't be back in time from their hikes in Switzerland. It's the Jungfrau this year."

"They ought to be here for Celia, but they do love their mountains."

"I'm hoping that everybody here gets along."

"Who are you worried about?"

"A couple of the names on the list don't particularly like some other names."

"I doubt it will come to fisticuffs."

8

Open Wide for the Doctor

1964

The university accepted Graham's monograph on Wingrave Prosper for his thesis and he was now the holder of a master's degree in fine arts. A New York publisher of fine art books paid a modest advance for the manuscript, but the editors wanted major changes, additions and expanded descriptions of Wingrave at work and his techniques. They would take the responsibility for tracking down the needed paintings and having them photographed for reproduction.

The publishers wanted to include more of the black-and white photographs of the painter at work and with his family, and the society photos in Los Angeles and New York. Graham scoured through Wingrave's collection of them with a large jeweler's loupe, looking into every corner of the prints. He could imagine himself actually in the photos as he studied the details—where people were standing, body language of the others around Wingrave, what everyone was wearing, shadows of other people out of the picture frame and who was looking out of a dark window in the background. Everything jumped forward with the magnification, became alive.

This was the process Graham learned while writing this first biography—to study all the photographs in minute detail. There was an untold story in every photograph—a hand around a waist, a clenched fist, eyes looking where they should not—and it could only be revealed under a glass. He found one photo that caught Wingrave peering with an intent eye past Dolores to an unknown woman, another with Mikal sad while the others laughed and one with Karl sitting high up on the steps away from the rest, looking apart and alone. Each held a clue to the whole story.

The Wingrave Prosper book was released in October and Graham got good notices. One reviewer said that it was a clear picture of a troubled man and another wrote that this was the well-told story of how a painter of the famous rose to the top. The publisher was delighted with the sales figures and expressed interest in any new biography that Graham would write. An advance of five thousand dollars was promised. What could be a better road sign for his career, to start now the grand walk towards the city of gold? The publisher sent a list of artists' names for possible biographies and encouraged Graham to continue his doctoral studies as he wrote. He only needed to decide which of the names to take on.

The Vietnam War grew more important in 1964 and Karl, remembering the Korean war draft, thought it was just a matter of time until he was called up. Since he had taken the year off to write rather than continue his studies, he would be in the high-risk to to be drafted category. To avoid the dreaded infantry front line, Karl chose an enlistment of three years wherein he could choose which branch he would join.

After basic and advanced training, he was sent directly to Vietnam. The war was in its beginning skirmishes and its full extent was hidden from the public back home. Karl wrote to Graham about his life in the war zone, driving ammunition and supplies from southern depots north to the troops near the Seventeenth Parallel and the intense bombing when they arrived there. Driving supply trucks was not the specialty he had been promised, but it proved too difficult a bureaucratic maneuver to make the change. His letters said he was not in real danger, not the same as the infantry at the front lines, and most of his days passed without an explosion or a gunshot. But Graham knew that nothing was really safe for a soldier.

Graham was 4-F from a childhood bout with scarlet fever, weakness in the lungs and heart making a man ineligible for service, and he was still in graduate school. He thought many times about traveling across the Pacific to Saigon to meet Karl, to have a week together in the capital. The lack of a love partner at home fed his imagination, made a few nights in a steamy Saigon bed seem desirable. It was possible then, the war more serious in the north, many civilians taking refuge in the south. Visas were available for ordinary tourists. But Graham's call to see his Karl was not strong enough and the window closed for non-military travel.

Coming home on an accrued leave in 1966, Karl went to stay first with the family at El Molino. They all noted how thin and wiry he looked, strained and distracted. Celia was home as well, starting to paint her canvases in the log cabin. Brother and sister spent as much time as possible together, often walking up the road to their favorite valley overlook., the same place she had asked Graham to come to her bedroom.

She felt her brother's back, how solid he had become. "Karl, I worry about you."

"No need. Army feeds us well."

"You know what I mean. The danger."

"Danger is there, without a doubt. Several guys in my unit were killed, just before I left."

"I don't know what I would do without you."

"Graham would take care of you."

"Not in the same way."

"My beloved sister—I clearly see us both in our eighties, doddering around El Molino. I will survive."

She kissed him on his ear, held him close for a few minutes.

"I'm going out to see Graham," he said. "Be with him for a while."

"I wish I could go, too."

Karl drove over to stay in the staircase apartment with Graham, who was finishing the work on his doctorate of arts. At first the two men felt awkward, the years apart a barrier. Graham ran his hand over Karl's chest and back, felt the hard muscles of war. Karl had always been fit and full, but this new firmness had a depth that both scared and excited him. In two years Karl had grown a separate, new self that he would never know, with visions he could not share. How quickly it had happened, he thought. Would there be other Karls to deal with when he came home again with the wounds Graham could not see?

"Can we still be lovers?" Graham asked.

"I think so. I want it to be so."

"Let me just hold you for a while."

"Shouldn't I open wide for the doctor?"

"Bear with me."

When they lay next to each other, what Graham was afraid of, that the gap had grown too wide, proved not to be the case. He was still able to please this student prince who had become the warrior, to caress the places he remembered, to make joy, to turn the real present into sensual illusion. Behind the soldier's façade was the man who had come to him so often before, the man with the worried eyes. The hardness was only a Roman soldier's breastplate fastened on the surface; there was a warm-blooded man underneath.

After they made love, Graham held Karl's head close to his chest. If he kept him close enough, perhaps it would shield him from the tropical danger that awaited. Graham sensed that this was the dynamic that would inhabit their togetherness should it last, that he was the keeper of the hearth and home, and Karl would make the difficult sorties out into the world. Graham had become Penelope to Karl's Ulysses.

"Are you happy?" Karl asked.

"A worried happiness, at best."

"I'll be back in one piece, I know."

"You'd better. I wouldn't survive without you."

"Remember our time immemorial," Karl said.

"I'll try."

But Graham could not bring himself to try telling Karl the real news, that in three months' time he and Celia were to marry. He knew it would spoil the idyll, this beautiful homecoming. He suspected that Celia had not had the courage to discuss it with Karl either, the two of them afraid of wounding the brother.

In trips back and forth between the staircase apartment and El Molino, while Karl was away, Graham came to think that the only way was to marry. There were a few notable exceptions, but he knew that the world of that time would not let a man live with another man without bringing grief down upon them. There was an unspoken disapproval from both his father and Wingrave, although both men stepped back from criticizing their artistic sons. To be taken seriously, a man must have a wife and Graham loved Celia, almost as much as he loved Karl.

When Graham and Celia had discussed the idea of marriage, he asked her, "You know that I have made love to Karl?"

"How does that change us?"

"I wonder about my own motives. Am I just reacting to Karl's being away for several years, trying to fill the loneliness?"

"I don't know. Are you?"

"Can I make you happy and still love Karl?"

"I don't see why not. Our sex is great. You are a good provider on that score."

"Wingrave says I am a greedy man hoarding away two of his children."

"There would be nothing wrong with your continuing to love Karl."

"It seems I have to make a choice."

"It will be all right, Graham. Karl will accept us. Stop worrying."

There was time to make sense of it, after Karl came back for good from Vietnam. They made the arrangements for a small wedding at El Molino, family and a few friends in the garden of the big house. No priest or church service. Celia said she would not agree to obey.

As the time for the furlough at home approached, she asked Graham, "What about Karl? He arrives on leave next week."

"I can't figure it out. Do we tell him or wait?"

"If we wait, he'll have a happy two weeks at home. He needs that."

"We're cowards. I'll force myself to tell him on the last day."

And now that he was with Karl on the last day, Graham knew he could not look at those eyes if he told. He could imagine them with a wet fullness, not real tears, then see them change as Karl's protective mind covered the hurt and summoned words to say how happy he was for the two of them. It was betrayal from his best friend and his favorite sister. A letter would wound Karl less and feel different from the treachery it was. As Karl's taxi pulled away, written phrases were already coming up in Graham's head, the long dependent clauses and the subjunctive mood to shelter and soften the truth. *Dearest Karl, since Celia so often says with some authority that you and she might be but one person, differing sides of the self-same coin…*

9

His Back to the Chateau

24 July 2011, 2:30 PM

I hear the caterer's van park at the side of the house, from where both the kitchen and the back portal are accessible. I go to meet them in the kitchen as they carry in trays of partially prepared entrees, bowls of sauces and a basket of fruits and herbs. Lilli, who had worked for us before, is the captain and she introduces the five others, all in black trousers and shirts: Margo, Vanessa, who will bartend, Cathy, Candy and Josh. They carry the tables and chairs to the back portal and bring the glassware into the kitchen.

Walter Burley's is now an established catering firm, cooking dinners and serving them with panache for twenty years. From a small start he has collected a first-class cadre of chefs, waiters and assistants to craft and present a dozen large parties each summer weekend. Few talked directly with Walter now, his captains conferring for menus and arrangements, like the pope relegating mere bureaucratic matters to his cardinals.

I want to see if the six eight-foot tables marry together into the long table I have envisaged, so I watch as they set them up. The twenty chairs on either side look comfortably spaced, no elbows hitting elbows, so I give the go-ahead to lay the white tablecloths. We discuss a sample setting—small and large forks on a napkin to the left, knife and spoon to the right. But they seem to know all of this already.

Since there is not an exact center place to twenty people in a row, I look to a spot about center where I will sit, ten to my left, nine to my right. Celia is just across. Is it better for me to sit with my back to the house, looking out? I think so. There must be something written dating from medieval times in the voluminous French books on fine etiquette that the lord should have his back to the chateau, ready for combat should it occur, sharpened sword near his fighting arm. A table in the open was open to myriad possible dangers. Ladies should sit towards the middle, knights at the ends where they can rise up with clenched fists should danger approach. But we'll trust there are no such incidents in this modern gathering of peaceable friends. I'll spread the knights about where I choose in this time of relative peace, French etiquette aside.

I consult my plan of the seated guests as Josh, Margo and Cathy smooth the cloth so it appears as one long piece of fabric, and they sit down at the end to fold the stack of napkins. Jullian Closson is perfect seated next to Celia. Jullian composed a song cycle about a woman painter who everybody supposed was in fact Celia. But both the women insisted that it was a universal tribute to the difficulties of all creative women who struggled to succeed. Music is wonderful in its ability to be ambiguous, to not speak the whole truth. Carolyn is Jullian's partner of many years and I have seated her across the table, down on my left. At venues across the nation, she often plays the intricate cello concerto she is known for, the one Jullian wrote for her.

Next to Carolyn is Hilliard Milano, the architectural photographer. They should have plenty to talk about, both loving Italy and things Italian. Hilliard photographed Celia and me for his *Artistic Couples* book, four pages of us lounging about El Molino, looking as artistically fetching as we could. On Jullian's right I have Johannes Adler, the art historian and longtime friend from our university days. He continues to write books on the great movements of art, his last one titled *The Renaissance Eye.* Johannes can deliver entertaining anecdotes from the world of Vienna and Berlin, but he can be ill tempered at times. And he can be a trial for attractive and athletic young waiters at our winter restaurant dinners together if he chooses to extend his Malacca cane. I recall Johannes gave Jullian's song cycle a rave review in the local art magazine, so that pairing will go well. Carolyn Aarp, the painter, will be next to him. Since she is a modernist and he an unvarnished traditionalist, there could be a spirited but harmless banter between them.

Blaine, a lawyer who works with the pueblos is across from Sybille Latimer, whose mother I am sure was a Crow Indian. There are many injustices for them to dissect. Sybille's husband, Quattro, is an architect and I have remembered to seat him well away from Hallston, Blaine's partner, who hates everything about Willy's steel and glass houses. Now that I can see the list seated around me at the table, which people are next to what people, I think I have done all that I can to make a pleasurable evening. The ones who dislike each other are not so far apart that they cannot glower back and forth, but not close enough to actually throw insults. A little drama is not a bad thing if the combatants are kept well apart. The mere rattling of swords can be oddly compelling, the easy digestion of a rich meal assured with the added adrenalin of discord.

Joseph McLarry, also a photographer, was in Vietnam with Karl and they still attend veterans' events together. I think Joseph's years there left a deeper mark on him than on Karl. I have seated them together as I know they feel safe in each other's company, like back-to-back soldiers in a restive valley.

There are three couples who live up the road from El Molino whom I have divided among the next rank of seats, and beyond those are all the rest. Juan Carlos is at the far left end, next to a young man he will surely find attractive. My now middle-aged nephew Parchment is at the other end next to the youngest women I could find on the list, and his cousin, Dominique, is on his other side. Parchment's shy demeanor will charm everyone around him, so there is no worry at that end of the table.

I still have a hard time thinking of Paloma and Juan Carlos as a couple, a married couple at that. Theirs may have been a case of marital musical chairs, they being the only two left when the band stopped. Celia observes that they are happy, the way they treat each other tells her that and I must not speak aloud my thoughts. I am fond of Paloma, a gentle soul who wants only good for those around her. I can see that where she seemed destined to be the spinster sister, caregiver for the dying mother, the marriage to Juan Carlos took her in quite another direction and gave her a higher standing in the extended family. My uncharitable thoughts make a guilty cloud, then pass over and move on.

10

Family Money

1967

After the news of Celia and Graham's marriage reached Karl, he had a difficult time accepting it, drinking into the early hours, worrying his Army friends. If he and Graham could not live together, there had to be another way. At a bar in north Saigon, he met a young woman who listened to his stories, his woe, perhaps not the whole truth, but for certain the whole unhappiness. If the man and the woman together was the answer back at El Molino, it might be in Saigon too. Even though Karl was about to be rotated home in a few months and discharged, he asked the personnel office for an expedited permission to marry. There followed a small ceremony with her aged parents and a few of the men in his unit. Most of the group at the time supposed that the bride was pregnant before the nuptials, Karl stepping up for the age-old punishment. That appeared to be a wrong assessment in the months that followed, as Karl grew disillusioned, unhappy with himself, and made plans to leave Vietnam without her. The papers he filed for annulment were short and to the point, an unjust but easy way for a soldier to erase a mistake. What was based on a lie could be undone with another lie. He left her a pile of cash and returned to an Army friend's house in La Jolla to plan his future before returning to New Mexico. He did not want to face Graham and his sister just then.

In the same years, Wingrave had second thoughts about how he had treated all his children. The volcanic ups and downs of his career were slowing down, and he regretted the early decision to send the boys and girls off to boarding schools, military schools, distant colleges—anywhere to get them from underfoot. His plan to make up for this was to give each of them a house and land, giving them roots in the El Molino compound. At his studio

Graham asked Wingrave about his motives. He wanted to leave a legacy more substantial than just his canvases, he answered, a mark on the earth that he had been a caring father, even if he was not.

"A family should live together," he said at his studio. "Otherwise, they drift and lose their centers. This will give them all a place to come back to, or never leave if they choose."

"Don't you think it's more the American way to move far away, start a new family, forget the home-place?" Graham asked.

"But my children won't move away. Its because I have made them all cripples in one way or another. Roberto takes no joy in his marriage or work, Artemis is like a nun in her life at Mills, Karl obviously has something wrong in the head since Vietnam, Celia is almost crazed with ambition to best me, Mikal is a handsome weakling and Paloma will stay a spinster, unloved and unhappy."

"Aren't you being too hard on yourself and them?"

"I don't think so. A famous father is a curse, like binding up their legs, making it impossible for them to walk away. Even the Garcia money hasn't helped, making them more dependent than independent."

"It's not that unusual, Wingrave. Many have survived strong fathers and gone on to happy lives."

"Your Celia will, and perhaps your Karl. You picked well."

"Wingrave, I didn't pick, I've just followed my love."

"Perhaps and perhaps not."

It turned out to be a more complicated project for Wingrave than a quick gift. Uncle Parchment pointed out that the land was the Garcias and that Wingrave, a mere in-law, could not give it away without first buying it. Many hundreds of thousands of dollars changed hands, Wingrave paying his personal funds into the Garcia family trust. Wingrave knew that Parchment had been waiting for this moment, watching the dark blossom of dislike come into full bloom, its petals happy at last.

Wingrave contracted with Juan Carlos to look after the design and construction of the houses. Roberto, Artemis and Celia each were deeded an acre of land and a house, and Paloma and Mikal would share a single house on an acre. Karl was given the acre with the old log house, with Juan

Carlos overseeing the refurbishment and additions. El Molino resounded with construction noises from the summer of 1968 to the following summer.

Graham and Celia moved into her house, she working in the small separate studio. Celia rankled, however, at the minute size of her studio, supposing it was really a comment by Wingrave on how little he respected a woman who wanted to be a painter. The small space was good enough for the little still life and the flower paintings she might produce, like a cozy kitchen for a woman's work.

Celia dreamt of a large, high-ceiling studio for the future she had in mind. If nobody else would do it, she would have it built herself. She met with Roberto at the Great River National Bank to borrow the money she needed. He told her that her request surely would be approved, but she must get Graham to co-sign the note.

"But I'm borrowing this money, not him," she said.

"Married women can't borrow on their own."

"This married woman will be the one who pays it back."

"My board would never agree."

"Graham doesn't have any family money, and you know perfectly well I will receive the Garcia trust money in a few years, pay you back then."

"My hands are tied."

"You bankers are such pigs."

"Why do you need another studio, anyway?"

She would not ask a husband to sign her note, even her Graham. She knew that Artemis had already received her disbursement from the Garcia trust, her thirtieth birthday the day for vesting. It was a simple matter for the sisters to agree to a short document, and Celia had her money. The new studio was larger than her new house and small studio combined, an expansive ultra-modern painting space, storerooms and offices. Graham wondered if Celia had paced off Wingrave's studio in secret to make sure that hers was larger than his. It did not resemble her father's, but was a timbered structure in-filled with large rectangles of glass, as light and open as his was heavy and dark.

With few changes to the small studio except the bookshelves, Graham moved in and started writing. He had decided to take Andre Derain as the subject for his next book. With what information he could collect from the Santa Fe municipal and New Mexico state libraries, he wrote the outline, noting where he needed to go for interviews and the information he wanted to uncover. It was certain that he would have to go to France for research, but only after he exhausted all the stateside sources. TheUniversity of Texas had a few letters and documents from his first galleries, so that would be the first trip.

Juan Carlos transformed Karl's log cabin into a well-furnished *garconnière*, everything in place for the returning soldier. He added on a couple of bedrooms, bathrooms and a kitchen, leaving the cabin itself as the place to write, whenever Karl the novelist-to-be chose to take up residence there. Graham thought that Juan Carlos spent more time on Karl's house than any of the others, his way of giving evidence of his long-held love.

Karl did not return to El Molino that summer or the next. His patriarch painter novel, *Living with the Monster,* came out in November, a novelist's career well on its way. He wrote to Graham that he was living with a lover, another Vietnam vet. In time, he wrote, he and Harlan would drive east to El Molino and have dinner with him and Celia, catch up on the unknown years. Meanwhile, he was sending them his favorite statue of Buddha Holding Back The Sea as a house-warming gift. The new novel about the war was proving difficult to write, may not come to completion soon. Did books about war take more time to gestate than books about fathers? How long did Tolstoy take? Please write back and tell me how you are.

Graham remembered one of his favorite professors saying that it was never wrong to put personal feelings into words, even if to cast them to sea in a bottle. The thoughts he had been living with needed to be put down on paper. Graham was not unhappy being married to Celia, but he knew life felt incomplete without the other half of this curious creature. If he described it in words and sent it off, the letter jut might drift ashore. He sent this letter to the La Jolla address:

> Dear Karl: I wanted you to know that in marrying Celia I was not abandoning you. Your father says that I am a greedy man, and maybe he is right, because I want both Celia and you in each of my days. You've found someone else to love, but we know that can change. When it does, come back to me and El Molino. There is an empty part of my heart that only you can fill.
>
> Yours,
>
> Graham

11

A Complicated Machine

24 July 2011, 2:40 PM

The afternoon becomes cloudy with a monsoon storm threatening to upend our preparations for the party. I know that this is a summer pattern and quite often the storm dissipates as the evening hours approach. A crash of faraway thunder makes me question Lilli about what we should do if there is a downpour.

"We could move the tables into the house, like we did last time," she says.

"The tables are out of the rain but it would not be a pleasant place to eat in a heavy rainstorm."

"Let's wait a bit, Graham. See what the storm does."

I remember building the portal for just such a problem, to provide a place out of the weather to have summer parties. Juan Carlos helped with the design, a porch wide enough for a single long table or half a dozen round tables seating eight. The advance check for my biography of Bonnard just about covered the costs and we had our first event that year. It was a small dinner to celebrate the book. There were also storms that evening, me bringing out shawls for the women.

Rain is the subject of, or at least the inspiration for, Celia's new series of paintings. I walk over to her studio as the first light drops are falling. She is sitting in a chair studying the canvas on the easel, a seven-foot square of swirling lines, narrow lines, covering most of the white space in a baroque pattern. Rain in a windstorm is what you might think it was, but Celia is always quick to say that it is only an idea, not a representation of anything real.

"What do you think, Graham?" she asks.

Celia needs no one else in her painting world, no one except the voices in her head that tell her where to go. Sometimes they speak so softly she cannot understand. She has included me in her process over the years, knowing that I will give the abstract answer to her nonobjective question. One of the secrets to our life together is that we do not abandon each other to these lonely stretches of art. I can ask her about a paragraph that does not seem to work, or she can ask me about the strength of a line or whether the rhythm of the painting is off.

Chinese-like, cryptic comments are the best. An off-hand, casual observation was not possible and nothing concerning the actual paint, if it is right or the technique, or how well paint is applied. What Celia wants is to know if she is going in the right direction and that there is another person who cares about it. It is the child within the artist, needing approval but not wanting it to be granted too quickly or with too little thought. Literary comparisons, meteorology, engineering or music are good sources for metaphors.

"I like the syncopation, those small pauses."

"They are good, aren't they? I want to use them more often."

"For the whole series, then?"

"If I can. They would tie the lot together."

I have watched in the past as she took an idea, expanded it, questioned it, refined it or divided it, and turned it into a beautiful completion. No other painter today can make a canvas shimmer with color and light the same way, an energy that is built in by the mere juxtaposition of colors and shapes that do not agree with each other. With Celia as conductor, they meld without giving up their differences. I do not understand her whole process, but I have great admiration for a finished piece.

Karl is more introspective in his work. He wants nobody there when he is writing, no person, lover or not, looking over his shoulder. A new page is a new tender piece of skin without the ability to protect itself, a newborn to be sheltered from the burning rays of the sun. When a book is at last done, all put together, is the time for another to enter in. *Here it is, the best I can do, what do you think?* Even at this stage he is defensive about his offspring—any criticism must be mild. Happily, he is a good writer and seldom goes off onto awkward peninsulas. His sagas have expanded in scope with many characters and many themes, folding back upon each other in a grand contrapuntal design, returning at last to ground. I am not sure I have the ability to edit what he has done.

My love for Karl has never competed or negated my love for Celia—each reinforces the other. I see Karl's face when I make love to Celia. His body is a complicated machine; I still learn its many functions, and perhaps it is why I still take such delight in sex with Karl. Did that tender and responsive spot move around to a different part of his body since the last time, demanding search and rescue? It seems a game of chase, the real Karl hiding in a deep shadow or around a corner, and I am quick to saddle up for the hunt.

From the beginning I found Celia's body more difficult, even more complex that Karl's. There were so many more working parts that needed attention, but it is amazing when they all sing together. She responds differently, no sudden burst of light, but a steady glow, brighter and brighter. Sometimes we make love in her studio, dropping our clothes on the floor in the rush for that growing brightness. I wonder if the act of artistic creation is parallel to the sexual act, the studio a natural place for both.

Celia returns to the canvas, reinforcing an existing portion of the design, using a long-handled brush with a narrow bit of bristle. I know that these are the finishing touches for this painting when her obsession comes into play to make every inch of it just right. I have brought over several of my manuscripts to read aloud to Celia, this one a curious take on Cezanne's feelings about his father. I wonder if something like it resonates in Celia, who never reached a smooth place with her own father. For now, I can see that it is better to sit in silence and watch.

12

Pueblo Shadows

1971

It snowed on the late winter day Karl showed up back at El Molino and he made it clear from the very beginning that he did not want to discuss his time in Vietnam or La Jolla. Both Celia and Graham tried to sound him out, but he changed the subject every time. He moved into the log cabin house waiting empty for him for so many months. Juan Carlos was delighted to show him around, to point out how the heating and plumbing worked, how to light a fire in the river-rock fireplace, where the blankets were stored. Juan Carlos was happy to have his long-departed hero back in Ithaca.

Karl had always felt content here when it snowed, the still air and the piñon smoke making a house more protective, more house-like. When Juan Carlos left him alone and he was looking out at the swirling white, he thought it was a good omen, this snowy welcome for the prodigal. He could see the new tracks of the resident fox at El Molino, circling a discreet distance from the house towards the river. He supposed it was a vixen, hunting for a morsel for the cubs.

Graham never felt jealousy or unease over Juan Carlos's infatuation with Karl. They were boy adventurers together, he was sure, like his own time with David Lawston. Karl had moved on, found another love, lived another life, but Juan Carlos had not. Since Graham knew the delight he himself felt at his lover's return, how could he not approve of how it made another happy as well?

Roberto, who did not have to serve in Vietnam, appeared to be glad to have his younger brother back from military service, stopping by the log cabin to chat for a while almost every day. Graham wondered if Roberto, like

Wingrave, was expiating guilt from things left undone—like not loving or protecting a younger brother enough.

There was still snow on the ground when Roberto invited Karl and Graham to fly with him one afternoon. Roberto had discovered the ruined pueblos of the Galisteo Basin and how they became so visible from the air, particularly as the sun got low and the shadows lengthened, even more apparent with a covering of snow. He took them low over Pueblo Blanco, an arroyo coursing through its middle; Pueblo Colorado, huddled up against the safety of red cliffs; and then low again over Pueblo Shé, said to be the largest ruin in the valley. The shadows brought up the room-blocks, plazas, turkey pens and circular kivas in sharp detail, where little would have been visible from the ground. Graham thought about how this land had nurtured people for so many thousands of years, El Molino only the latest incarnation of closely spaced houses, clans and families in agrarian juxtaposition.

"Graham, do you want to see Rancho Garcia?" asked Roberto, turning off to the east. "Uncle Parchment lives out here all the time now. I'll buzz the house, let him know we came by."

He flew the airplane low over a cluster of buildings in the middle of a cottonwood cluster, the headquarters of the Garcia sheep operation. On the second run around, they could see men waving in front of the buildings, responding to Roberto's wagging up and down of the wings. One of them was presumably Uncle Parchment, the abbot in charge of his circle of secular monks.

Farther north, there was a circle of stones on the Galisteo Creston, also deeply shadowed, from which could be seen all of the valley's pueblos, perhaps used for shaman bonfires on particular nights. This was the ceremonial center of the whole basin, Roberto said. They headed north across new subdivisions, back to Santa Fe.

"While we have the sun, would you like to see El Molino from the air?" Roberto asked.

"I'll bet we can see Celia at her easel," Karl said.

"And Wingrave. I've seen him before in the big north window."

They looped around the town and then followed the river up to El Molino. Celia heard the plane and came to the door to wave. Roberto took them in a circle around to see Wingrave's studio, coming lower so, as he suggested, they could look down at the old painter at work just inside his window. As they raced over his roof, El Molino appeared established and warm to all three men, smoke trails from the chimneys in the late afternoon sun, a treasured home-place. After they landed at the airport and were driving in the slow traffic back into town, Roberto asked Graham about his next book now that he and Karl had both skewered Wingrave.

"Do you really think we skewered him?" Graham asked.

"He has become very contrite, trying to make up."

"Maybe it's time for all his children to forgive him."

"Not me. It feels too good to hate. Again, who's next for you?"

"Andre Derain. He was a minor French painter, just now appreciated. His daughter is alive still in Collioure, on the south coast, and I want to talk to her before it's too late."

"You're leaving soon? Olivia and I may be back in Frejus for the Concours. We can have lunch somewhere again. Just let us know."

"I'm going too, Roberto," Karl said. "We're both writing new projects."

Graham was glad to be going away. He and Celia had reached a plateau in their marriage where each questioned it, wondered if a mistake had been made and if there was anything to do about it. They were not unhappy, but were wary of the torpid cloud that had settled over their time together. It was, in fact, the classically bad seventh year of their marriage. She encouraged Graham to go, saying they could rethink and rework when he came back at the end of summer.

He told Celia, "Karl is coming with me. He wants a new place to work, as well. The Vietnam War book is going slowly."

"You can be boys again. Find what you lost," she said.

"I'm not sure we can be boys again, but maybe we can find something."

"I love you, Graham. Let's leave it at that."

◊◊◊

Karl and Graham took the transport from the airport into Paris and rented a car again at the Etoile garage. This time Karl circled only once on the outside lane around the monument, resisting the inward push and turning off to the south. They stayed one night in a noisy roadside hotel along the Rhone, neither of them getting much sleep. In an unspoken agreement, both of them had come to the decision it was not the place to start their love again. They left early, and it was afternoon when they arrived in Collioure on the Mediterranean coast, checking into a small *auberge* on the main street.

Both of them had sex on the mind, the desire building up like storm clouds as they drove south into the moist coastal air. The research could wait for a night, while Graham explored the body that had given him so much joy so many years before. How much time was it since that guilt-painted parting at the end of Karl's furlough?

Afterwards, Karl said, "Thank you, that was wonderful. But let's take it slow. We have all of the summer to repair."

"And maybe all of life, too."

"I feel the immemorial clock is going again."

At the small museum in the town centre, Graham asked where the artist Derain had lived. The receptionist there gave him a tourist map that illustrated which paintings were painted in what houses, with their street numbers. He knocked on the doors of houses nearby asking if there was a grandmother or someone who would remember, identifying himself as *le biographe officiel*. He had been wise enough to ask for a letter in French from the publisher, but most did not want to see this verification of his status, encased in stiff plastic like a large driver's license. At the sixth door there was success. The grandmother there had helped her own mother cook for the artists, Matisse, Derain. Graham asked if she might talk about her experiences.

Mais, oui...for a small fee. Graham and Karl were shown into a back room facing the garden to meet Madame. She was a sharp-minded old lady in her nineties, now savoring the role as one of the few left who could tell the story. She said that Derain's daughter, with whom she used to play, was dead now for three years. They were too late for her tales.

"So you want stories about the painter Derain?" she said in French.

"It would be wonderful, whatever you remember."

"I remember it all. Robin and I ran through the kitchen day and night."

"Did you watch him at work?"

"Hours and hours. He was a genius."

Graham realized that all this woman's stories were well-rehearsed, but he recorded them nevertheless. When he came back the next day with flowers and a bottle of Armagnac, he got more of the same. He came to know that the birth pangs of great art were not clearly seen by a small girl from the kitchen door, but her tales were a start for his book.

One name led to another, and Graham and Karl drove all over France to talk to each of them and to the sources Graham had set up in advance. There was a man who remembered working for the Kahnweiler Gallery in Paris when Derain exhibited there, a professor who wrote a book about the London paintings, another who was an expert on his ballet designs for Diaghilev and several others. These witnesses were quite a bit younger than Graham's first nonagenarian, and each held a small piece of the story. Despite a post-war period of collaboration disrepute, Derain came to be well regarded by most Frenchmen. Graham wondered if it took the excellence of Derain's art to overcome his countrymen's doubts.

In Chatou, just outside Paris, they found what they thought was the pastry shop of Derain's father. At 64 Grand Rue in Chambourcy, they peeked through the gates of Derain's last home. Nobody living nearby could remember him personally, but most neighbors had stories told to them by their grandparents.

In another commune of Paris, Garches, Graham talked with the man who said he was there on the day when the near-blind painter was struck down by a speeding truck in 1954. Later that day, Graham talked to another man who said Derain was a passenger in a nighttime car wreck, the fire from the car lighting up the sky with vivid yellow when he was a boy, the whole town running over to watch. Graham had already written in his notes about a third man who saw a German limousine strike him dead, his white cane flying as the merciless car drove on. Despite such contradictions, it could be safe to write that he died in a traffic accident.

With that, Karl drove them back into central Paris for a few weeks of other pursuits at the end of August. The Hotel des Saints Pères had a vacancy, all of the city having gone south on holiday, the concierge said. It was a small hotel in a converted pair of townhouses, an easy walk to all the Left Bank.

After the men took this opportunity for an unrushed afternoon of love, they walked over to a bistro on the next street. Only a few tables were occupied.

"Your book is coming along, I think?" Graham asked.

"The trip has been good for me. I have sixty pages total."

"I've watched you writing in the early mornings, new pages each day. I haven't asked about it because I know that bringing up the Vietnam years is difficult for you. I have tried to be quiet."

"You don't need to be quiet. When I left Harlan this spring, we had just finished the worst of a lot of bad fights. I waited in Arizona for my black eye and other bruises to get better before coming home. I was ashamed."

"I wondered if that might be the case."

"It was not meant to be. Harlan was a bully, a very sexy bully, and Vietnam only made him worse."

"Did you fight often?"

"All the time, usually just after we had sex. I thought it was part of our getting over being soldiers, to wrestle, to yell at each other. It got rougher and rougher. When he really beat me up, I left."

"Karl, I'm so sorry."

"I'm very lucky to have you to come back to. Thanks for your letter."

Graham saw that Karl had been burying remembrances about Harlan and the war. It was that ability that made Karl a survivor, to move along from unpleasantness like the Buddhist monks who could stop a cut from bleeding with their minds. As a boy Karl learned to walk away from Wingrave's abuse in the mountains, and there must be many Vietnam days he still needed to erase. The stubborn memories remained, bringing up the nightmares that woke both of them, Graham enclosing him until they returned to sleep.

The men stayed on another week in Paris so Graham could consult the archives of the galleries that sold Derain paintings. Karl worked on his book in the small library room at the Saints Pères or at morning tables in the nearby cafes while Graham sorted through the ribbon-tied boxes of letters at the Bibliothèque or the archive vaults. After their afternoons together, they had dinners at the bistros in the area. This was the end and highlight of their summer, the misunderstandings and hurts of the last years repaired, love and sex reinvigorated, a promise for their future. They were ready to take on whatever waited for them at El Molino.

13

Right Beside You

24 July 2011, 3:00 PM

I am the perfect husband for Celia—most other candidates would be crushed under the grinding wheels of her ego. The world knows her now, magazines and cable art shows calling every week for interviews, high-dollar collectors asking us to join them for lunch at local restaurants—they have traveled all this way to meet the painter personally. It was hoped that with the purchase of *Grey Lines No. 7* for so much money there came some proximity privileges as well. I keep the walls high and very few get through.

Celia has had a lover for decades now and she loves him much more deeply than me. Of course, he is Art. I have always understood that her work came first, even in those first tentative years of our time together. How often I have reported in my books about the disappointed wife of a painter, how unimportant her beauty was, how low on the ladder was her place. Unhappy spouses are a given in the annals of art.

I do not know if Celia has ever had a living and breathing other lover, clandestine meetings away from El Molino, but I doubt it. There was never any indication that such was the case during my many trips away. When she discovered painting, it became a vast world where she could travel with impunity, fly on its morning wings to the uttermost reaches, see wonders that others could only imagine. It took her breath away more than any mere human could have. I have seen in other painters that same intensity of purpose focused down to a laser dot while the frustrated spouse languished in inattention. Matisse certainly, Bonnard at times and Picasso repeatedly. *Why don't you come up to bed, dear, leave the easel for a while? What fun is our bohemian life if we never go anywhere?* But that is not the case in our life at El Molino. Celia learned that I am immune to the artistic radioactivity that surrounds her, able to walk right into the reactor without ill effect. I expect that many other men might have ended up being burnt toast.

There are those who criticize me for standing off to the side while she basks in the light. I am thought of as the Milquetoast helpmeet, holding the scarf. Ours is a fair arrangement, however, that opens up much for me, grants me the same freedoms. Without hesitation she gives me Karl and our love. In our months away from El Molino, I cannot imaginee that Celia has ever looked away for long from her canvas in sadness, wondering where we had gone. If there was ever resentment, it vanished without a trace.

I can see that Celia is ready for me to read to her. Without looking my way she asks if I am still there.

"Right beside you," I answer.

"I always feel good when I know you are there. Am I like a headstrong young girl wanting her father to witness her ice-skate or dive from the high board? Watch, Daddy, watch?"

"Exactly like that."

"Is it monstrous?"

"Not to me. It is the child within, still there."

I have brought some pages from several of my current projects about Cezanne. In them I wonder how the disapproval from his father affected his work. Does a layer of parental censure stay with him his whole life, making him work harder, longer hours? Or did he decide that he could never erase that dissatisfaction, so he moved on to please only himself? He did not write often to others on the matter and his contemporaries did not address the problem in their writings. It may not be possible to find something so abstract as an odd passage in one of his paintings. I suggest this parental condemnation may be the engine that drives many artists, the endless quest to be loved for what you do, to make good. These are the gears that never stop grinding.

"Does any of that ring a bell?" I ask.

"Certainly. I can still see Wingrave coming by and looking at a new canvas on my easel. Silent. Unsmiling. No comment at all was so much worse than a bit of harsh analysis."

"Does it still hurt?"

"Only a bit."

"But you've gone well beyond that and bested him in his own world."

"I had to."

"That's what I believe Cezanne did, even though in his mind Aix-en-Provence was always his father's home, not his."

"I thought that El Molino was always more mine than Wingrave's."

I stop reading for a while and just watch Celia at her work. The fight with her father is still right below the surface, the force that drives her forward. Her slim body is always active, moving up and down the ladder, reaching high for an upper section and bending low to finish the lines at the bottom. No doubt this has contributed to her preserving a young figure and countenance. Anybody seeing her walk along a street in New York or London would think she was in her middle years, the salt and pepper hair an early family trait. Her face is unlined, only the barest trace of the wrinkles at the ends of her eyes. She moves quickly and gracefully, like a well-tuned athlete.

14

Magnetic Storms

1971

Celia observed that Graham returned a different, happier person from the Derain summer with Karl. His long face was not pulled down by sad expressions like before, when they both began to think that their marriage had no hope. Odd how a single summer could make such a difference, she thought. It was also odd how letting go made things more firm. Both her men seemed better, more palatable for their time away.

She had paid off Artemis for the studio loan with her distribution from the Garcia trust, her vesting age of thirty attained. Money was never a concern for Celia, and she was now more aware that there were goals other than financial. The local Ludlow Gallery showed a first collection of her paintings, fourteen in all, to good local reviews and a well-attended opening night.

These were bold paintings in strong, dark colors—zigzagging lines across the canvases inter-filled with cross-hatchings and cross-braces. The pictures seemed to portray the steel girders underneath bridges, one bridge overlapping another. People at her opening asked if they represented bridges crossing to other worlds, hope in a dark world, but she had already learned to remain noncommittal about the meaning of a canvas.

The excitement of the exhibit galvanized her work in the studio for the rest of the year, with the lights over the easel on well into the night. Graham thought that the success of the exhibit gave her a new energy, surpassing what had always been there. Victory begat victory, the rich getting richer.

Karl's patriarch-painter novel had not sold well in the past year. Then the announcement came that MGM purchased the rights to adapt *Living with the Monster* into a screenplay, improving the sales and bringing a second round of reviews, many better ones this time. There was no timetable for the actual filming of the work, but the mere purchase of the rights brought a glow of happiness to the publisher's cheeks. There was no obligation for Karl to participate in the writing of the screenplay, but he could confer after it was completed. In other words, he had no control whatsoever over any part of the film. The disbursement from the Garcia trust last year and the royalties and film options this year gave Karl a solid financial footing. A scion of a rich family, this was the first he felt the full harvest of his own accomplishment.

Graham continued to work on the Andre Derain manuscript throughout the winter and he delivered the finished work to Mallstone Books in May. It was scheduled for fall publication when all the technical problems for illustrations and copyright matters were resolved. This was Graham's second book and he learned the mixture of satisfaction and loss in a work completed. It now belonged to others—those who corrected it, rearranged it, printed it, placed it on shelves, sold it and reviewed it. It would never come home again or remain the innocent offspring like before. His fair-haired son had left the father who raised him, back for visits but never with the same closeness.

The studios at El Molino stayed active well into the night hours, as if demons were dancing behind all four of those making their paintings and books. Even Wingrave had fallen into step, finishing the last of a series of paintings commissioned to illustrate a heavy new book on the Greek myths. His young models came and went at all hours, always a few sporty cars in his studio parking.

Graham wondered if productivity in the arts was a cycle, like the magnetic storms streaming down from the sun. He would check to see if there were similar patterns in his biographical subjects, years when all the Post-Impressionists brought forth hoards of new work, and the opposite, when little was done. Was it all just a matter of astronomical tides, when electric energy coursed across the universe and the artists of the world picked it up, sensitive receptors that they were? And conversely, there must have been slack times, periods of low energy when the artists laid low on their studio sofas, backs of their hands to the foreheads, complaining of sore joints and deserting their easels? High tide, low tide, high tide. Surely there was more to it than that.

As spring approached, the Vietnam novel was coming together in Karl's house, a thousand words a day, four perfect manuscript pages with his side-bar drawings—depictions of tropical birds, rain clouds, weather reports, smiling women, bullets, muddy combat boots, land mines, Anderson, Ripcord and bottles of 333 beer. It was now a steady march forward, the whole book already composed in Karl's head. It only needed writing down.

Graham grew out of the post-partum depression that came from sending off his manuscript and spent most days in his writing studio, doing the first research outlines for a biography of Odilon Redon. The painter would be difficult to portray, certainly more complex than Derain. Redon the man verged on the mystical or delirious, and his paintings remained an ill-assorted grab bag all his life. Born in 1840, he survived only into the first decades of the twentieth century. Graham decided that his biography could be less chronological and more amorphous, mirroring the untraditional work of the artist himself. How he would actually do this was yet to be known, perhaps more like Karl's early Cezanne stories than an organized essay working stolidly from premise to the ending proof. Scenes from Redon's final weeks could be interlarded with those from his childhood, like a bulletin board of unrelated photographs.

Into this maelstrom of creativity, Mikal returned home from university. For most of the last ten years he had been away from El Molino, first at military school in Culver, then various colleges and universities. He had graduated from Princeton, but just barely, with a degree in history. The best looking of the sons, he had the Prosper beauty like Karl and Celia, but was a lighter version of their brunet sultriness. He was taller than any of the siblings, a natural athlete. Karl said that Mikal would always rather do something than think about something.

Although he was half owner of the house with Paloma, he asked Karl if he could stay with him at the log house.

"I'll clear out the second bedroom."

"I want to get used to El Molino again."

"You've been away a lot. Just take your time."

"I thought I might buy a horse, ride up in the foothills. You remember our Homer when we were kids?"

"A good idea."

"Other than you, Homer was my best friend."

"What about the Vietnam draft, Mikal? You could be called up."

"The university doctors said I have a weak heart."

"I don't believe it. But maybe it's better that way."

"Vietnam was tough on you, wasn't it?"

"Still a few scars, but my trip to France with Graham helped."

"Can I go next time?"

"You'll have to ask Graham. It's fine with me."

Karl felt a pang of sadness for his brother. He looked strong and *sportif*, but he was the most vulnerable of the family, both physically and emotionally, even more so than Paloma. Vulnerable to self-doubt, inaction, fear of not succeeding and all the other sharp-edged gifts from Wingrave. Mikal idolized Karl when they were younger, always sitting beside him at family dinners, walking near him on country outings. His innate good cheer masked a near terror of being alone. Karl wondered what awaited Mikal, whether he could in fact make El Molino his home again. His disbursement from the Garcia trust was still several years away, but he would need little to live on until then—and Karl could help with that.

15

Waiting for the Visigoths

24 July 2011, 3:30 PM

I stop reading from my manuscript and watch as Celia paints the convoluted lines of this new painting, angling down for a while, then curving back up to the left, circling around, angling the other way and finally back into the original line of descent. It is not an angle of repose, but an angle of action, like a stop-shutter photograph of the arrival of wind, rain and dust. There are many more convolutions to go, each a matchstick-thin sliver next to its neighbor.

There is a strong linear quality in all of her paintings, a technique that she took for herself early on. I have resisted putting this into words with her but her current works resemble weavings or tapestries. Is this the female part of her work, the work at the loom that women do all over the world? I know that she would be angry to be compared to women cross-legged in front of a half-woven rug, the female spinning her web. She was quick to object when an old, award-winning writer called her one of the best woman painters in the world, intending a compliment. It might be very dangerous for a young reporter to make a similar remark, for as far as Celia is concerned being a woman has nothing to do with being a painter.

The painted lines are there, nonetheless, for whatever they signify. I had not thought about it before, but the lines have been becoming thinner and thinner as the years go by. Would the lines disappear entirely in the last paintings, morphing into clouds of pale color? She finishs the next line, from top slowly down, curving around and then to the bottom. As those who wait for the pause in the singing to leave an opera, I decide that this is the time to depart.

"The caterers probably need me," I say as I stand.

"Who is coming, dear? I'm afraid I haven't paid attention."

She comes down from her stepladder, puts her brushes on the table and sits in the chair next to me. The inevitability of the party had entered her mind, and that maybe she should take an interest in the small details, a world so different from the clean purity and grandiosity of her tumbling lines.

"There'll be forty guests. Jullian is next to you on the right, Karl on the left."

"And you?"

"Right across. Dolores on my right, Carolyn and Hilliard down on the left."

"It will be fun to talk to Jullian. This is a very French table, both of us in the middle."

"You might want to know that Jullian has won another prize for her cello concerto. I haven't heard from David Lawston, but I'm leaving a space for him in case he arrives at the last minute."

"David. Your old inamorata."

"Unkind of you. It was so many years ago. The spark is long gone."

"We'll see. Who else?"

"Sybille, Carolyn Aarp, Johannes Adler, young Parchment and his friend who owns a winery."

"Who's in the kitchen this time?"

"Lilli. You remember her from last year."

"Good, I like her. Everybody remarked on her food."

"And five others, all attractive young people to wait on table. Walter Burley knows what we like."

"You're a good host, Graham. Thanks for not making this a surprise party."

"I don't like surprises either. Six-thirty is curtain time. Cocktails and hors d'oeuvres."

I walk back across the lawn to the portal with the table, now set with silver, napkins, glasses, unlit votive candles and the ten bouquets from Juan Carlos. There is a hush of expectation about a set table, waiting for the invasion of guests like Rome waiting for the arrival of the Visigoths. All is quiet now, not even a hint of the horses' hooves in the distance or the clang of swords.

16

Matching Gray Overcoats

1973

The pattern of life at El Molino was of separateness, each part of the Prosper family living in their own houses and studios, creating projects and, as the weeks went by, seldom getting together. Each could have been in a separate state, miles away. Of course, there were always the winter feasts, Thanksgiving and Christmas, when the extended family gathered at the old house. Lovers, spouses and friends were included, but during an average week there were no parties, no get-togethers. With some surprise then, Graham got a call from Wingrave, inviting him for cocktails at the studio. Five o'clock. No, neither Celia, nor Karl, nor Mikal were to be included.

Wingrave heard Graham's footsteps and came to the door. He was now well over seventy years old, with few traces of slowing down or giving in to the process of aging. Graham had forgotten how dramatic the interior of his studio was, the outside Craftsman style with its dark shingles and deep overhangs making one think it was small and low. The peak of the ceiling must have been twenty-four feet high and the north studio window came right up to the crossbeam, the view across a meadow with foothills and high mountains beyond. Wingrave's easel looked insignificant against the window, rising to barely a third the height of the glass panes.

One after another, Wingrave's studio cats were named Caravaggio. The current one was a mouser like his forbears, a broad-headed tomcat with short black hair and yellow eyes. There was a row of small canvases hanging beside the window with the portraits of the earlier three Caravaggios, all black and yellow-eyed.

While Wingrave mixed a scotch and soda for each of them, Graham walked over to the easel. On it was a full-length portrait of a woman in a white dress, standing against a wall of ivory-white damask drapery. Her long auburn hair was tied simply with a ribbon and she stood with her hands at her sides, one holding a wildflower. It resembled a Whistler portrait that Graham remembered from the National Gallery. Karl had mentioned that a woman had been coming to Wingrave's for sittings and he was now finished working from life, refining and embellishing. The portrait was the striking result of a painter working at the zenith of his abilities, paint applied with a bold sureness. The deep red hair shone as it moved as if in a breeze.

"It's beautiful, Wingrave," Graham said.

"Almost done. A few more hours on the fabric highlights."

"You are undiminished. Are you calling it 'Symphony in White'?"

"A good eye, Graham. Whistler did it first, but maybe I have done it better."

"Who is she?"

"Her husband owns my New York gallery. This is to be his birthday present to her."

They talked some more about the painting and Whistler. But Graham knew that this was not why Wingrave had summoned him for a cocktail. Wingrave stood up to get more ice, freshen their drinks.

"So, Graham. I want to leave this studio in my will to you. You can use it after I am gone, make it your own."

"A surprise, Wingrave. Why?"

"I was a son-in-law in the Garcia family, just as you are in the Prosper family—not an easy place to be. I think this will establish you in the eyes of the others as the head of the family when Parchment and I are gone. Like passing on the orb and scepter."

"Surely it belongs to Roberto or Karl?"

"No. I have already provided houses for them, as well as Artemis and Celia. Mikal and Paloma will get other bequests as they grow older."

"I'm trying to think whether or not I want to be head of the Prosper family."

"You are, merely by your nature. It's not a matter of want."

"May I tell Celia?"

"No. I want it to be unexpected. I bought the land from Uncle

Parchment when we built the houses, so it's free and clear from the Garcias and their lawyers when I go."

"You're the picture of health. Death will be a long time away."

"Who knows?"

As Graham walked back, he knew that he had grown weary of El Molino and its little dramas. He was anxious for it to be summer, when he and Karl could pursue the trail of Odilon Redon, trying to pry out an anecdote or first-person observation that he might use. It would also mean that the two men would be together June through August, a time for love without another Prosper eye watching. He was about to talk to the travel agent about plane tickets when his studio phone rang before he could pick it up. It was David Lawston.

"Graham, Marjorie is dead."

"Oh, David. How awful."

"She was hiking up near Mount Wilson. Fell four hundred feet."

"I'm so sorry."

"The funeral is tomorrow. Will you come, be with me?"

"Of course."

David met him at the airport and they drove straight to the funeral. Most traces of the Balboa Island young man had gone, replaced with a grown man whom Graham would have turned his head to notice on the street. Graham kept looking his way as they drove, hoping not to make David feel uneasy.

For Graham the beautiful small church in San Gabriel now meant death. A large group of their friends was there, men and women whom David, Graham and Marjorie knew in their Pasadena primary schools, and the other professors and their wives from Caltech. The recessional organ music brought up tears. The whole assemblage walked behind the hearse over to the burying ground next door and watched as the mahogany coffin was lowered into the perfectly cut grave, the trappings of death a professional enterprise in Southern California. Graham tarried with the other mourners, promised to come back for a proper visit, answered questions about his books, disclaiming any notion of fame. New Mexico was so far away, so different, they said. How could he have so completely given up all his friends in Pasadena?

His father and Aunt Ella waited until all the others had gone. They looked the same as he remembered them, in their matching gray overcoats for the unseasonal chill. Ella asked if he had time to stay with them for a while. His old bedroom was ready and they could catch up.

"David asked me to stay with him," Graham answered.

"Of course. We understand."

Ella could not hide the hurt that welled up in her eyes. Graham tried to remember a time when he had not wounded his aunt by his neglect, leaving undone those things he ought to have done. That happy time must have been when he was quite small, when she took over the Christmas dinners, baking the Swiss plum pudding with the hard sauce that gave him a headache. He was a good boy back then and she was a happy aunt.

Graham could smell Marjorie on the pillow in David's bed as they lay there waiting. They had turned out the bedside light and were silent. There had been no tears, but Graham knew that David would mourn Marjorie in a personal way when he was gone. After the two men made love, after the reborn memories of roiling nights at the beach, Graham knew that this was not a place for him. He had forgotten how overpowering David's body was, so much larger than Karl's. His chest was still firm and his warm breath had the same allure, but too many years had passed. There was no flame in the embers, no wind to bring them alive.

"Can you stay on for a few more days, Graham?"

"My ticket is for tomorrow."

"Maybe you can come back. I've missed you so."

"I've missed you." It was what David wanted to hear, and maybe what Graham wanted to say as well.

When he arrived back at El Molino, Celia knew what had happened with David without their talking, but Karl did not. It was better to say very little, and that in platitudes and clichés. Celia always knew it when he withheld the truth, but it did not matter. Mikal asked if he could come with them to France, but Karl told him it would be better to wait.

"We have to drive all over. Maybe next year when we'll stay in one place."

They did drive all over France, starting in the Medoc. There they visited the vineyards at Peyre-Lebade, source of several iconic Redon paintings, the chateau already converted into one of the Rothschild Estates. Then down to Languedoc, where the abbot of Fontfroide showed them the library decorations of *Night and Day*, long panels amid the bookshelves.

Afterwards, they drove to Brittany and finally to the village of Bievres, southwest of Paris, where Redon lived his last years. None of these visits were productive for anecdote or interviews. Graham was now fully convinced that his first approach to this Symbolist painter was correct—an unstructured book, without a timeline. How else could he depict the painter of such different motifs as smiling spiders, Cyclops, Oedipus, Standing Buddha, Sitting Jesus and flower-covered walls?

Back at the Hotel des Saints Pères, the men settled in for the month of August. Graham searched for what he could find at museum libraries and archives, which was little and unorganized, like the man himself. Maybe the Redon book was a mistake, but he pressed on, hopeful that something could be salvaged from the summer. Could he write a whole book about the decorations at the abbey? They were the most memorable part of the summer, commissioned decorations that rose to the level of art. Decorations of Bonnard's and Vuillard's had done the same, become important paintings in themselves. Maybe that was the book, decorations that rose to become art. There must be many more.

Karl had a good start on his next novel, an extended Hispanic family saga of the past century, a story very similar to the Garcia grand-uncles' and their shady dealings at the statehouse in Santa Fe. Karl could remember Uncle Parchment's many accounts of the family forays into the gray area of quitclaim deeds and land condemnation, the Garcia mother lode. He did not need the exact details, because the novel would be disclaimed as a work of fiction, no basis in fact. All of old Santa Fe would know the truth, though—a young half-Hispanic writer exposing his own family, paying back some long-held grudge.

"Will Uncle Parchment be angry?" Graham asked at their favorite bistro as their first glasses of red wine arrived.

"I'm pretty sure yes when he sees the cover with a large, be-wormed apple. The working title is now *Rotten to the Core*. Wingrave will give it a chuckle since the Garcias were always mean to him."

"No more kisses on the cheek from the extended family?"

"I'll be an outcast and a traitor. But it is a rollicking good story."

"What was the worst thing the family did?"

"I think it was the pueblo land they deeded over to themselves in the 1880s. Parchment said it was several hundred thousand acres."

"The pueblo people didn't complain?"

"No, that was the tragedy of it. The few that weren't dead of smallpox had walked away to Zuni. They wanted to forget the old lands and the misery. The Galisteo valley was a land of unhappiness. The acres were there for the taking."

"And what are the pueblos called now?"

"El Rancho Garcia."

That night Graham disclosed to Karl his night with David Lawston. Karl said that Celia told him that she supposed something like that would happen, that Pasadena was a dangerous place for our Graham.

"Your Graham says that it probably won't happen again."

"Probably?"

"The heart can't promise."

"It doesn't matter, Graham. I'm not jealous or upset. What I know is that David needed you and you went to soothe him—to help him grieve. That is not a bad thing."

"I much prefer your body, by the way."

"Just to keep the record straight, I reserve the right to stray myself sometime."

"Sometime? Jesus."

17

Marsala Sauce

24 July 2011, 4:00 PM

The kitchen has worked well for us since we redesigned it. The house that Juan Carlos designed for Wingrave had an adequate kitchen, what any homeowner in the 1970s would want. As our collective incomes rose over the years, Celia and I decided to completely enlarge and improve it. Again using Juan Carlos for the designs, we pushed the west wall out and made a country kitchen big enough for a central table and chairs, a corner fireplace, a six-burner stove with separate wall ovens, and French doors opening onto a vegetable plot. That garden is the one that I have time to tend myself, planting half a dozen different types of lettuces, herbs, spinach, onions, tomatoes, turnips and a few rows of corn.

I don't know where my love of vegetable gardens came from. At my family's house in Pasadena, circled with overgrown camellias and leggy hibiscus, there was not an edible plant in sight with the exception of the grape arbor in back. Perhaps I picked up the gardening fever in my travels. When Karl and I were spending so much time in Paris, we returned day after day to the rows of espalier pears and apples in the Luxembourg Gardens. After that we stumbled upon the potager just east of the main palace at Versailles, with its long rows of root vegetables and lettuces, onions, garlic and more espaliers. Civilization seemed to demand a vegetable garden within walking distance from the source of power. The neater and longer the rows, the higher the civility. I was hooked.

Remembering that grand vegetable patch when we reworked the kitchen, I added the vegetable rows just outside the French doors from the kitchen. Even in winter, I can pull up a few carrots and onions or cut some chives from the bushy row. The espalier apples against the adobe wall require pruning, a mindless task for my odd hours. In summer, there are lettuces and a row of cabbages, looking ever so pleased with themselves. Just like them, I am proud of the potager and the thrifty stamp it puts upon our otherwise overgrown garden.

When Celia and I are alone in the house, I usually cook the dinner. Our housekeeper, Pallida, is there during the day, preparing the lunches that she brings to our studios in baskets. But she leaves for home about four in the afternoon and we have the house to ourselves. I am not an elaborate cook, or a fine one, but I can pull together a pasta dish tossed with fresh vegetables and herbs, a salad and perhaps a baked apple for dessert. We savor the time to discuss the day and our current projects, linger at table with the last of the wine.

Today our kitchen is cleared as if for military action. Trays of entrees and desserts are spread around with waxed paper covers, and Lilli and her helper are washing vegetables. They have brought a basket of many different vegetables, ready for any suggestion or addition.

"Tell me about the chicken paillards," I ask.

"They are partially cooked boneless breasts, simmered in stock actually, sliced open and stuffed with cheeses and prosciutto, and we will grill them at the last minute to a nice brown crust. The red pepper and tomato coulis is to be drizzled on top, with a topping of a blade of salt grass."

"They won't be dry, will they?"

"They shouldn't be. But we can prepare a white sauce with a touch of Marsala to be sure, drizzle the coulis on top of that."

"I like that idea. What else?"

"You said you wanted carrots among the vegetables."

"I really like the way they look, and, just as important, the way they taste."

"We'll simmer them, leave them slightly crunchy, toss with butter and parsley."

"And the rice?"

"Rice pilaf with a smattering of wild rice for looks."

"I'm getting hungry already."

18

A Thin Book

1975

Karl gave Mikal a gift of two horses, Homer II and Rio, so the brothers could go riding together in the foothills behind El Molino. Karl hoped that it might bring back the time when they were closer, when the stables were full and the whole family rode up into the hills on summer days. It was one of the good memories, the children racing ahead of Dolores, looking like the Queen of Spain on a horse, and Wingrave. Mikal now spent most of the day grooming the animals and bonding with them, even sleeping in the stable when Homer II had a respiratory infection.

There were only finishing touches left for Karl's book, and when his books were complete he always felt restless. Even the horses could not allay his malaise. He spent more and more time in the few bars that Santa Fe had at the time, including the Senate Lounge. It was a disco and the meeting place for gay men, many coming up from Albuquerque and down from Taos on Saturday nights. Graham, although he often was asked to join Karl, never felt comfortable there and always asked to be left out.

Besides, Celia was pregnant and Graham felt a rush of responsibility for his upcoming role as a father. The worlds of his two loves never seemed farther apart and more in conflict. Karl took an attraction to Fred Barrister, a baritone with the Santa Fe Opera who was overwintering in New Mexico. He came many nights to the log house, where Karl installed a new Steinway for him. Mikal, who was not happy with the new arrangement, spent nights at the bunkhouse in the stables, much to the pleasure of Homer II and Rio.

As her time neared Celia's doctor told her that they were going to have twin girls, and the full reality of parenthood loomed. There was an extra bedroom in their house which Juan Carlos readied for the girls, in shades of blue despite their gender. Juan Carlos said as long as he was asked to bring things together, pink was out. A local artist painted great banks of cumulus clouds and flocks of migrating birds on the wall beside each crib.

And the question of names for the girls arose. "I don't like the women's names in my family—Dolores, Efrimelda, Paloma, Artemis and Benefacia," Celia said.

"Ella, May, Estelle and Dorothy from mine," answered Graham.

"Let's send a questionnaire to our friends."

"I'll get it ready today."

It might have appeared unfeeling for them not to come up with the names themselves, but the bohemian disregard for convention appealed to them. They laughed and laughed as they thought of the names for the friends to choose among. This is the card that they sent out:

WE NEED YOUR HELP

The twin girls to be born to Celia Prosper and Graham Obermann on or about 28 September need attractive names.

Theodora
Beatrice
Brunnhilde
Oratoria
Boadicea
Calliope
Gertrudis
Innesfallen
Diadem
Caterina

Mendenhall
Chesterilla
Springalla
Infloresca
Frankincensa
Courtney
Fallbrooke
Ludmilla
Persephone
Tatiana

Sylvana
Irmalinda
Farthingale
Tutu
Warroad
Thankful
Turalura
Inspirata

Select two...or write in your choice:

Dolores was too distressed to call Celia on the phone but wrote them an immediate letter, accusing them of disrespect for the hallowed state of motherhood and ignoring the many lovely family names available. Paloma and Artemis thought it very amusing and chose names from the list. Roberto thought it was not amusing, did not choose. Mikal did not understand. Wingrave made no response at all. But their friends came through, ignoring the facetious suggestions and writing in (they must have conferred among themselves) with Morris and Margo. The parents were delighted. Morris and Margo it would be.

The twin girls were born on their appointed day, and from the start they were healthy girls, happy in their own company. This was just as well, because Celia was an impatient mother, not really content being with infants, even her own. Anxious to be back at the easel, she let Dolores interview the candidates for both a nanny and a cook. A very suitable Hispanic spinster was found for each position, Lucy for the nanny and Pallida for the cook. That winter Graham and Celia established a pattern of being with the twins for an hour before dinner, then having them whisked away to the nursery as the sun set. The English way of child rearing was reborn on Upper Canyon Road—love, but not too much.

Celia returned to her studio with a vengeance, going there early in the morning and staying until nanny time. It was not that she and Graham were unloving, but that their other loves were too strong. Whereas most couples took great pride in creating children, Graham and Celia put them on the list of their real creations—but well below their paintings and books. It would prove lucky that Margo and Morris were twins, looking after each other as soon as they could in this odd household and all but raising each other.

Graham decided to convert his Redon book from a biography to an entire volume about the decorations at the abbey library. The abbot had given him all the back-and-forth correspondence regarding the commission, and the archive at the Art Institute of Chicago sent him a bulging file on the matter. To Graham, the abbey murals were the high point of the artist's life, and more than any single other painting they displayed his genius for symbolism and ambiguity.

It was a thin book, but Mallstone Books accepted the manuscript with enthusiasm and hired French photographers to capture the murals in close detail from many angles at differing times of day. The editor wrote saying that this was surely the future of artist biographies, dividing out pieces or eras of a painter's life and subjecting those to microscopic scrutiny. He asked Graham to consider other books that might parallel this idea and please notice the increase in your advance check.

Spring found Karl and Graham waiting for the start of Fred Barrister's concert of art songs at the Loretto Chapel. The baritone would sing Schubert and Benjamin Britten with piano accompaniment. The audience was small, filling only the front rows and a sprinkling of seats behind, where the two men sat.

"Fred's worked hard all winter on these songs," Karl said. "He'll hate it that so few people have come."

"I never much liked art songs myself, too many herzen und himmel hochs," Graham said.

"An acquired taste, I guess. Like Fred himself."

"I haven't seen the two of you for several weeks. How are things going?"

"Not well. I'm a bad lover."

"Why do you say that?"

"I've fallen out of love. Fred doesn't interest me anymore."

"Did you have a fight?"

"Not exactly. I've wondered if any performer, particularly an opera singer, can ever get off the stage. He needs constant adoration. Even after making love, he waits for my applause."

"Wasn't that all there when you first met him, before he moved in?"

"I'm stupid, Graham. I should have seen that, but I didn't."

"It doesn't make you a bad lover."

"I've been putting it off. After the concert, I'm telling him it's over."

"Will Fred be upset?"

"I don't think so. He has his sights on someone with the Met in New York."

"Maybe you and I should spend the summer in France."

"Could we? I've made a bad mistake."

"The music is starting. I'll buy our plane tickets tomorrow."

19

Dependent Clauses

24 July 2011, 4:15 PM

As I leave the kitchen and walk across the living room, I see a copy of Karl's latest book on the side table. We have each written many books over the years, our writing lives intertwined and supportive. We have been equal partners for so much of the time, reading each other's manuscripts, commenting and making suggestions. Karl said he often got ninety percent of a new book written in France, the last ten percent in the log house during the winter. Even this summer, after Celia's party, we plan a couple of months of writing in the South of France.

It has been an arrangement that has worked so well for both of us, leaving El Molino and all its responsibilities for the summer in Europe. I am still envious of Karl's ability to write his books by hand, a simple stack of yellow paper notebooks and a good pen the only requirement anywhere in the world. I, on the other hand, always have to cart around the portable typewriter with ribbons and carbons, and in the recent years a laptop, portable printer and extra batteries. Whichever way, we usually finish the summer with our books almost complete. Maybe this was part of what made our attraction to each other last—that love was a treasured side dish instead of the featured entrée. By not putting our whole weight on the durability of love, we were able to glide through the difficult patches, our work more important than the sex. Successful night vision for the soldier, Karl told me, depended on his not looking too long at the same thing, lest it erase itself from the eye.

I open Karl's book and ruffle through the pages. It is the novel that he wrote last summer about a man and a woman who find love more delectable in its second recasting, "mature fire" as Karl calls it. My writing is more straightforward, no lingering dependent clauses and paragraph-long sentences like Karl's. He is a florid writer, his mind taking the reader through divergent pastures which at first do not seem to relate to the story but slowly make sense, giving a broad understanding on several levels. His reviewers often refer to his grandiose, baroque style, delighting the reader with an ornamental procession of words. His publisher now incorporates the sketches from his manuscript pages into the printed volume, and they have become an anticipated feature of his books, sometimes utilized in the design for the cover.

I sit down to read a few pages and remember the hot days on the Cote d'Azur when Karl read out loud this section from the manuscript to a group of us after dinner as the air cooled. The narrator of this book, a journalist, was hoping to start writing novels, a solitary pursuit unlike the camaraderie of story sessions with other journalists and editors in the newsroom. It proved to be more lonely than writing tomorrow's lead article. I think Karl has caught the idea of an older man coming to grips with a second career and a second love, each with their problems.

There will not be another love for me, I am sure. Where would I find another such multi-sided creature, a precious stone with myriad facets? When something happens to me, I have separately told Celia and Karl to go on, to find new loves. They both have replied that they would carry on alone, but I have my doubts. Being loved and loving is too much a part of them, too vital to their creative days. If it is not me beside them in the difficult patches, they will find others to warm that chair. I wonder if they will share a new companion as they have shared me.

Karl continues to fill my sexual imagination, always a new part of him to discover. It must be what the geishas were taught with care, to parcel out delights in slow procession, to lengthen the sensual night. I have become complicit in this, not rummaging around for secrets beforehand but waiting for Karl to reveal them in his own way. I am the audience and he the impresario. It is only recently that I realized I have been doing the same for him, waiting with impatience to disclose when the time was right. The compulsion to have an answer to the mystery remains, to see the smile behind the fan. It may be the engine of love.

20

Blood Orange Sauce

1978

In the months after it was published, the book on the Redon decorations proved not to be a bellwether in the world of writing biography. Reviewers were unanimous in deriding it, one saying it was a thin book in every regard, from ideas to the actual prose. Another called it stilted and academic, so unlike Obermann's previous work. What is the world coming to when a respected art historian picks a subject of which he knows nothing and writes even less about it asked a third.

Henry Mallstone wrote Graham personally to explain that the reviewers were wrong, as usual, and we on the Avenue of the Americas still love you—we hope that you are still interested in your idea of a book solely about Bonnard's landscape paintings from his house Le Cannet. A thoughtful good offense remained the best defense. In a perverse response to the bad reviews, sales of the Redon book remained quite healthy throughout the winter.

Fred Barrister, the baritone, stayed on for a while, trying to rekindle a life with Karl. By the following spring he had moved on, the harmonies of the Prosper family proving too complicated for his well-pitched ear. Karl and Graham spent the winter retuning their life together. Without mentioning it to Karl, Graham concluded that Karl's forays with other lovers, first with the Vietnam War veteran and then Fred Barrister, were his response to the developments in Graham's and Celia's life that threatened him, made him feel unloved. Their marriage and then their becoming parents each brought up a new person for Karl to take into bed. An action would always get a reaction, the laws of physics working the same way in matters of love. Graham was learning that he must take more care with this fragile brother, unlike his very strong sister.

Mikal was excited to be included in the next French summer, finding a neighbor boy to tend the horses while he was gone. The three men flew overnight to Paris, rented a car and drove south along the Rhone and then eastward over to Cannes. Graham was eager to drive by the Bonnard house even before they looked for a place to stay. It was the weekend of Pentecost when the French close up all businesses, a bank holiday to celebrate the arrival of the holy wind. Young girls in high-necked white dresses crowded the street in front of the chapel on the way up to the Bonnard house as the church bells gathered the faithful. While they waited for the street to clear of the giggling cygnets, Mikal asked Graham what it was about the house he wanted to see.

"I've read that it had been boarded up for twenty-some years while the French courts decided about the estate. Mostly, I want to see the view from the house."

"We're going up and up. There should be a great view."

"He painted sixty versions of that view. Sometimes with the horizon blending into the sky and others with a misty mountain range."

"I think we're there."

From where they parked on the street they could see that the house was metal-fenced and boarded up. It looked derelict and unloved. How could the French allow this disrepair, this falling down of such a historic and artistic site? They walked behind the house, higher up on the hill so they could see over the house. Graham began to understand Bonnard's appeal for the long-distance view across La Cannet and Cannes, orange-red roofs dotted amid the abundant green trees, old date palms high above the other trees and a purple ridge of mist off in the distance. Like the paintings, there was a mystery alive in the very view.

They drove to Mougins, twenty minutes away, where Karl had found an ad in the *Nice-Matin* of a house for rent. *Whole summer rentals given preference*. The address proved to be off the main road on what seemed a farm road, at the back of 1920s villas and mansions with wrought-iron gates. Agrarian France stood just behind, small fields of shrub-roses amid the unpruned olive trees, clusters of farmhouses along the road. Karl knocked on the door at the address in the listing. A middle-aged woman, still pretty as a schoolgirl, answered the door. When he asked in French about the rental, the woman broke into a broad smile and responded in machine-gun verbiage, gesturing off towards another house farther up the road. Graham understood most of what she said.

"It's not this house," he said to the mystified Karl. "It's the one over there. She will walk us over and show it. Are we Americans? she asked."

"I hope that's not bad," Karl said.

The rental house was not at all similar to the thin walled villas on the main road. It was a true tile-roofed farmhouse at the edge of a terraced olive grove, the yellow-ochre stucco falling off in places to reveal the thick, well-laid stone walls beneath. There were river rocks placed here and there on the roof tiles to keep them from blowing off in the mistral winds and wide stone chimneys stood like bookends. The spring grasses were knee-high and moist as they walked over. The woman opened the door and waved them in. There was a heavy aroma of wood-smoke and wax, the furnishings a mix of antique fruitwood and rustic. There were three bedrooms, one primitive bathroom, a large kitchen with a dining table and a separate sitting room. The ceilings were low and beamed with square-adzed logs. All the rooms at the rear of the house had a door to the outside, to a grassy terrace above the rows of olive trees.

The woman said that her name was Marie Laure Moreau. She and her sister owned the land and they needed the higher rent of the summer so they could make it through the winter. It was no longer possible to make much money from the family olive trees, but they sold the rose blossoms for perfume. If they wanted, she could cook their evening meal for added money. The rent seemed reasonable, but not cheap, for such an unspoiled house and land. Karl said he would take it and paid Marie Laure with a check for the whole summer.

He introduced his brother, Mikal, and his friend, Graham Obermann. Graham and I are both writers, want a quiet place to work on our books, he said.

"But no," Marie Laure said, switching into a singsong English. "My sister is the writer, too. She will be delightful. You will have aperitifs with us tonight? Six o'clock."

The men chose their bedrooms and unpacked their suitcases. Karl's room had its own writing table beside the window and Graham took over the library table in the sitting room. Mikal left open his bedroom's door to the outside as he went out to explore the olive terraces.

"I'm glad Mikal came with us," Graham said.

"Thanks for including him. I'm feeling more and more responsible for him. I didn't know he was so helpless in the world, such a child."

"I can see that now. He's a sweet man, though."

"I've wondered if there are learning disabilities. No one noticed when he was growing up."

"If not the brains, he has the Prosper looks."

"Haven't you noticed how people here look longingly at him, not at us?"

"We're chopped liver. How did that happen?"

Graham started to work that afternoon, writing his impressions of what he had seen at the Le Cannet house. They were fresh and easy to write down. The horizon, the sky, what the nearby houses looked like, the roof colors, the palms, the colors of the Esterel mountains off in the distance. He tried to capture the caught-in-amber quality of the place. Perhaps this book, like the Redon decorations, also should be more subjective, more concerned with unique aspects of the painter rather than the exact chronology and all the facts. He could already see a dozen or so chapters. The Horizon. The Black Clouds. The Mountains Beyond. Faces in the Foreground. The Lack of Mist. It would be necessary to talk to neighbors and people who remembered details. That would come after he finished this outline.

As it got to be six, they walked over to the sisters' house. It was also a farmhouse, but one brought further into the twentieth century. The windows and doors looked newer, the roof not weighted down with rocks against the wind.

"This is Francoise," Marie Laure said.

"Welcome. My sister says that two of you are writers. Alas, we live so far away from the city that I haven't heard of either of you before." Francoise's English was better than her sister's.

"Not surprising," Karl said. "I am a new novelist, but Graham is a well-reviewed biographer."

"Biographies are hard to write. So many facts to honor."

"We both write about artists, painters."

"As do I. Novels about French artists and their loves. How love can transform art."

"Francoise's books are very popular," Marie Laure said. "She works all the day and some nights, too."

"I've had some success. That's why we can live on here," Francoise added.

"They call her a modern Georges Sand."

"I can't wait to read one of your books," Graham said. "Which do you suggest?"

"*Mais non*, they have not yet been translated to the English. German and the Portuguese, yes."

"Karl and I can read French better than we speak French."

"Then I'll give you this one," she said, picking up a volume from the sideboard. "*L'Hôtel du mon rêve.*"

Thus the Mougins summer began. Karl thought that it would be better to turn in the expensive rental car and buy one instead, since they would need a car for the whole summer. The Citroen dealership in Cannes was glad to oblige him, a bright yellow Deux Chevaux, four doors and room for five passengers if you were French and thin. It was the newest color, the dealer said. They might be able to send it home after the summer, Karl said, to give the people back in Santa Fe something to marvel at. Otherwise, they could sell it or maybe the Moreau sisters would let them park it until next year. Anyway, they had this glorious, noisy stick of butter with wheels to ride about in for the whole summer, to unroll the canvas top and tease the admiring local population.

When Graham described his book to Francoise, she had a few names for him to interview, friends in Le Cannet who knew Pierre and Marthe. With an eager, early start the next day, he started on the list. There was a neighbor, a boy before the war, who chopped firewood for the couple's fireplaces. Another neighbor, now in her eighties, could remember Bonnard sketching with a pencil behind the house, huddled there in all weather. She never saw him with a *plein air* easel, though—just the small notebook. A third neighbor had photographs of the painter and Marthe sitting in the garden with their dachshunds under the mimosa tree in bloom—alas, only in black and white. Of course, Monsieur Obermann could use the photos in his book, for a small royalty. The neighbor also said that others might say the Bonnards were friendly, good citizens, but they were not. After all, they were artists.

Graham promised each of the neighbors that there would be a recognition in the forward pages of his book. He kept Celia up to date on his progress with weekly letters, single-spaced on the typewriter. She seldom wrote back, but he did not waver from a letter written every Monday, before any work began on his book. He did not want the other half of his love to fade away, perhaps a wash of guilt at his happy summer away from El Molino and his sensual nights with Karl.

As the days grew hotter, the men drove in the late afternoons, after their writing hours, to Juans-les-Pins to swim several times each week. The Garden Beach Hotel rented them the chairs and umbrellas for the three or four hours of their stay. They chose the three chairs most free from bird droppings and ran into the water. Mikal was the best swimmer of the three, coursing out into the bay with a strong Australian crawl. Karl and Graham swam back and forth in front of the hotel, the waters of the Mediterranean cool as they talked about their writing day. From the afternoons in the sun, all of them were turning a deep brown color and they talked about how in shape they felt, how agreeable their life in Mougins was.

"Mikal was the family jock when we were young," Karl said as they sat under the umbrella, watching him swim away from the shore.

"He still looks fit, running every day," Graham said.

"He loved running up along the river, far from the house."

"You guys had an enchanted boyhood, despite how much you whine about it. Horses, a beautiful house, running in the hills, a talented father, a rich, aristocratic mother, and lovely sister."

"We are shits to complain."

"Joking. I know there was another side. Do you think Wingrave diddled Mikal too?" Graham looked over to see Karl's reaction to his obvious tease.

"Too? I'm not so sure he diddled me."

"Whatever. The full truth might call it a molesting, you boys the victims."

"We survived it."

"Mikal is content when he's here with you. He doesn't even seem bored with us writing all day."

"I've noticed he's taken to driving Marie Laure to the market in the mornings."

"I can hear when they leave. Your yellow car is not a good getaway number—sputter, cough, sputter, cough, varoom."

"But so very stylish."

"Mikal's coming back in. He must have swum a couple of miles."

Marie Laure proved to be an excellent cook, her stews and gratins heartier than the fare at the local restaurants. She personally shopped for their meals—lettuces and fresh vegetables from the open-air market down the hill, meats, wines and cheeses from family shops—while Mikal waited for her in the Citroen. The rhythm of the days had established itself, built around the importance of the two books under way. There were usually enough leftovers for a quick cold lunch, each man rooting around on his own in the kitchen. Work was more important than a fancy mid-day meal. By four in the afternoon, Marie Laure was busy back in their kitchen, her soft humming heard throughout the house.

On bad-weather days, Graham drove over to Le Cannet to observe and photograph the view from above and beside the Bonnard house. Graham had learned to take quite acceptable photographs, professional enough to be included as illustrations for his books. He saw the changes in the sky, the deep black haze that built up over the Mediterranean and the mottled clouds that blew onto shore. Many of the symbolist oddities in Bonnard's landscapes, accepted as his inventions, were there to be seen in real life. Graham was able to divide Bonnard's landscapes into a group painted before Marthe died and a group after. As he looked through the lens he saw the black shadings from a passing cloud that often filled Bonnard's mid-grounds, not purple like the others, but black and ominous. It might be too simplistic to identify grief in the blackness, but he knew that a telling book was possible.

As the end of August neared, the men asked Francoise to join them for one of Marie Laure's meals. The table was set up on the first terrace, a white tablecloth and votive candles for the occasion. They started with a fish and potato soup and progressed into a series of Marie Laure's gratins, a squash and corn kernel one, a tomato and cheese one with anchovies, an onion only one, and a sausage and Swiss chard one. It was getting dark as they finished, sipping their inky-black Nicoise coffees.

"Marie Laure has become very fond of all of you," Francoise said. "She imagines that you are lost members of our family, cousins we never knew we had."

"We are the family of writers ... except for me and Mikal, of course," Marie Laure said.

"So the two of us have talked," Francoise continued. "We wonder if you might wish to buy this house? We need to sell it, but we couldn't see anybody else living in our grandfather's house."

"I would love to buy it," Karl said, almost before she could finish. "I've got the extra money now, but it would have to belong to all three of us, Graham, Mikal and me, if we can take title that way. Of course, it does depend on the price."

"Splendid. It will be the good price for you. Thirty thousand dollars. I will set it up with the lawyers. Marie Laure has promised to look after the house during the winters, when you're back in the states. Like she always has. You don't need to worry about its being a burden."

Karl opened a new bottle of wine and proposed a toast, struggling in his French to construct a sentence about a new family of three writers and their brother and sister, happy in two houses for time beyond time. After applauding his linguistic lacework, the sisters walked back to their house and Karl turned to the other two, all in smiles.

"I'm so happy," he said. "What a great summer."

The next afternoon he telephoned Roberto at the Great River National and made arrangements for payment to be sent when Francoise's lawyers requested. Roberto said he was envious, the summer back in Santa Fe was dry and windy. In spite of the rumors that French real estate transactions were studies in Byzantine unhappiness, the check in U.S. dollars arrived without a bump and the deeds signed. The *Mas Moreau* was now theirs, along with a hectare of olive trees, each tree denoted separately on the deed with a man's name—Patrice, Hectaire, Henri, Victor, Georges and so on. This year's crop of olives and roses, however, would belong to the sisters. Karl had already left the office of the notaire when he wanted to ask why the trees did not have the names of women since they were bearers of fruit.

That week Karl finished his novel, spending a full hour drawing the finis page with an ornate stage curtain and footlights. The book concerned a selfish young baritone who made the life of his lover unpleasant as they travelled together between European opera houses. The baritone comes to an unhappy end, his dalliance turning into marriage with a beautiful but bad-tempered Italian soprano, famous for her sharp renditions of the *bel canto* repertory. The narrator, not unlike Karl, is overjoyed and finds a new friend, docile, broad-shouldered and handsome, on a voyage the long way home through the Suez, Indian Ocean and the islands of the Pacific. Another steamy Prosper tale of love lost, love restored. Karl hummed under his breath as he wrapped the manuscript for *The Curse of Perfect Pitch* in brown paper and twine, ready to be sent off to the publishers in New York. Fred Barrister would find himself very sorry that he toyed with affections of that attractive local novelist at the Senate Lounge.

Mougins now would center their summers, a place from which they could foray out for research, interviews or pleasure trips. The Hôtel des Saints Pères in Paris had served them well for the same purpose, but Mougins was more comfortable for their long days of writing. It was a very urbane, small town, home to many artists, expatriates and the world-weary and Picasso had lived just up the road, For the nights when Marie Laure did not cook, there were a dozen restaurants within a half hour drive.

She cooked for them on their last night in Mougins before they were scheduled to fly back to New Mexico. Again they were out on the terrace as the sun was setting.

"Mikal, you must come back for a Cote d'Azur winter," Marie Laure said.

"Isn't it rainy and cold?" Mikal asked.

"Only for a few weeks. By the end of January sunny weather returns, and gardens start to come into bloom. Spring is very early here."

"Maybe I will. I hate the winter snow in New Mexico now."

"It will be too cold to swim, but beautiful for the walks."

While Marie Laure cleared the table and stayed in the kitchen to prepare her famous soufflé especially for their departure, Karl poured them all another glass of wine.

"Mikal, I believe you've found yourself a sweetie-pie," he said.

"Who?"

"Marie Laure. You both have secret smiles and laughs when you're together."

"Oh, Karl. That's not so."

"May loves October in the South of France. Nothing wrong with that."

"She's just a friend. Francoise can be crabby, and you guys are always working. She's fun to be with."

Graham realized that Karl had stumbled on an obvious bit of truth—that Marie Laure and Mikal felt left out of things, the writer siblings in both families getting the limelight. And they were uncomplicated souls, quick to see the good. If Mikal were the middle-aged man and she the young beauty nobody would think again. People were lucky when they found an empathetic heart, someone who understood. It was not Graham's role to make fun of Mikal, only the task for a brother.

"Karl is way off base," Graham said. "Pay no attention to his teasing. It's always good to find a friend, Mikal. You don't have that many in life."

Marie Laure arrived with the Grand Marnier soufflé before the conversation could continue, but it did not go unnoticed that she served Mikal the first and biggest portion, pouring on extra spoonfuls of the blood orange sauce. Graham thought he could imagine the animated scene if Mikal announced his intentions back at El Molino, the perfect culmination for a routine family dinner. Dolores would hold back tears while Wingrave and

Celia held back their laughter. The others would look down at what was left on their plates.

When Graham returned to El Molino, Celia was overflowing with stories of her work, the new canvases, the New York gallery people who made a special visit and their promise of an exhibit in the fall of next year. Margot and Morris were now three years old and happy young girls. Lucy brought them over to the studio for a one-hour visit every afternoon to watch their mother at the easel. Life still had the cool overlay of British upper class at El Molino, where no crisis in the nursery impinged on the adult lives at the other end of the house. That's a lovely poem, dears, now let your beloved Lucy take you to bed.

"Since you're back, we'll alternate afternoons with the girls," Celia said.

"What fun," Graham said, with little conviction.

21

Scarab Eyes

24 July 2011, 4:30 PM

I put down the book of Karl's I have been leafing through. His novels tell a great deal about him. He is a romantic, through and through, respecting those characters who make a success of love and life. Those who do not get a range of punishments, like marriage to an irritable Italian or assignment to consulate in the Upper Congo. The hearty and loving always prevail and the mean-spirited get their reward, as Jane Austen might well appreciate. Most of reading America must have felt the same way, because his books sell in the millions, a large photograph of the handsome author always on the back cover. I wonder how it is that Karl and I have been in love for so long. Perhaps ours is a country-dance, one coming forward with a bow, the other retreating with a smile. Backwards, forwards, always on the move. Where will you go next, my love?

I understand better why Celia and I have stayed together. There is a true electrical difference between us, like negative and positive ions, one always a challenge to the other, sometimes with almost a buzzing sound. If I describe a scene of joy and happiness in one of my books, she will suggest that there is sadness lurking in the corners, the possibility that things are not in the full sun. We do not argue about insignificant household matters, but only the very important concerns of aesthetics. Have I gone too far here, should you stop the painting where you are, could I improve this section or is it wise to leave this subject unresolved? She can hear the words I cannot and I can see the painting matters that pass over her head. Maybe we really are that consummate artistic couple that Hilliard portrayed in his coffee table book, both of us looking prescient and mysterious as we lounged about this very room. Move over Clara and Robert, Frida and Diego.

This living room has served for many years as our private gallery for Celia's paintings and sketches. I keep at least two of her newest series hanging in the two places of honor, above the Chinese altar table at the end of the room and between the windows on the west wall. The LaPlace Gallery has complained, wanting the new pieces sent without delay to New York, but we allow them to move on only when our room is finished with them. Perhaps her paintings are like the green pears grown at El Molino, needing time inside the house to ripen to their succulent best. They are perfectly lit by overhead spotlights dimmed so the paintings glow ever so slightly lighter than the walls. Juan Carlos has become a master at lighting, spending hours correcting details each time we change the canvases. Celia and I often have cocktails in the room, savoring the new pieces before I start to prepare our dinner. She says she practices just glancing at them as she walks through, a snapshot for her right brain to absorb and critique.

I pace around the room, correcting the placement of furniture—adjusting a pair of chairs too close together, turning on the table lamps, opening a window, moving the Buddha Holding Back The Sea a bit forward and pushing back a bowl full of Egyptian faience scarabs that has worked its way too close to the edge of the altar table. I think of our time in Thebes, Celia ill from an innocent-looking but powerful tomato salad while Karl and I hired a car and driver for the day. We drove out along the Nile to the lesser pyramids, the ones built of mud bricks now melting away, with stone retaining walls where crocodile and ibis glyphs are still visible. The next day Celia was still sick in bed, so Karl and I hired a felucca for a trip along the river to an abandoned terraced garden with palm trees and overgrown flowering shrubs, fragrant in the hot air. While the felucca men waited for us at waterside, Karl and I found a secluded stretch of grass on a terrace of palms to make love. We stayed until sunset, sailing back to a dock filled with Eye-of-Horus and scarab vendors, pushing and imploring. The gauntlet along the dock left me the proud owner of a basket full of the turquoise-glazed beetles of all sizes and many happy vendors, counting their one-dollar bills. I think of that palmy terrace of Thebes and the water aromas of the Nile every time I come near the altar table, the scarab eyes looking up at me as I pass.

The living room is all in order for the guests who will arrive in a couple of hours. We will have cocktails in this room, with Walter Burley's servers passing trays of canapés and refilling drinks. The sound of voices will grow louder and louder, Jullian sitting down to play something obscure at the piano....a song and dance from Mompou, perhaps. I will prop open the French doors to the terrace for a fresh breeze, the evening promising to be cool. But now all is silence, with a sense of readiness and waiting.

I suppose if I had lived in ancient times I would have made a decent oligarch — not a thug or a bully, but a benign leader looking after the well-being of everyone on his island. I do that very thing here every day at El Molino, ensuring the placid progress of our lives. I'm the one who hires all the people who work here, pays them when Fridays come around, supervises how they rake the gravel driveways and prune the fruit trees. If a roof leaks, I call the roofer. I hire the man who brings the apple-wood down from the orchard prunings, ten separate loads for all the houses, stacked neatly away from the rain, I see that the chimneys are swept of the black matter before the winter. If a tree falls in a windstorm, I find a man to cut it up and haul it away. El Molino looks as pristine and groomed as when I first saw it, maybe even better.

I wonder how that has come to be. Uncle Parchment's death left an opening, a power vacuum, that none of the other men wanted to enter. In his time, Wingrave rarely left his studio, Roberto lived elsewhere, Karl was not interested, Mikal was too young and none of the Prosper women chose to step up. It was left to the bookish son-in-law to take over. Who would move into my place when I was in the camposanto? Probably nobody. Would the roof leaks go untended and apple trees unpruned? A piece of land needs an oligarch. On a recent day Karl, afraid I was growing heady with my powers of husbandry, said that they were lucky to have their persnickety old poofter. Faint praise lives a good life at El Molino.

There is a rumble of thunder in the distance and a light sprinkling of rain. I am hoping that the storm will follow the summer pattern and disperse by the time of the party. As if my thoughts were heard, there is closer clap of thunder, the rain clouds moving our way.

22

La Colombe d'Or

1980 and 1982

The book on Bonnard's Le Cannet landscapes earned rave reviews from the same critics who panned the Redon book, the tides of biography at full flood. Insightful, intriguing and well researched, they said. Mr. Mallstone proposed a book tour for Graham, two weeks in the United States and two weeks in Europe, where the French and German editions were already starting to sell. Graham asked Celia if she would like to join him, a continental vacation, if on a somewhat frenetic carousel. Celia declined, the new series for the London branch of LaPlace Gallery only halfway completed. The studio was where she traveled to other lands, she said.

So Karl joined Graham at the end of his European book tour in Germany. There was a museum exhibit of Bonnard at the Haus der Kunst in Munich. The bookseller was located in the next block and Graham's short lecture and book signing were well attended. Bonnard was already on the minds of Munich's citizens.

Karl was at the end of the waiting line. "There's a good restaurant a short walk away. Ox-tail soup and perfect schnitzel, they say. Listo?"

"Am I? Let's go."

"I've rented a car for us. Tomorrow we can drive south, five hours over the Alps to Venice. By Friday we can be at the *Mas Moreau.*"

"That sounds so great. This is definitely the last ever book-signing. Why do I have a rich, novelist lover if not to live off the largesse?"

It rained the next night in Venice, a downpour starting as they carried their suitcases across the Accademia bridge, following the walking directions to *il pensione*. Only a hundred steps from the far side of the bridge, the friendly old man at the car park said, where poets and artists languish. In its rooms people fall in love again. Still a bit out of breath, they dried off instead in the spare-furnished room. A recommended restaurant was close nearby so they borrowed an umbrella from the *signora*. Few other diners had ventured out, theirs one of three tables that watery night. Dinner was a sautéed small fish from the lagoon, head and tail still on, fat green beans, rice from the Po and a strong, aromatic white wine.

Again the night rain brought up nightmares for Karl, the never-forgotten war surging back to life. They both wrenched awake with Karl's single yell and Graham put his hand over on his forehead, cool against the heated skin. After ten minutes of this silent laying on, Karl fell back into sleep. Graham wondered what it was in his hands that could soothe his lover, was it some odd form of the *chi*, more healing than the warlike variety? This assuaging *chi* had worked since the nightmares began, leading Karl to safety back from the humid, deafening jungle. Karl always said that he drove a supply truck in the war, never seeing any real action, but Graham knew there must be more to the story, more than that one terrible night in the rain.

On the first of June, Sunday afternoon, they reached Mougins and the farmhouse. The green bloom of spring was past, the grasses under the olive trees turning to summer straw. While Karl had a novel under way, Graham thought he might recuperate, read some other writers' books for a while before starting his next project.

Mikal had been there a month already. He was reading a newspaper at the kitchen table as Marie Laure prepared the dinner for the expected arrival, a couple content in their own company. He got up when he heard their rented car park behind the canary Deux Chevaux.

The three men and Marie Laure had a slow dinner together, each reliving the time they were away from each other. Graham told them of his book-signings around Europe, the worst at a shop in the bookseller's quarter near the cathedral in Cologne. The first buyer in the line bought all three dozen of the books, asking to have them all signed. The people behind him in line complained but he was adamant. When Graham left after a half hour or so, he passed on the next block another bookshop with a window-sign in German—*Bonnard's Le Cannet Landscapes, Signed*—at twice the price. When Graham went in the owner said all was fair in Germany's market economy.

It was obvious to Graham and Karl that Mikal and Marie Laure had been having a good time together. They smiled at each other as Mikal talked about driving again over to Marseilles for several nights, where the seafood is the best in France. Then they came slowly back through Avignon and the Vaucluse, Aix-en-Province, and a couple of days at the Colombe d'Or in St. Paul de Vence, where the restaurant walls were covered in Post-Impressionist paintings and the water in the pool was a crystal emerald green. Graham wondered if it was just Mikal's trust income being put to such admirable use or were there nibbles into the principal.

After Marie Laure left to go back to her own house, Karl asked Mikal, "Are things getting thick between you and Marie Laure?"

"I guess so. We have a lot of fun together."

"The difference in your ages doesn't bother you?"

"It bothers some other people."

"What does Francoise think?"

"Marie Laure says that even though Francoise makes fun of us, she is jealous."

"I can imagine. Where do you think it will go from here?"

"We might get married. Next year or after that."

"Why wait?"

"She says a long courtship is the Moreau family way."

"Well, god bless." Karl knew that there were several more unusual arrangements in the Prosper family besides an older woman with a younger man. It would not do to throw stones for fear of the large, unprotected panes of glass closer to home.

The design of their summer returned in the next days, Karl writing in the mornings, often right through the noon hour into the late afternoon. He went deep into his fictional world, peopled with the characters who could appear more real than those around him. While he was immersed in it, the universe of his novel glowed with an intense sense of life. And when he stopped writing for the day, it was an abrupt, almost dizzying jolt away into the here and now. It must be how people with multiple personalities must feel, he thought, ripped away from one life and plunged without notice into another.

This would be one of Karl's most popular, well-reviewed books, a story of a brother and sister. He strived to make it a story of all brothers and sisters, but he could not help but make it very like Celia and himself. Although the brother was a writer and the sister an artist, very different pursuits, they struggled with an enduring rivalry for the love of those around them. It was a classic story, falling into place in its entirety in a single summer.

Graham had hoped to spend a month or two reading and resting, but the clarion of writing could not be ignored, particularly while Karl was so involved in his own work. This writing in tandem appealed to both men, as if they were pulling along a large object in unison.

Describing the ambiguous paintings of Paul Signac was slow going for Graham. It was an illusive story, the painter working in many different studios, converting his sketches to elaborate large canvases both in fauvist and pointillist styles. Graham had reproductions of all the paintings, but it was difficult to discern the long line in his work—influences as variable as Gauguin, Seurat and Monet. Graham wondered if the theme to all of Signac's work was a shallow restlessness.

Francoise and Marie Laure invited the three men over for a Sunday lunch. When the sisters cooked together, it was often more refined, traditionally French than when Marie Laure cooked for the men. Lunch was a quiche Lorraine, a green salad with butter croutons and a rice timbale, and the wine was a white Chateauneuf-du-Pape. Graham put their thoughts into words, asking how they had been so lucky to rent and then buy the *Mas Moreau* and meet such endearing culinary talents. Glasses were raised, toast proposed, and the conversations divided the table.

Over the years Graham had come to respect Francoise's opinions on French art. She and her sister as girls had met many of the painters who kept houses in the Cote d'Azur, where pursuits of the intellect were respected. Although the sisters came from a respected family of farmers and olive orchardists, their father was an outspoken anarchist between the wars, a discomfort to his own agrarian father. Painters and writers came to his house for smoke-filled evenings of rebellious talk. The eldest daughter, Francoise, was included at the table, she just old enough to absorb their ideas—on the need to oust corrupt officials, on what governments ought to be, on the folly of war, on what art was, on what music was and on what it meant to be a French intellectual. She accepted early on the importance of this spirited discourse. To question an idea, take it apart, regard it from various angles and resolve the questions that arose was the only correct way to converse.

Graham read her novel, *L'Hôtel du mon rêve,* and found it unlike what he expected. Perhaps the design for all French novels was different from those in English, merely opening up the roof of a house for a while then closing it. A single slice out of a life could make the whole book, nothing much happening, no disclosures at the end, like a salt-grass field in the Vendée, featureless, windy and flat. English-language publishers, both British and American, required the protagonist's character to change, perhaps grow, as a great challenge or moral battles endangered it, and then to digest those changes as the drama concludes, storm seas calm once again. Despite a few unhappy endings, were English-speaking writers more optimistic about the possibilities in life, that people could change for the better? Were the sunny uplands a possibility for everyone? Did the French, on the other hand, expect little from human nature and even less from the lessons of life? Francoise's novel was a slow-moving disappointment, gloom at every turn. It was too early in their friendship to discuss it, so he switched back to asking about his current book.

"What do you think of Paul Signac?" he asked.

"Second-rate Fauvist, but the best of the second," she said.

"I'm writing about him."

"Marie Laure told me so. Why?"

"I'm looking for the common thread among his paintings. A theme, if you will, to organize the book."

"I like his coastal paintings the best. Antibes, Saint-Tropez, even Constantinople."

"I'll take a closer look at them."

"I've read that he had his own small boat, sailed the whole Mediterranean shore making sketches. It is well-known that he loved the water and towns by the seaside."

The next day the structure for Graham's book was clear, an armature waiting to be encased in clay. He also had the title: *Sailboat to Byzantium—The Coastal Paintings of Paul Signac.* It was not exactly from Yeats but close enough. Francoise, always the source for anecdote, knew some people for him to interview, starting with an old painter in Antibes, who as a boy adored Signac and may have even gone sailing with him. There was a woman in Villefranche whose mother rented a house to Signac, sued for damages when it burned down, and a couple who lived in the converted Signac studio, still standing in an unstylish inland part of Saint-Tropez. They were all an easy day's drive in the canary with wheels.

◊◊◊

The three acres beyond the camposanto at El Molino made up the apple orchard, two hundred trees planted by Dolores's father in the 1920s, to honor a dead brother from the Great War. They were old trees now by modern orchard standards, but still producing a profitable crop in the years without a late frost. Graham had once asked Dolores about the orchard and her dead uncle.

"They were small trees when I was a girl. Uncle Maclovio was Parchment's older brother, killed near Nancy in the Great War."

"He was not married?"

"No. He was just twenty-two or -three, I think. He had great promise as a painter, everyone said. I was just eight when he died. I remember he was more handsome than Parchment, but that's all. There are many of Maclovio's paintings out at the ranch house in Galisteo."

Graham suspected that the Garcia family, Dolores's family, harbored many generations of single, artistic uncles who chose not to marry or, perhaps, married only to please the elders, not a guarantee of spousal happiness. Were there as many spinster aunts who chose horseback riding and other manly pursuits over the tedium of the kitchen and the folding of linen? Did the genes that made Celia and Karl come down through the Garcias, blossoming in odd generations and avoiding others?

"How did Maclovio die?" Graham asked.

"A German bomb. Parchment took us to Nancy on our grand tour, and we went out to the battlefield, ten years after the armistice. We thought we came across the very crater, covered with grass and flowers. Wingrave was the one who found it on the map."

"And the apple trees were planted as a memorial in the late twenties?"

"Right after we got back from Europe. The whole family helped. The bare-root saplings were about four feet tall. The men dug the holes and we girls planted them, spreading out the roots. It took about a week."

In their winters at El Molino, Karl and Graham started to take on the renewal of the untended orchard. Since vital pruning had long been ignored, they started work on thirty or so trees a year with helpers from the Galisteo ranch. Opening up the centers, pruning away the water-shoots and top-dressing the root spread with dried sheep manure from Galisteo, the men slowly brought the orchard back. This was the last year of their revival project, and only a light, maintenance pruning across the whole orchard was needed.

At the end of the last day the whole crew—Karl, Graham, Young Parchment and the Galisteo men—were sitting along a fence having a beer to celebrate. Graham thought the orchard was the best part of El Molino, trees now well-formed with the grass underneath making the first green of spring. There was something right about man and trees working together to provide food for El Molino, bushel baskets of the best, unblemished apples for the dozen houses and piles of the pocked ones for cider or a treat for the horses.

"Can I take over the orchard now, Uncle Karl?" Young Parchment asked, his second year of helping the older men. They had taken a warm week in February to finish up the pruning, stacking the sawn limbs and branches to the side. The Galisteo helpers would collect and split them for firewood, enough for all the houses at El Molino.

"I suppose Graham and I are getting too old for this."

"I've been reading about orchards. I'm sure I can do it."

"I know that there are trees several hundred years old down in the town, but these Spitzenbergs may not have many more years," Karl said. "You might think about planting new trees in that open land."

"I will—maybe Granny Smiths and Fujis and Galas. And what about grapes? I've been reading about those too. There's a professor up at Los Alamos, a friend of Mother's who knows about soils, said there is no reason why these decomposed granites couldn't produce a superb white burgundy. The original Chardonnays."

"Don't you think there is too little land, without cutting down the old trees?"

"We have two empty acres. There's a famous two-acre vineyard in Burgundy, one of the best. La Romanée Grand Cru."

"You have been reading."

"Eighty-seven hundred bottles in an average year. A ninety-year-old woman runs the vineyard, with only her two brothers in their eighties as helpers."

"Go for it, Parchment. Karl and I will pay for the vines," Graham said.

"When can we expect the first bottle of El Molino White Burgundy?" Karl asked.

"Six years. I can manage the two acres by myself. And the orchard. I know I can do it with just a little help from the Galisteo men."

Graham could see that this excited Parchment like nothing before, a venture of his own. He had drifted after the death of his father, his mother Olivia moving away from Santa Fe with a new husband and all but dumping Parchment at El Molino. Olivia's mother, the famed aviator, gave him flying lessons, but he was a lackluster pilot. He completed preparatory school, but made no plans for college. When Graham helped him plant a vegetable plot, Parchment found how much he liked to work with the soil. He supplied the extended family with corn, squashes and heirloom tomatoes for the summer months. This would be a major jump ahead for him, directing the orchard and a new vineyard at El Molino.

23

Disinherited Dowagers

24 July 2011, 4:45 PM

I check the portal to see if the rain has blown in on the table. The young waiter, Josh, is already there, wiping the few raindrops off the chairs. Another helper, Candy, I believe, is walking around the table, straightening the knives and forks, adjusting the spacing between the chairs. The redolence of rain is strong and I can hear the faraway thunder of storms coming our way.

It is a handsome table, but I notice for the first time that it is angled across the centerline, slightly askew from the portal, perhaps eight inches off. It is impossible to correct at this late time—another little gift from Allah, who shows us once more that perfection is his alone, that we must learn to live with imperfection.

The silverware on the table comes from all over the world, trips with Karl where we searched the back streets for antiquarians on the days when we were not writing. There were never many sterling pieces to be found at one time, six forks tied together with a ribbon or a stack of spoons with differing initials that could be easily stashed away in airline luggage. There was a set of forks and knives with the engraved initials *R de R*, from a shop in the Loire, perhaps lifted from a chateau in the deep pockets of a disgruntled scullery maid. A dozen spoons came from a Santa Fe friend who collected them in small towns in Sussex and Kent, selling them on the front lawn on his return home to pay for his English summer idyll. A great many forks were discovered at Mrs. Bishop's shop on a back road in Barbados. She sold crystal and silver from English families who came to grief on the island, her cats watching from on high as we inspected the backsides for London hallmarks. Three knives were side-by-side in a shop window in Bergen, and coin-silver forks, easily bent, waited for us in a Zurich shop window. Several full settings came from the slender old shopkeeper in Sena Plaza who went by the name of Rare Things, his shop and himself—good Philadelphia fiddle, thread and shell. There were a few pieces of hotel silver with the plate wearing off, *Le Splendide* in block letters on the handle, and stout knives from an old painter's estate sale, her too-distant relatives too distant to attend.

Each piece jogs the memory of our summers driving the Citroen about Europe and elsewhere. How often Karl and I thought that we had discovered the secret to joy that the rest of the world did not know, laughing at our luck. We alone knew the answer to the riddle, love watching us with pride from the back seat. Karl wrote ten novels in our summers together, and I got the better portion of eight biographies finished. Still we had time to poke around for such treasures as spoons and forks, to have bistro dinners with sliced black truffles and several thousand glasses of country wine. We drove the coughing yellow apparition as far north as Norway and east to Turkey, discovering the coast of Antalya when only the fishermen still owned the waterfront, disinherited Polish and Russian dowagers sunning among the houseplants on the few apartment balconies. The Citroen in the ship's hold amused the Greeks greatly as we ferried from island to island, sputtering across the hilly uplands to the best beaches on the far side.

And at El Molino I have the very real reward of the unmovable feast of a life with Celia, each of us in our studios during the day, a coming together at nightfall. Starting when our girls were nine or ten and home from school, we had dinners at the kitchen table. Celia spoke to them in French, asking them to respond, and I read aloud from my latest chapter, picking sections that might appeal. We listened about the injustices of their lessons at school and asked if the Sisters of Loretto discussed matters of art as well as those of faith. Of course there were evenings of discord, but I remember us as the Family Beautiful, everything in its place. Both Karl and Celia accuse me of remembering nothing but the better parts, winnowing out the chaff.

I wonder why memories are so close this afternoon, as if a thick layer of nostalgia comes down with the rain, bringing along the aromas of the past. I think I can smell my childhood, the very distinct scent of chalk and erasers, and the vinegary bosoms of the teachers. There is a hint of the malodorous soap Father concocted from a Swiss recipe—a long-simmering dark-brown mess on the stove, astringent and animal. Jacaranda trees, everywhere in Pasadena, bloomed for months on end, intensely sweet but not pleasant. And I am sure there was a whiff of David, musky and inviting like a fresh-turned garden. There are so many remembrances in the simple smell of rain.

24

Succulent Beetles

1983

This summer would be different from the others. At Mougins, Graham worked on his article for *Art News*, an analysis of Bonnard's color techniques. Karl finished his first non-autobiographical novel, a poignant bi-racial love story with his central, recurring family only in the side plots. Mikal kept them company, as well as taking Marie Laure on day-trips along the coast.

Celia flew to England for her solo exhibit at LaPlace London in August, with Karl, Graham and Mikal driving up from Mougins, all four staying at Brown's Hotel. They had the night before the exhibit to themselves, dining late in a nearby restaurant. Graham noticed that the three Prosper siblings still turned heads with their beauty, diners at adjoining tables fascinated, as if unable to identify the homeland of these foreigners, so different from the long-toothed blandness of the English. It was midnight before they walked back to the hotel and went to their rooms, thinking about Celia's reception the next night. It would surely be triumphal, the LaPlace people having already sold the majority of her paintings.

◊◊◊

Early morning in Santa Fe, Wingrave arrived at the usual hour in his studio. The north window light was the best at this time, cool, without the yellow distortions that a direct sunlight could build up later. He heard an airplane overhead, the distinctive sound of a single-engine Cessna. It would be Roberto again and he would zoom down on the studio, annoying the neighbors, prompting calls to and from the sheriff. Roberto had been doing this all week before he went to work at the bank—close flyovers of the studio, rocking his wings as he swooped down. The studio window was high enough for Wingrave to see the cavortings from his easel, and he wondered about his eldest son, what an odd adult he had become. Were he and Dolores responsible for the choices of their children—two or perhaps three of them homosexual, another so obsessed with flying that he endangered his own career at the bank, another a prim philosophy professor, loveless, unattractive, and Paloma, the sweet one, so shy that she hid away, peeking through the curtains when the suitable young men called? Could the parents have caused this or did curious offspring just turn up, like stunted cornstalks in an otherwise healthy row or a single apple branch with small, variegated leaves?

Roberto banked and set up for another loop, the engine sound at first a long way off in the distance, then growing louder and louder. Wingrave turned with brush in hand to look up at the plane, wings rocking, and the dive seemed to be aimed right into his easel. The noise became a roar, and Wingrave turned his whole body to see Roberto plummeting directly at him through the window, large shards of glass and splinters of mullion flying inward. The studio exploded in gasoline-fueled fire, parts of the roof blowing into the air, yellow flames high in the sky, and in the midst of the inferno, there were more explosions from the cans of turpentine, alcohols and thinners. As the wooden structure, integrity gone, imploded upon itself, the trees and grasses near the studio started to burn, a half an acre ablaze. High-octane fuel and painter's turpentine intermingled, father and son dead already in the flames. The fire made curls of dark, black smoke mixed with strands of white smoke from the trees, a horrid wall of patterned marble several hundred feet high.

Paloma and Dolores were shopping in town when they heard the explosion off in the distance. It was merely a sonic boom, said one of the other shoppers, so many military planes overhead now. When the women finished their errands and drove up towards El Molino, they could see the flames and a great mushroom cloud of black smoke. The fire trucks were already there, but there was nothing the firefighters could do except let the flames burn out and prevent the fire from spreading. Juan Carlos joined them and the three watched from the main house portal for hours, speechless as the flames and smoke died down. The telephone in the house kept ringing and ringing, but no one had the heart to answer. Dolores went to her room, leaving the other two on the portal.

"Should we call Celia and Karl?" Juan Carlos asked of Paloma.

"It would ruin Celia's opening night. And Karl or Graham could not help telling her if I talked to either of them. And there's nothing they can do. We'll call tomorrow."

"They will all be devastated."

"It was surely an accident. Roberto just lost control," Paloma said.

"We'll never know for sure."

"Uncle Parchment will not have heard about it, out at the ranch."

"I'll drive out and tell him," Juan Carlos said. "He never watches television and seldom picks up the telephone."

"Ask him to come back for the funeral. I will call Father Diego and set it up for day after tomorrow. Only us in the chapel, then to the camposanto."

"So soon? Won't they want to come back from London?"

"We can spare them if we get the funeral over with."

"What about the family cousins in Santa Fe?"

"We'll do a large memorial later, in the cathedral, for the Garcias and the others. Now, it's just us."

They did not call Celia in London that night, to ruin the elation of her first European exhibit. Nothing more could be done for Wingrave and Roberto, what was left of them soon to lie on the tables of the medical examiner. After Juan Carlos drove out to the country, Paloma went inside to knock on Dolores's bedroom door. There was no answer, so she decided to watch the television news in the living room.

Famous painter dead in plane accident. Reporters have already interviewed the neighbors who had complained in the past, claiming that something bad was bound to happen with such a hothead pilot trying to be a jokester. Another neighbor thinks he heard the plane engine stall and all control of the dive lost. It will be a long investigation, says the nightly news.

There was a late afternoon light in the canyon as Paloma walked around the fire-trucks and the still smoldering studio to the camposanto at the far end of the property. The gate complained with a screech, and she reminded herself to put a can of sewing machine oil into her pocket for the next visit. A noisy gate at a funeral would not be right. This was where the two men would be buried, next to each other for eternity. Paloma wondered if Roberto intended to kill his father, a parricide, or was it as the news reports had it, an aviation prank gone terribly wrong? An accident rather than a murder. Would Wingrave and Roberto hate being there forever, side by side, or would they patch their differences in the slow time of underground? Paloma was sure that the sooner they were in their graves, the sooner the questions would stop.

◊◊◊

The next morning the four in London were having a festive, post-exhibit breakfast in the dining room at Brown's, the maroon curtains pulled back to let in the morning sun. Paloma decided to speak to Graham, her brothers and sister more the ones at risk. Graham picked up the discreet note on a waiter's tray—a telephone call for Dr. Obermann. He was gone for five minutes and returned with an expression that all the siblings noticed.

"The worst sort of news, I'm afraid," he said, gently touching Celia's arm. "Wingrave is dead. Roberto crashed his plane into the studio, killing himself too."

"Oh, lord," she said, placing her hand across her eyes.

"Was it murder?" asked Karl.

"Paloma thinks it was, but the authorities have it as an accident," answered Graham. "She thinks it is better to leave it that way."

"I think an accident is better, too," said Karl.

"And the funeral is tomorrow. We could all just make it, but Paloma says we mustn't try to come back for it. There will be a memorial service later, for the whole family."

"Can they get the bodies back for a funeral so soon?"

"I asked that too. She says that Uncle Parchment arranged it, and they all believe a small funeral is what's called for. And, by the way, Caravaggio has survived the fire. They have seen him hiding under the willows, but he eludes capture."

"I'm going to call Paloma. Excuse me," Celia said.

Later that morning, rather than sitting in the gloom of their rooms, they walked around St. James and Green Park. They sat for a while by the lake with ducks and swans, then walked over to Westminster, sitting in the back pews to listen to a choir rehearsal, Handel echoing up into the empty cathedral. A boat tour of the river was just boarding and they were the last four aboard. It was a warm day and they sat on the top deck, floating under the bridges and past the waterside taverns and apartment blocks to Greenwich. They had an hour to walk around the grounds, lying on the lawn under the horsechestnut trees, clocks marking the quarter hour, the smell of new paint from taped-off benches. It was late afternoon when they returned to the hotel.

Graham wondered if they had made a mistake not flying home for the funeral. Would these deaths always lurk on their minds like roiling clouds on the horizon, no visual memory of the dead inside their coffins and then being lowered in the ground? It may be what funerals were intended for—to place punctuation at the end of the sentence, paragraph, chapter and book—that it was over, this was the end. Period.

A quiet dinner in the hotel dining room seemed called for, rather than one in a fancy restaurant. It was an introspective meal in the now dark room, curtains pulled against the summer evening light and the raspberry-shaded lights at each table giving a dim upwards glow. Celia seemed the most conflicted about her father's death, he for so long the devil she hid away from in her girlhood nights, she never disclosing what had happened. She could not even tell her brothers, who had suffered in similar but different ways. Wingrave was the evil master she must surpass, if not in life then in the world of art. Since he was now gone, had she won the race? It did not seem so, only that he no longer wished to make battle.

Graham thought about an Emily Dickinson line of *All but death can be adjusted*, but kept it to himself, and Karl remembered the snowy nights on the mountain, the son both attracted to and fearing his father, a forbidden secret between man and boy. He had long ago forgiven his father, the maltreatment forgotten, and a pleasant memory of childhood love remained. Why had Roberto reacted so differently to the same misuse, his very soul twisted so far out of shape? Did the brothers' minds process the same information in different lobes, one on the demonizing side and the other on the assuaging side?

Mikal was the one who best put their thoughts into words. "I think Wingrave hurt Roberto more than the rest of us. It must have been really hard for Roberto to keep his hate down inside, hidden away, building up. It just snapped into the open. If we had one or two demons, he had a hundred."

◊◊◊

In the late morning camposanto, the iron gate now oiled and silent, there was a small group of mourners. The brick-walled family cemetery had been blessed by the old French archbishop, he giving the Garcias the young boxwoods and yews from his own nursery garden. They had grown to over shoulder-high along the walls, dark and green. The priest said the Latin words to bless the coffins of the two men, killer next to killed. Artemis was the only out-of-towner at the ceremony, everyone in black. Uncle Parchment brought in three ranch workers to dig the graves and to refill them, tipping them each with the traditional large silver coin.

Paloma thought about how she and Celia played in the burying ground as girls, hiding from each other behind the boxwoods and sitting on the round-topped stones, waiting still and quiet for magpies to hop over the wall, root around under leaves for succulent beetles or crunchy grasshoppers. Despite their being dressed in black for the ceremony, today the magpies were standing off, too much somber activity in their favorite picnic grounds.

Parchment noted that the iron gates for the camposanto had grown rusty and thin, tilting away from plumb in places. Was it time to replace them, to see the family headstones guarded for another hundred years? He would call the ironmongers while he was in Santa Fe, ask them to match exactly what was there. Would there be any Garcia men left when this new gate rusted and fell over, only the gnarled boxwoods to keep out the coyotes? While the ranch hands covered the coffins with dirt, the black-clad family and priest walked back towards the old house in groups of two and three. They stopped talking as they skirted around the charcoaled remains of the studio, only a chimney of scorched river-rock remaining and the pervasive smell of burned wood. A cold supper had been set up on the old house portal, bows of black ribbons tied across every window.

On the walk back to her house after all ceremonies were over, Paloma saw a sparkle in the willows near Wingrave's studio ruins. It was the framed photograph of the young lieutenant, blown clear of the exploding house. She wiped off the glass as she walked and decided to hang it in Karl's log house. It held more memory than she wanted to confront. Caravaggio, now accustomed to his loss and sensing the start of a new chapter, followed her at a discreet delay all the way to the log house, his home in the brown-shingled studio no more.

25

A Clicking Sound

24 July 2011, 5:00 PM

Everything in the kitchen apparently in order, I return to the studio to sit silent, watching Celia at work. She is a tall woman, with all the grace possible from a long frame, but the seven-foot square canvas is too much even for her outstretched arms. She stands in front of the painting on a low ladder, extending her arms to reach the upper corners. The canvas is filling with pale color, grays and blues alternating with milky whites. If it is, as I suppose, a rainstorm, then it is a windy winter storm, the icy strands encircling in the gusts and intermingling as they descend. It is beautiful, shimmering as a translucent curtain with light from behind, ordinary colors engorged with a sparkling life of their own. Despite many efforts to copy her technique, nobody can. It is obvious to collectors and curators when they see a Celia Prosper canvas on a gallery wall that this is important art and there is nothing else like it.

Although her paintings seem to have a rushed, urgent look about them, her work is slow. A single canvas can take a month or more, first with the full covering in color, then repeated refinements, smoothings, adjustments and re-workings. The patterns go around to the sides of the canvas, as if the piece was cut from a quarry wall and polished up to a finish. Every corner is inspected and re-polished, rotten-stoned and rouged, until a part of Celia's brain registers its approval, almost independent of her surface thoughts. She has often said to me that she can hear a clicking sound when that happens, and nothing more is ever needed. When a panel is finished, it glows with a *sprezzatura*—as if it were done on a single sunny afternoon, coming like a wisp of fog right out of the painter's mind.

The ladder makes a strained creak as she works on a section to the far left. It is an old ladder that we had specially designed and built for her, giving her a stable platform instead of a narrow step. The old carpenter, a Garcia family friend, beaded the edges of the steps and sanded the handrails smooth as moonstones, proud to be a supplier to a Garcia studio. He always admired Dolores Garcia's beautiful young daughter, Celia, and could now provide her with a crafted work other than those carved frames for her early sketches.

Often the only sounds as we are together in the studio are my breathing and the ladder's creaking. She comes down to refresh the paint on a brush, then walks up the two steps to continue. It is a vanity of mine to think I have been included, surely by the old gods, as the favored witness to creation. Like a courtier in a royal bedroom, bewigged and buckled, I wait in silence for the sounds of birth.

Today it is Celia most often on my mind, even though the images of brother and sister always mingle together. I create a fanciful story of other times, ancient times, when a commemorative coin might have been minted for this birthday occasion, the oligarch father commanding a special large size, more gold than usual in the alloy. Golden, heavy, with a deeply reeded edge, it portrays a handsome woman with banded hair and a thundercloud background on one side, and on the obverse, a full-lipped athlete's profile within a wreath of olive leaves. Citizens stand in lines for their dispensation, a single free coin for each resident family in honor of the royal twins' attainment of maturity. All the city will hide the coins away in hinged boxes with their other valuables, to remember this high-placed sister and brother and this day when all the shops are closed and linen banners hang across the streets. Precious water is released to flow down the streets and cool them on its way to the harbor. The coins travel father-to-son, grandmother-to-granddaughter for dozens of generations, surviving wars and fires, buried in an earthquake then unearthed, finally spent for food in a desperate time and surfacing today in a fine antiquarian shop in a London arcade. The brown ink, handwritten price tag says—*The Sibling Drachma, No Coin More Rare, From the Ancient Aegean, Ten Thousand Pounds.*

She must have heard my thoughts as she turns to look at me. "You're still there. So quiet."

"Daydreams."

"Of your party?"

"Of gold and oligarchy."

"You're such an odd one."

"Would you like for me to read?"

"Please. Who's the painter now?"

"Braque and his birds."

"Oh, good."

I have a running start on the book about Braque's bird paintings, how the image took over his later years and defined him. The painting I keep coming back to is of the large white bird returning to the nest, a swan or a goose, still free from the earth but about to make connection with the three eggs below, no legs outstretched. Is it sky and freedom relinquishing itself to house and earth? Why should it give itself up? Is it self-immolation? These are the thoughts that have been filling my head when matters of food and table are not there. I start to read the first chapter as she paints.

26

A Glass of Retsina

1988

Both Karl's and Graham's books have been published, the Signac selling well to university libraries and professors, the brother-sister novel high on the best-seller lists. Karl's career as a writer had taken to the stratosphere, each new volume awaited and adored. Even though his novels featured narrators from his own life—the patriarch painter, the money-grasping uncle and the Vietnam vet—the sub-plots were peopled with young people in love, bittersweet and temporary. Readers loved his minor characters and the problems they created for themselves. There were many variations, sometimes with the happy endings, sometimes not. From the beginning homosexual love happened, but to secondary characters on the unlit porches off the main dance floor. Later Karl would bring these into the lighted room, dancing in full view, holding hands on the boulevard, but in 1988, a man and a woman was the thing. Hollywood certainly thought so, buying each new Karl Prosper book without worry.

If Karl's books were on the boil, Graham's were on the simmer. A good run for him would be thirty thousand sales of a single volume. Mallstone Books was proud of its art professor, but their advertising money was spent elsewhere. Mr. Mallstone phoned him at least once a year with the message that he would always have a home at Mallstone Books. Graham guessed it was a comfort that whatever he wrote would be published, even if few read it.

This summer's biography would be of the painter Chaim Soutine. Graham and Karl rented a modern flat in the Montparnasse quarter of Paris, the stomping grounds of Soutine and his close friends, Modigliani among them. No one would have survived there who knew the two, but Graham wanted to absorb the flavor of the area. He had read that Soutine painted a hanging beef carcass there so slowly that the neighbors reported him to the police for the stench. He drank and caroused with friends, but painted with a daily fervor despite hangovers or sickness. Albert Barnes of Philadelphia, always on the lookout for new genius, bought sixty paintings directly from his studio. Soutine on that fortuitous day hired a taxi to drive himself and his friends drinking all the way south to Nice. Graham thought that Soutine had the classic bohemian gloom mixed with an appealing *joie-de-vivre.*

Montparnasse had changed since those artistic years. It did not matter to Graham, who looked up the old addresses and asked questions of the neighbors, taking photographs as he went. Apparently all the artists, all their friends and all the friends of the friends had moved on. There would be no interviews or anecdotes from the Fourteenth Arrondisement.

They took the train south, arriving in Mougins on the first of July. The Deux Chevaux was washed and ready. Mikal had come over early to oversee the construction of the swimming pool on the second terrace and to continue the slow-moving courtship of Marie Laure. Karl thought that she looked younger, prettier and now tanned, but that was what a novelist would think. Graham found her cooking grown better and better, surely a few stars above the now famous Moulin de Mougins.

The four of them had a dinner on the terrace, windless and warm. Mikal, also deeply tanned, asked them about Paris and they asked the couple about their trips around the south.

"I expect we'll be here until the end of October," Graham said. "We've both a great deal to write. The two of you can have the swimming pool every morning."

"Good. That's when we usually use it."

"No tan line, I expect?"

"You'll embarrass Marie Laure."

The engines that turned their summer paradise started to hum again. Mornings at their writing tables, typewriter clacking on one and Karl's scratching away on the other. The new swimming pool tended to call them away, cool waters besting a sense of accomplishment.

Graham had come to believe that his method of writing resembled rock-climbing, going up a cliff face without ropes. It was slow and dangerous, in the sense that a mistake could send him almost back to the beginning. First his fingertip needed to go in a far crack, another finger tip in the next crack, then another until all fingers had a firm hold. A single foot could then go over to the ledge, then the whole body, pulling over and up. Another, higher crack then asked for that single fingertip, then the second one beyond and so on. Clambering slowly but surely up, never looking down. Sometimes he would hang on a ledge without an obvious way ahead, thinking—where does this book want to go from here? Then, almost like magic, another high crack would materialize—fingertip, fingertip, foothold and up. The only difference was the cliff-climber might fall to the valley floor while Graham would only fall out of the chair. Death versus a nasty bump.

Karl's writing process was more straightforward. He could pick up mid-paragraph where he left off the day before. Graham thought that he had the whole book in his mind before he started, every subplot and minor character fully rounded. Karl denied it, claiming he worried as he went along, revising and expanding in his mind. It was a matter of not wasting paper, waiting until it was ready to inscribe.

In early October the three men drove to Brindisi for the ferry to the Greek mainland. Graham wanted to see the real Mount Parnassus, just above Delphi. Winter storms often held off until November, giving cool days and waters still warm from a summer under the sun. It was doubtful that any light could be shed on Soutine and his art from viewing Mount Parnassus, but Graham wanted to include an expositional paragraph about it nonetheless. After docking on the western coast of Greece and a drive of a few hours, they booked into a taverna with rooms right on the Gulf of Corinth. In front of the taverna was a sandy beach, where the men went for a swim after a day exploring up the hill to Delphi, and Parnassus above that. Tourists must have gone elsewhere, because terrace, mountain and beach were all but deserted.

Their days settled into an ebb and flow beginning with a swim in the morning, writing reserved for the afternoons. Mikal swam faster and farther than the other two, often coursing out of sight around the headland enclosing the bay. Graham and Karl would regain the beach, lie in the sun until he came splashing back onto shore, breathless and excited. Even the first cloudy day did not seem threatening enough to cancel the swim. When Mikal had not returned, the men decided to walk up to the terrace to start lunch, wait for him there with a glass of wine.

This time Mikal did not return. He could have come ashore farther down the coast and was walking back along the path, which he had done before. After an hour, their worry increased. When the tavern keeper said that autumn storms always brought strong currents, Graham asked him why they did not warn their unsuspecting guests, foreigners who did not know the local ways. He only pointed to a sign in Cyrillic Greek at the beach and shrugged with his hands out.

They drove down along the coast, but found no sign of Mikal. The captain at the police station spoke some English and explained that the November storms had come early, with their strong seaward riptides. The brother could already be swept out of the Gulf into the Ionian Sea. A Patra fisherman from across the gulf, leaving shore in a dinghy, had also disappeared. The boats they sent to search for him would also look out for the brother. This is all we can do, he said.

It was not enough. The expected storms came from the north, filling the whole week with rain as they waited in increasing despair. The Gulf of Corinth waters turned to a dark gray with whitecaps on the endless row of waves. At first Graham and Karl were paralyzed with sadness, not moving from the room except to walk to the police station for news. Nothing again. They walked back in the rain to the taverna with the official words in their ears that after a week he is surely dead. Bodies seldom were recovered, the captain said, because the sea has her ways. He was sorry.

"I made a mistake in bringing us here," Graham said as they returned to their room.

"The mad thought keeps coming to me that some old god took him away, to be his lover."

"We came too close to Mount Parnassus on a foolish mission."

"It's not your fault, Graham."

"Let's leave now. The police know how to contact us if anything happens."

"I feel sure that nothing will happen."

While packing up their bags, including Mikal's clothes and shoes,

Graham thought that shoes were the most personal parts of clothing, more full of the lost spirit than the shirts or shorts, more like the man that was. It would be better to spare Karl the touch of his brother. They loaded the bags into the Citroen and drove along the rain-soaked coast to the port. As they crossed on the ferry over to Brindisi, Graham watched from the outer deck as the sea threw its waves against the ship. If you have Mikal in your dark arms, our beautiful Mikal, why are you so angry?

He had never confessed to Karl or Celia, both of them away at a family gathering in California, about his days at El Molino with Mikal. The younger brother, arriving home without notice from a university holiday, wanted to be a part of what his siblings had. Graham did not resist when he walked in one night. He now remembered Mikal as the source of an intense love, undiluted by experience of the world. He had an electricity that came in waves out of his body, stronger and unrefined. For a few days Graham thought that Mikal might be an unexpected answer, a man with a quality of robust and innocent sensualness that neither Celia or Karl had in such abundance. But the lust and delight burned out quickly as a pine-wood fire, and it remained an untold secret. It stayed as a memory often in their eyes when they looked at each other across family dinner tables in the years afterwards. Graham could imagine Wingrave, if he knew, saying *How many of my children do you want?* Two was just right, Wingrave, three too many. Graham wondered if there would ever be a time he could reveal that week or would the guilt stay on in his mind like a recurring song? His thoughts switched as Karl came up beside him on deck and they both looked out at the horizon.

They had not called anyone in France or El Molino about Mikal's disappearance and death, the telephone not the right way for such news. Now they faced the task in person. Marie Laure, expecting them, was in the kitchen filled with succulent dinner aromas when they returned. She collapsed, choking when Karl told her. Karl held her as they were both on the floor, rocking her slowly back and forth. He had feared she would accuse them, blame the two for not watching out for Mikal. But she stayed in a trancelike state for days, not leaving her own bedroom.

"Does it seem like a myth?" Francoise asked Graham. "A story from the other world, told again and again?"

"In some ways. The Corinth police captain said they would recover no body. They never did."

"It must have happened many times before."

"That's what Karl and I have come to think. Some horrible black force taking away beautiful young men, perhaps every October."

"Zeus. Poseidon. A water beast," she said.

"I am so sorry I took us there. An aesthetic whim turns into the most unreasonable death."

"Perhaps in one way it is better. How could he and Marie Laure have lived for very long together? It was an unlikely dream."

"Death is never the better way, but I've thought the same thing."

The two men boarded the train to Paris and flew back to New Mexico. Graham knew it was Paloma who would take the death hardest there. Mikal and Paloma were the youngest, boy and girl together, the closest friends among the six. Although Mikal stayed in Karl's house, he trusted Paloma the most for his inner thoughts. Karl said he could not be the one to tell Paloma. It was just sunset as Graham knocked on the door of her house, knowing he could not put it off until the next day.

She did not fall to the ground like Marie Laure, but stood silent with her head down. Graham closed his arms around her, standing with her for several minutes.

"Tell me how it happened," she said.

Graham tried to include all the details. The daily swim, how far out Mikal always went, usually returning while they were at lunch, the rainy day, the unknown currents, the long wait for news, the drives along the coast, the coast-guard search boats and the final certainty. He left out Marie Laure's collapse.

"So you did not see him go around the headland?"

"No. We had already gone back to the taverna."

"Were you making love while he drowned?"

"Paloma, no. Why would you ask such a thing?

"You and Karl were supposed to look after Mikal. You knew he could not face life on his own. He was a child. You abandoned him."

"It was an accident. The currents swept him away."

"It will take me a long time to forgive you. Our helpless Mikal."

Two weeks later, Graham and Karl had a private ceremony at the camposanto, with Juan Carlos and Celia. Dolores had been asked, but declined when she heard there would be no priest attending. Karl asked Paloma and Artemis, but they also declined. There was a carved headstone that Karl had arranged for and Juan Carlos installed—a newer, whiter marble than the others.

Mikal Prosper, Sweet Brother, Taken by the Gods.

They each read a poem and then shared a toast with a glass of retsina, pungent and bitter, to remind them of the villainy of a whole country, Greece. Karl and Juan Carlos walked ahead as they took the path back to the houses. Celia put her hand on Graham's arm as they walked.

"Paloma says you and Karl were making love when he died."

"She's wrong."

"She's probably striking out, trying to find a reason."

"I know. Karl has a great hurt, too. Perhaps greater."

"And you?"

"Of course. The pain is more when the beautiful die."

27

The Phonograph Needle

24 July 2011, 5:10 PM

I finish reading aloud to Celia the chapter from the Braque manuscript, a discussion of his time painting with Picasso. Their friendship was important to both painters, almost a love affair as they explored the new lands of Cubism. I am writing in detail about it, how it probably was not a literal affair, but an aesthetic one. However, I ended the chapter with an anecdote that Picasso repeated several times. Picasso went to visit Braque in the hospital, but was not allowed to see him. "The nurse wouldn't let me into his room. She said Madame Braque was with him. She didn't realize that I am Madame Braque."

Celia continues to paint, but she is amused. "That should appeal to you," she says.

"It does, enormously."

"There's another famous quote from Picasso, isn't there?"

"He said that Braque is the wife who loved me the most."

"Collectors of expensive art don't like to hear things like that. Queer things."

"Isn't it fun to make them hear it?"

I wonder if it were at all possible that Picasso and Braque were lovers, queer lovers, comforting each other with sensual hands, laughing as they finished their sex, feeling so full of luck that they had found one another. Braque was the taller of the two and perhaps he carried Picasso to bed with his short legs kicking in faint objection, a scene from the better pages of Balzac. If the rafters had eyes and could tell us the truth today, it would explain a lot of questions curious writers have about the sameness of their Cubist canvases. For a while, they were the same person, bodies and minds intertwined, painting very nearly the same paintings. It would explain the bitterness of the rift that grew between them later, oddly wide for a mere aesthetic difference. I remember Karl and me laughing that way, breathless after sex. We lived within a solid fortress of secret sex, an oaken door keeping out the disapproving world. Did the two painters have a similar safe place, even for a short while, where their bodies touched as they laughed?

"I wonder what people think of us," Celia said.

"Does it matter?"

"It has worked so well for us, for so many years. Maybe someone should document it."

"Like me?"

"Like you. Who can tell the story better?"

"I'll think about it. I see invasion of privacy issues."

"Nonsense. It would be published after we're gone. And it would be instructive to others, let them know that there were others just like them."

"Let me think about it this summer."

"And I have all your Monday letters in a drawer over there. Should I instruct the girls to have them published when we're gone?"

Of course, I answer that it is a splendid idea. The letters, now forty years of them, would tell the whole story of Karl, Celia and me. There must be numerous unsavory anecdotes in the letters and it would be only right to leave them in, unbowdlerized. The wholesome, honorable and bold with the lascivious and the merely petty. The letters would document how the love embellished the art. Knowing that we are loved gave all three of us a solid ground to start from, a place from which art can grow.

Celia's interest returns to the canvas as she reaches up to start another thin line from the top. This one is bluer, bolder than its neighbors, a division or frontier in the middle of the painting that I will always see and remember. Would somebody else in the future also hear our conversation recorded in that line, know that a man came into the painter's studio and distracted her with tittle-tattle about the lives of others? That they laughed together? That they loved each other? Like a chromatic phonograph needle picking up the sounds in the grooves? Maybe all paintings could be listened to instead of just looked at, a storm outside the studio windows imbedded in this bit of black and a singer's high voice next door, coming through the thin walls of the Paris atelier, caught up in that band of yellow? Touch it and hear the voice, vibrant again.

I make corrections to the chapter, the reading out loud having disclosed awkward phrasings and words that seem to rub on each other. It is a good thing to put my writings into voice, to pay attention when I stumble across a passage. Spoken words can have a validity that rises above words on a page. They can come to life, be drawn out for emphasis, a normally quick vowel given several milliseconds more of life. Or they can be clipped with a razor, lending the meaning a sharper importance than is really there.

I think again about Braque and Picasso. There is a photograph of Picasso wearing Braque's military uniform, the Spanish pacifist masquerading as French soldier for the camera. Picasso appears to be engulfed, an impostor swamped by the larger man's uniform. I remember when Karl was on leave from Vietnam and we had our bittersweet week together. It was an odd, sexual experience to put on Karl's uniform, almost exactly my size, and both of us laughed as I progressed. The faded fatigues, combat boots and black beret—and then came a passing cloud of unease when I was fully uniformed, standing at mock attention beside the bed, my arm cocked into a salute. There was something improper, unsuitable about it, a matter of unworthiness, persona and shadow, primordial and deep. I was the poseur and the fraud. We both stayed silent as I undressed—knowing that I had ventured across the line into the unacceptable, not a matter for laughter.

28

Bedside Glass

1990

Graham wondered if death came in cycles, like a sudden onslaught of high waves against the shore. The three deaths in his life made him think that it did. He hoped that it meant there would follow a long period when there were no gatherings at the camposanto, no new head stones to be commissioned.

Mallstone published the book on Soutine, one that would always remind Graham and Karl of their long days in Greece. The book was like most of his others, selling well but never taking fire. Graham had already started the next project, expanding the magazine article on Juan Gris into a full-length book.

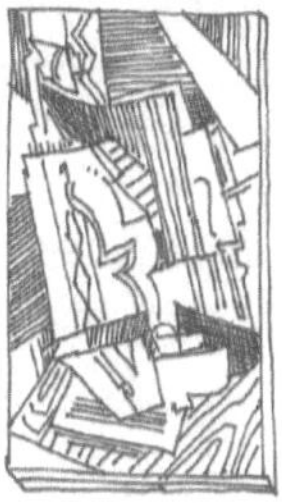

He watched in silence for ten minutes in Celia's studio, her current series constructed from horizontal lines a full inch wide. There were the colors of earth, but mixed with many parts of white, a whisper only of terra firma. Graham saw a repose in the paintings, as if layers from the sky were settling to the ground with a slow resolve, closer and closer together. Celia had become one of the darlings of New York, the LaPlace private plane arriving at the Santa Fe airport at least once a year to retrieve her work. The gallery workers enclosed the precious paintings in protective wraps and returned with them to the city the same day. After a few weeks, this new series would also be on its way eastward.

The current Caravaggio had moved over to Celia's studio. He was a curious cat, preferring to be underfoot at the easel, sometimes the recipient of a dropped blob of paint. The official greeter of the studio, he deserted the easel location for any seated visitor, rubbing with disloyal energy on Graham's leg.

Graham asked, interrupting her concentration, what she thought of Juan Gris.

"Odd color combinations for a Cubist, more energetic, as I recall," she answered.

"That, and his patterns. Do you like those?"

"Better than Braque or Picasso. He felt at home in Cubism, not impatient to move on to new ideas."

"I think that shows in a painter—being at home in his work."

"Is he your next book?"

"I think so. Karl and I will be leaving next week."

"Karl is still sad about Mikal."

"I'm hoping a few months at Mougins will change that."

"I'll miss you, Graham."

"Are you asking me not to go?"

"No. I didn't mean that. Just that my work slows down a bit when you are not in that chair."

Graham was eager to get Francoise's take on Juan Gris. Her insight gave him the direction and title of the last two books, but he had several interviews elsewhere before they could move in for the summer in Mougins. They checked into the Hotel des Saints Pères for a few weeks in the first of May while he consulted the gallery archives in the national library. Gris's son, Georges, was still alive and agreed to an interview. Sons, Graham had found, seldom have as much information as daughters, but Georges came up with several amusing stories.

There were former employees of the gallery surviving in Germany and available for interviews. The papers of Curt Valentin, German owner of the gallery that showed Gris paintings, were stored in a museum library in Dusseldorf. Still, after their trip to Germany, Graham had no strong direction for this book.

By the middle of June, they were settled into *Mas Moreau*. With

Marie Laure, they held a ceremony for Mikal in the olive trees with the same poems they had read at the Camposanto and a white marble stone of the same design. After a few weeks Graham found the time to discuss Juan Gris at dinner with Francoise.

"Really better at Cubism than Picasso or Braque, don't you think?" she asked.

"I think so. Celia says he was 'at home' in his art, unlike the others."

"I think so, too. He never gave Cubism up, refining it, expanding it. Strong colors and inventive designs."

"Twenty of those brown, gray and white cubist paintings of Picasso can be a bore, no? But not twenty Gris paintings," Graham said. He remembered his early disappointment with the sameness of the Cubism of Picasso and Braque, one very similar painting after another.

"Quite right. Gris was more inventive."

"Could there be anyone left in the village of Ceret that knew him?"

"I don't think so. But most people think that his Ceret landscapes are among his best."

Graham knew what he already thought was right—that Gris, by staying with Cubism, polishing it, improving it, became the best of the lot. It would make the other art historians angry, but he had his approach. By the end of the summer, he had finished his text for *Juan Gris, The Best Cubist.* They stayed on for a few weeks in September, Karl still in the middle of his book. It was a good time for them as lovers, Graham observing how Karl's body had seasoned to a sensual fullness, a man in his full prime. His flesh had the same delicious firmness as a ripe plum, bouncing back when pressed.

Death was not done with Graham. His father called from Pasadena—will he come home for the last days? There was a week or so left, but nothing more. Even though he had not been the obedient son, Graham knew he must do this.

His father did not look ill unto death, only much thinner from the growing tumor inside. His color had always been robust, perhaps a gift from Switzerland—like his lack of humor and life-long, world-coming-to-an-end pessimism. Graham helped him into a chair on the back porch, facing the garden and the overgrown grape arbor. For a moment he was sure that if he hugged his father for a long enough time, a restoring power streaming outward in tides from him through the thin body, a loving embrace at long last, that death would slink away and his father would become well again. He knew it was wiser not to test that power but to sit down beside his father instead.

"Thank you for coming, son."

"I apologize, Father."

"It has been hard since Ella died."

"I know. I was in France at the time."

"She loved you so much. Like her own son, she said."

"Would you like for me to stay for a while?"

"Very much."

"I thought I could read to you from my latest book."

"I would like that."

That one week turned into another, and another. The cloud of guilt dissipated somewhat as Graham cared for his father, the few weeks at the end so much better than a surprise notice of his death, a telephone call in the night from the housekeeper. Time stood still as he read from his book, and two more of his books, and two of Karl's, and he kept the bedside glass filled with water. In the last few days, he washed his father and helped him eat. This was what he should have been doing all along, the care of a dutiful son.

"Are you happy with your Prospers?"

"I think so, Father."

"You have become a substantial man, Graham."

"It doesn't seem that way."

"Ella was very proud of your accomplishment. She read all your books and gave them as gifts to our neighbors."

"I miss her."

"I also, son."

After the funeral, Graham went through the house and the loose-leaf books of stamps and boxes of coins. The county museum would be happy to accept them with a few pages of the Tanna Tuva stamps put aside, the ones with the big white musk ox and the camel racing a locomotive that he remembered from his youth. These were the stamps that brought the Obermanns to America, supported them, and sent the son to university. Graham tripled the amount of his father's bequest to his housekeeper, a gentle woman from Mexico. He found a Greek coin in the box full of them, a smooth gold circle with a man's head on one side and a woman's on the other. Brother and sister. Or was it husband and wife? He put the coin in his pocket.

The lawyer came to the house. For a fee, he would be able to file the will and see things through, California a superb state for probate, statutes governing all its possibilities. Please sign permission here to sell the house and dispose of the contents that you do not wish to keep. Are you sure you have taken all the pieces that you want? It was the rare clear day as he flew out of LAX, the plane circling out across the water and back over the valley of his youth. He wondered about David Lawston and thought he could identify his house as they crossed above, red tile roof and double palms in the front yard. He should have invited David to the funeral and asked him to share the sadness, but it might have opened a sensual chapter Graham had no place for now.

29

Great White Bird

24 July 2011, 5:20 PM

There is a passage in French that I want to read aloud to Celia, one of the few that Braque wrote. The painter trusted that his art would speak for him, that mere words were awkward and incorrect. Despite the many months of my residence in France, there are insufficiencies in correct pronunciation. Celia ignores the minor mistakes but interrupts when I go too far afield. At the finish she says that I am much better, but not there yet. I am certain that I will never be there.

"Most of the people in France that I interview switch the conversation to English."

"I can understand," she replies from her ladder.

"Am I that bad?"

"Not really, but I remember the sisters at the academy swatting us with a ruler if we spoke like you just did. They said it must hurt to speak good French. Not like Italian or Spanish, languages you can slither with ease into. French, not German or Russian, is the true language of pain and suffering."

I am usually with Celia during the winter months, the summers away with her brother. Karl and I plan to leave for France next week. There are many Braque sources lined up for me to interview, some of them in Paris, but also out on the coast of Normandy. His studio at Varengeville still stands, but it is owned by others. I will have to track down the current ownership of the atelier paintings, as well as the later bird paintings. It will be a busy time, but afterwards we have all of September and perhaps October at the *Mas Moreau.*

The birds of Braque excite me. They are both symbolic and real, flying with slow grace over the assorted objects Braque had strewn about his studio. Surely the choice of objects was not random, a meaning inside each one of them. I wonder what has happened to those objects, the actors in his dramas. And the great white bird, hovering just before landing, must be the emblem of arrival. Of better times, perhaps? These ideas will fall into place in France, now disjointed and not working together.

Karl will continue to work on his current novel, another French family saga in the Vietnam before Dien Bien Phu. It is a story with an eager audience both in France and the United States. Karl gets urging letters from his publisher, hungry for a regular supply of Karl Prosper sagas. His editor has been on talk shows in New York, hinting what little he knows about the new book. Karl's French families are all connected, readers hoping that this cousin or that handsome uncle, the one with so many lovers, survived into the current volume. It is certain that he picked up this idea from his own family, not only the Prospers, but the Garcias, Leybas, Montoyas, Padillas and the long-ago New England Parchments to call upon.

I shut my book and get up to leave. Celia turns my way.

"Cocktails at six-thirty," I say.

"I need to clean up and dress. I'll be there shortly."

30

Zadok the Priest

1991

Celia had decided long ago that Margo and Morris should go to the same Swiss school that she and Artemis attended—the Geneva Academy, run by the Ursuline sisters. The twins were about to turn sixteen, with one more year before university. Since Graham and Karl were leaving early for Europe this year, Celia suggested that the men invite the twins for a chaperoned week in Paris. They adore both of you, she said.

Karl's novels had been bestsellers in Europe and the twins were proud of their uncle, if somewhat unaware of the popularity of their father's academic biographies. The uncle met the girls at the Gare de Lyon, loading them and luggage into a taxi.

"First time in Paris," Karl said. "Are you excited?"

"We couldn't sleep last night," Morris said.

"The whole week is planned, down to the minute. Your father has the Van Dongen research to do in the afternoons, but I'm free to take you around. We'll go to a different restaurant each night."

"Mother wrote that we should ask for you to take us to Chanel."

"I've never been there, but yes, of course, I know where it is."

The girls were already booked into the Saints Pères, a room down the hall from Graham and Karl. Saying they could unpack later, he walked them over to the Boulevard St. Germain and found a table at Les Deux Magots. After a small and expensive lemon squash for each of them, they strolled over to the Seine and across the gardens of the Louvre. Several blocks beyond, there it was, Chanel, in the Place Vendome, still looking smart in black and white.

The staff were delighted with the girls and their perfectly spoken

French. Karl chose for them each a very long black-and-white striped scarf, despite the sales-woman's observation that it might be too formal, too severe for young girls. Something in mauve and pink, Monsieur Prosper, to not fight with the beautiful young skin—but Karl would not be put off. Morris knew immediately how to place it, circling it loosely around her neck, and with Morris helping, Margo followed suit. Karl was silent as he reassessed the wisdom of the sales-woman's remarks.

They wore the scarves to dinner at Laperouse that night, looking very sophisticated in their simple black dresses. The girls had the Prosper family good looks, tall and graceful for all their youth. Karl soon realized that there was a difference between the twins that he had not noticed before—Morris the more outward one, Margo the reticent one. Would that grow more pronounced as they grew older? It would not do to treat them the same. As they read the menus the first night, Karl asked Margo if she knew what she wished to eat, or did she want her uncle to order for her, to surprise her.

"I don't like surprises, Uncle Karl."

"I never did either when I was your age."

"Would the *poulet roti* be good?"

"I like everything I've had for dinner here. But *roti* might be more of a bistro dinner, so let's both have the *Poulet a l'Estragon.* Tarragon and butter. And a green salad to start."

"What about wine?" Morris asked.

"Your mother expected you might ask. From afar she says—no wine until you're eighteen."

"Even with some water in it?"

"Even that. She's cruel, your mother."

"She wouldn't know about a single glass."

"Mothers have a way of seeing across oceans and around corners."

Graham, at their dinners, asked the girls about the day's events with their uncle. Karl was giving them a view of the Paris he knew, the Paris of a bookish, well-to-do bachelor ‹‹‹ Hermès, Shakespeare and Company Book Shop, the Monets at the Jeu de Paume, the Palais Royale, a Folies Bergère matinee, the Petit Trianon at Versailles, Vermeer's *The Lacemaker* at the Louvre, the Rue de Bac antique shops, and back to Place Vendome for two small bottles of No. 5. Again, the saleswoman said, not at all suitable for young girls. Really, monsieur.

"And then we went with Uncle Karl to buy his new shoes," Morris said.

"The Ermenogildo Zegna store," Karl said, with a sheepish look over to Graham. "I ordered some sharp new oxfords. We could all fly home for what they cost." Karl seldom missed a Paris opportunity to buy a new pair of expensive shoes, one of his few vanities.

"They love him there," Morris said laughing. "They called him Zee Famous Novelist. We have all read books by Monsieur Prosper."

"Everybody responds to your Uncle Karl, even the Italian shoe-mongers," Graham said. He reached over for Karl's arm.

"Karl told us an awful secret," Morris continued. "That you and Mother were going to name us Chesterilla and Mendenhall if friends hadn't come to the rescue."

"It was innocent fun. We wouldn't have settled Chesterilla on either of you."

"I'm so glad."

"But Mendenhall is another matter."

"Dad, you wouldn't have."

Their dinners out were more Graham's time to be with the girls. Morris did most of the talking, with Margo watching more than entering in. Graham told them stories he had learned of the painters of Paris, including several on his current subject, Kees Van Dongen, at their dinners at Roger the Frog's, Taillevent and their three favorite bistros in the Saint Pères neighborhood.

Both father and uncle accompanied the girls to their morning train back to Geneva. Karl watched as Graham kissed each of them in turn, giving Margo a second hug. Perhaps he did understand the difference in the girls. At the street café afterwards, Graham asked Karl if he was exhausted.

"I should be, but no."

"Thank you. I couldn't have done it by myself."

"We may be a curious family, but they are my girls, too."

"I've got all the Van Dongen gallery material and the letters from his portrait commissions. We can leave for Mougins tomorrow. There's some more at the museum in Monte Carlo—we can drive over for the day."

Graham knew the proper approach for the Van Dongen biography, a focus upon the many portraits. It would prove to be the quickest book so far, *Kees Van Dongen, The Portraits of Women.* There still existed many of the Van Dongen letters to his friends describing what he thought were the secrets of his success—he elongated the women, made them thin and enlarged their jewels. Graham knew that was the lesser part of it, that Van Dongen also had a creative mind, using unexpected colors in the shadowed sides of faces and designing his canvases with strong diagonals.

At the first dinner at Mougins, Francoise brought up the subject.

"Van Dongen was not a good painter," she said.

"I don't agree. My book is just about his portraits of women, which are mostly excellent. Compelling, twentieth century portraits," Graham said.

"Why are you writing about him?"

"It's a story that hasn't been told. Most critics say right off the bat what you say, that he was not good. Like most conventional wisdom, it's erroneous. I'm taking a closer look."

"We used to laugh at his paintings back in my Paris years."

"Young university girls can be quite savage and quite incorrect."

"*Eh bien*, we were sharp-tongued and unafraid."

"Writing books on what everybody agrees about is not very interesting, is it?"

"We will see, won't we?"

Karl had been working on his novel of the death of a younger brother, a serious book for him. He worried that the happier subplots were not strong enough to balance the tragic drama at the center of the story. He was not a writer of tragedy, he told Graham, but he wanted to memorialize the dark weeks in Greece, to record them for others to know. A death that was read about, even in fictional form, was never forgotten. Everybody who knew Mikal would know that this was about him.

On hot afternoons, they returned to the beach at Juans-les-Pins for a seawater swim. Karl thought that the sea was more restoring, better for you, than a dip in the pool. The beach had a sandy bottom there, not like the hard-to-traverse small pebbles elsewhere. Both men swam out and coursed back and forth in laps along the shore, and returned to dry off in the sun.

Looking at Karl's body gave Graham continued joy, the firm ripeness of middle age even more enticing than the inexperienced smoothness of youth. Graham thought of the bronzes of adult Greek men they saw at the Louvre, small bulges on either side of the waists, which they had decided meant a healthy sex life. Karl's body was that of a mature, confident male with all the attributes of expertise in bed –a physical skill not available from the callow twenty-year-old, however attractive he might be. It was an ongoing conversation between the two men, which part of the body was the most sensual. The dent at the bottom of the neck, the impression above the lips, the line where the leg comes into waist, the back of the knee, the small of the foot and, of course, tits. Were there other places on Karl waiting to be discovered, where the mere light touch of the hand could start the overture?

The regular evenings with Francoise and Marie Laure had become a savored part of the summer at *Mas Moreau*. Both men discussed writing in general and their books in particular with Francoise. She was interested in their projects and could respond with expertise about technique and approach. This summer Karl was using many music metaphors in his novel. Who composed the most perfect musical description for an actual act of love, he asked, a piece that mirrored the first temptation, then the arousal, the pulsating rhythm of love itself, the pinnacle moment and the slow joyous decline?

"Something from Puccini?" she asked.

"Nessun dorma? Beautiful, but too sad."

"Verdi? An aria from Traviata?"

"Too fussy, " Karl said. "What about Berlioz *Symphonie Fantastique*?"

"Too violent, too obsessive."

"And nothing from Wagner, I suppose?"

"Absolutely not. Never a German."

"I disagree, "Graham said. "Handel was a German and a piece he wrote in London is my candidate."

"I can't imagine a rousing Handel chorus at my bedside," she interrupted. "How grotesque."

"*Zadok the Priest*. Do you know it?"

"Isn't that only for the English coronations?"

"There's a long introduction, straightforward chord progressions getting more and more insistent. Again and again. Orchestra stronger, the chords placed down with firm steps. Then Handel pulls back a little with some ornamental violin arpeggios, across a plateau with minor chords. Onward with the music growing, growing, up and up. Then, louder than we might expect, there comes the great outburst of the chorus, a fortissimo climax of a hundred voices, an explosion ... *Zadok the Priest*, they sing, culmination and the long, slow diminishing of the violins. The queen is crowned and we are complete. Warmth and happiness ensue. It is an act of love, beginning to end."

"*Bons, alors*, very pretty, but who would want to make love to the English queen with her purse?"

"You French can be so obtuse."

31

Sweetmeats and Puddings

24 July 2011, 5:30 PM

As I walk back towards the house, I think about my role in the Prosper and Garcia families. With my own relatives all dead, I have appended myself to these families, first as a mere son-in-law, then growing in influence and regard as the years went by. I have replaced Uncle Parchment as the man with the telescope on the high deck, guiding more than directing where we all are going.

The oversight of the family finances should have gone to Roberto, the erstwhile banker, but he put an end to that before it happened. The emotional and spiritual matters stayed with Uncle Parchment, who retreated like Hadrian to his country house, putting distance between him and the everyday quarrels. In time, Parchment went to his reward, leaving his Galisteo acres to Karl, and his patriarchal duties were ceded to me by acclamation. Dolores said she could not add up a column of numbers anymore, that they looked like chicken scratchings. I was not hungry for position and power—instead I had the timing to be there when the vacant position asked to be filled.

It is not a dictatorship or a kingship, but similar to a very secular version of the Bishopric of Wurzburg. I oversee the lands and moneys for a small group, assuaging their day-to-day tribulations, keeping enemies at bay and starting projects for the common good. Since nobody else wanted the position, the amenable atheist son-in-law stepped up. Let's overlook his godlessness, because he is good at the rest of it. The fortunes of the family are sound, the houses weather-tight, the driveways without potholes, the animals curried and the land productive. Fifteen hundred bushels of apples came from the orchard last year—thanks in part to Young Parchment, of course. No white burgundy, so far, but there are high hopes.

I suppose this dinner is, in fact, a project for the common good, a feast day to brighten the tedium of rainy days along the Rhine. A Prince Bishop needs to have a sense of such things, bringing food and entertainment to town just as village life is turning gray and lackluster. Boars on spits, the wine cellar doors open again, sweetmeats and puddings, music written especially in Italy, jugglers from Spain, with all of Wurzburg coming up the palace stairs in their finery—all from the beneficence of Graham, The Swiss Usurper. Such is life in our backwater principality, noted for the excellence of its poets and artisans.

My reverie is interrupted by what Karl said to me this morning. *Please come over about five, when the writing day is over.* I am late, but it is a short walk to the log house, the grasses wet from the afternoon rain.

He is still at work at the writing table centered in his living room and lamps with shades of green glass like a public library. His house has always given off an English country house quality to me, despite its being made of rustic logs. Perhaps it is the pervasive dark brown color—walls, floors, ceiling and all the furniture. There are waxed oak side chairs and pear-wood tables from shops in France, high brass candlesticks on a sideboard. Karl and I found the long refectory table, his writing table, in a shop in the Loire, a refugee from a nearby monastery of a height more suitable for eating than writing. We talked back and forth about the table before it arrived in the states, the monks who dined there on thin barley soups with brown bread, shepherd dogs underfoot waiting with patience for the dismissing bell. The remembrance of monastic life that might be imbedded in its wood appealed to both of us, perhaps a beckoning from a shared earlier life of simple faith and subservience—very unlike what we had become. Did a forbidden love live in that monastery dining hall, large fires giving bare warmth to the stone floors, a love unspoken but alive when we looked up at each other from our soup bowls? Christian brothers with quite unchristian thoughts?

There is a big difference between the houses of the sister, Celia, and the brother, Karl. From the few conversations we had about the matter, I put together a light-filled house for me and Celia. She had no interest in interior decoration but always went for the rooms with white walls and Gustavian furniture when we looked through books, and I proceeded from there. Ours could be a large summerhouse on an island out from Stockholm, washed-out colors everywhere, silver and pale gold, birch trees pressing against the windows. It was a good choice, because her paintings all but glow on the walls, our house bowing down to her art.

The dawn-like quality of our house brings me a great deal of intellectual delight, but Karl's rich, polished-wood, Rembrandt browns satisfy something deep in my soul. His house is encompassing and male, a protective darkness away from the world. If somebody asked me which I liked better, I would be hard-pressed to answer. An early Mozart concerto versus a slow movement from a Brahms symphony, I want them both.

The photograph of the young lieutenant remains on the wall where Paloma hung it so many years ago. I have learned to understand that Karl was the only one of his brothers and sisters who continued to love his father. By not harboring real or imagined injustices, he was able to go forward past forgiveness. To not blame somebody for their failings was one of Karl's best qualities. He could encompass the fact that someone else was not perfect and see the beauty of the remaining qualities.

I see the two stacks of yellow legal pads beside Karl, one with fresh, unwritten pages and the other with the growing novel. Sitting down in the chair across from him, I put my hand over on his. We talk for a while about his book, which he has detailed for me before—a young Frenchman sent out by his family to look after the plantation finds a love unacceptable to those back in Paris. The randy uncle has become the old man of the family, trying to make a place in its ranks for the young narrator. The war is yet to come, but signs of unrest are everywhere, a colony about to explode. But I feel he does not want to talk about his book.

"I sometimes think of Mikal when I come into your house," I say.

"It doesn't bother me anymore, his being here."

"He used to sit where I am."

"Late at night and when I glance over during the day, I sometimes see him."

"Not a bad spirit to be keeping you company. Remember the party tonight for Celia, cocktails start at six-thirty."

"Will you come over here after the party?"

"If I can. You know, it's Celia's birthday night."

"I feel alone."

"You're not alone."

When I put my hand again across for his, he turns up his palm. Is it that *chi* energy coursing out of the hand that makes it such a sexual connection? Two palms together can sizzle with anticipation. The squareness of Karl's hands has always both excited and soothed me when I touch them. He responds the same to my hands, I know. I wish we had more time this afternoon and do not want to leave him alone.

My two allegiances rarely make me decide between them, like today. Without printing out a schedule, we know in some ineffable way of our nights together. All summer in France I have Karl, and the rest of the year I vary between them. Most winter nights I spend with Celia, however. I know there must be jealous thoughts, but the intellectual part of our brains works to put out fires at the first sign of smoke.

I have been reading biographies of the Bloomsbury circle. Lytton Strachey, Virginia Woolf, Duncan Grant, Vanessa Bell, Bertrand Russell, Maynard Keynes and Ottoline Morrell. Excepting the infrequent argument, they were able to combine and recombine sexually for many years, in unexpected and perverse pairings. All this while they painted and wrote the many dozens of works that people still treasure. It is not a customary or popular way in Santa Fe, but Karl, Celia and I seem to have taken up its call.

I do not think any of Bloomsbury subscribed to such an idea as Celia's—that she and her brother, at least as far as I should be concerned, are but one person. I understand better the truth of such as the years have gone by. What Karl is, Celia isn't. The jagged break between them fits exactly together to make one coin. One side is not jealous of the other. When I kiss her, I am kissing him.

I have found in my writing about artistic circles that the marrying of one sibling because you could not have the other, for whatever reason, was quite frequent. Is it more common among artists and writers than the general public?

Bryon might have been wiser to not love his sister Augusta, but he did anyway. Sometimes a man would marry one sister when he nurtured a life-long love for the other sister. Or a woman would marry the brother of a woman she loved and could not have, approval of Sapphic love to come years later. In one case among my own Obermann cousins, a man divorced his wife to live with her brother. It did not always create happiness, this once-removed love, but it made a pairing where underground sensual rivers could be heard gurgling in the quiet hours, never entirely silent. So Celia's concept of unity is not without precedence, and I am the beneficiary of the great good fortune of not having to choose between brother and sister. I try to accept that they are but one person.

32

Ten Women

1994

Karl's publisher had started to print facsimile editions of his manuscript pages, full size handwritten pages with the drawings. They were limited editions, numbered and not signed, but fully subscribed. He was one of the three or four writers that the house claimed with pride in its promotional materials. Karl wondered if he could ever write a complete book at home in El Molino, his days at Mougins so much more productive than those at home.

The Van Dongen manuscript was delivered to Mallstone Books and Graham chose Modigliani as the subject of his next book. He knew it would be a much more difficult book than his others, so many earlier biographers having written on Modigliani. The rooms at the Hotel des Saints Pères served as base for Graham's research in the painter's Montparnasse neighborhood. It was walking distance from the hotel to the few people left there to interview. The son of the painter's landlord had several anecdotes, and a shopkeeper who was alive during the years of the Great War, she a child in her father's green-grocers, remembered Modigliani's visits. She owned a painting the artist traded to her father for cabbages and leeks. For a reasonable fee a photograph of it could be included in Graham's book. There were other grandsons and granddaughters of the painter's friends with bits of memories.

Graham received from one of these the name of a man in Nice whose father made the alleged purchase of ten of Modigliani's portraits just after the first world war, the painter all but destitute. It was said the portraits were still hanging in the family house in the Old Town, a few blocks back from the seafront, but it was also said that they must be forgeries. Karl and Graham took the train south and established themselves in Mougins, Graham hoping for a chance to interview the fortunate son, if he was still alive. The next morning he dusted off the Citroen and drove over to Nice.

The house at the address given was a four-story stone building with dark yellow stucco, black shutters at every window. Many new shops and galleries surrounded the building, but this well-kept house still appeared to be a residence, with a street number for identification. A courtyard garden to one side was shaded with fat-trunked date palms behind a high wall with clambered vines. The porcelain oval below the street number was written with *Pierre Duvallier*.

Graham knew it was bold to just knock. He introduced himself and explained his quest to the man who answered the door.

"You are an American, no?"

"But, an American with the love of France and art."

"I asked because few Frenchmen want to know of these paintings," Duvallier said. "Even the catalogue raisonné people did not wish to see them. Please come in."

"My source in Montparnasse says the paintings are among Modigliani's best," Graham said, deciding a bit of flattery would not hurt at this early stage.

"Ah, well. It may be so. Would you like to see them?"

"Most assuredly, sir."

They walked up to the main floor rooms of the house, the shutters closed but their slats opened to a hot breeze coursing through the house. The man opened a few of the shutters and turned to point his hand to the paintings on the far wall. They were in a line, six of them, all portraits of women. There could be no mistaking them for another painter's, and they were signed. Graham walked over to the first one, a head and shoulders of a woman with red hair. He was silent as the man watched him looking at each painting in turn. Celia came to his mind as he studied the last one, a woman with dark hair and strong eyebrows.

"Modigliani lived in a rented house across the street," the man said, pointing out the window. "My father bought paintings one at a time, when the painter needed money. I do not know what he paid for them, but Father was a generous man, probably gave the painter, his family and friends enough for several weeks of living expenses."

"This was in nineteen eighteen, during the war?"

"And nineteen nineteen, when times were even harder. Father bought other paintings from other painters, Roussel, Forain and Chabas, but these portraits are all but forgotten. The Modligiani women are his true inheritance."

"I heard there were ten in all," said Graham.

"Four are in the bank vault. They probably all should be there in safety, but I like looking at them."

"Tell me about this one on the end. Is it known who she was?"

"Portrait of a Woman is all it says on the back."

"It resembles the woman I am married to."

"Perhaps it is she from an earlier life."

"I wonder if we could include photographs of these as illustrations for my book? My publisher would pay a generous fee."

"I will consider it."

"Including them in my book might lend them authenticity."

"Perhaps. Many people say these are forgeries. I have no heart to fight the big museums and the Paris experts."

"We could find out for sure."

"That would be good. I think the reason that there are so many portraits together is because of my father's love of women. Modigliani saw that love, and when he needed more money for food he painted another portrait for old Monsieur Duvallier. He was a sure sale."

As Graham drove back to Mougins along the sea, he thought with amusement about the painting that bore a resemblance to Celia. If there was such a thing as former lives, had she known Modigliani, been one of his lovers? Did this past bohemian life explain her meteoric rise in the current world of art, a bank account of accumulated merit from a time before to spend so lavishly in the current time? Had the crowded nights in bars of Old Nice with bottles of country red wine, the choke of tobacco, questions about the role of the artist and the meaning of art given her an ability to see what others could not? Was this the step up, not given to others, that propelled her so quickly to the heights? Were all of today's successful artists only reincarnations of older painters, artists begetting artists down through time? Were there in fact only a dozen or so true artist spirits, living and working again and again, in one life after another? Did Giotto become Botticelli, then El Greco, Vermeer, Goya and finally Monet....changing styles and ideas as he went along, but the same perceptive person again and again?

That night Francoise was skeptical about the Nice paintings. Graham asked her why.

"There are so many skillful forgers at work. This would be a perfect way to introduce a group of forgeries masquerading as a forgotten bequest away from public eyes for so many years."

"You have a criminal mind. Pierre Duvallier seems the picture of truth."

"Why is it that the catalogue raisonné editors did not authenticate the paintings? What did they see?"

"I will let the publisher deal with this."

"You are Monsieur Duvallier's last chance. That's why he was so welcoming."

Graham had come to identify the great skepticism in the French character, strongly alive in Francoise. Their first response to any new information was disbelief. A well-spread negative rumor could clothe the Duvallier paintings forever in question, enough to discredit them in the suspicious eyes of the catalogue editors.

Perhaps an opportunity awaited in this national cynicism. In the following weeks Graham turned back to his notes for the book, the painter Modigliani's life a classic tragedy. The night after he died penniless of tuberculosis, his common-law wife leapt to her death, a jump from their fifth-story window in Montparnasse. Did the details of this sad life need telling again? By the first of September, Graham had his idea for the manuscript. He drove back to Nice for a final talk with Monsieur Duvallier.

"I have a proposition for you, sir," he said at the door.

"Please come in."

After they were seated in the second-floor sitting room, the shutters widely opened this time, Graham presented his proposition. He would title his book *Ten Women, Authenticating the Lost Modiglianis,* if Monsieur Duvallier would submit them to the close scrutiny of auction house investigators and university authenticators. His book would be more a detective story than an artistic monograph, an account of finding and validating these excluded paintings.

"They all must come here to do their work," Duvallier said. "I do not want the paintings to leave the house."

"That's fair."

"I have no reason to question them. My father was an honest man."

"Splendid. I will fly through London on my return to the states and set this up."

"In the end I may not want to give them to the auction house."

"That's perfectly all right. I also need for professional photographers to make a high-quality record of them."

"Why do you do this, Dr. Obermann?"

"I believe that they are authentic and I know it will make a thrilling book."

"Very well. Let us shake the hands."

Graham and Karl stayed for the necessary two days in London on their way back to New Mexico. Graham realized with some guilt that he had a book whatever the outcome of the expert investigators. If they were fake, he would track down the forgers and describe the shady world of art fakery. In his heart, though, he felt the Duvalliers, father and son, were simply honest men.

As the taxi took them back from the Albuquerque airport, Graham looked across the valley to the mountains, his home in the high air. He was always so glad it was still there.

Graham went to his house and Karl to the log house. There was a note on Karl's long table from Paloma, *Please come over the minute you return*. He knew fully well what awaited him.

33

Violet Blossoms

24 July 2011, 5:40 PM

I take a final look at the table as I walk back across the portal. Juan Carlos's flower vases sit in a long row down the center, each a summer clutch of daisies, heliopsis, spikes of lavender, chamomile, white and yellow yarrows, and variegated grasses. Juan Carlos has a good eye, the bouquets simple, unpretentious but festive and elegant nonetheless. The wine and water glasses are not in an exact alignment, but vary slightly back and forth, an agreeable evidence of humanity involved, definitely not a royal occasion with goblets in a laser-assisted row.

In the kitchen Lilli and her helpers are at work, cutting and dicing, arranging the platters of hors d'oeuvres and stirring a roux at the stove. There is a white porcelain sample plate for me to see, the grilled chicken paillard on one side, a ribbon of white sauce across it at an angle with apostrophes of the tomato coulis. A mound of the rice pilaf adjoins, with green and yellow vegetables next. The sautéed carrots in parallel rows complete the place.

"You're a genius, Lilli."

"It has good color, doesn't it?"

"May I taste?"

"No, Graham, you'll just have to trust me. The real plate will be warm and succulent."

"Only a nibble?"

"Out of the kitchen."

I can smell the orange zest cookies I have requested in the oven. It is an aroma from childhood—Aunt Ella cooking them for my return from school in the later years, the only nephew home for a week or so. Father wrote to complain that they so seldom saw me in my graduate years, the Prospers in Santa Fe taking all my time. We look over at your empty chair at family dinners, he said, now just Ella and me. It is as if a giant hand plucked you up and out of our lives. We hope that the Prospers are good people and treat you well. Your corner bedroom is always made up and ready should you return.

I missed Ella's funeral, Karl and I so far away in the south of France, the complications of last minute travel more complicated back then. I could picture it anyway, only a few mourners at the family plot in the San Gabriel churchyard. Father would be bereft, now all alone. I was too far away, in spirit and in life, to be with him. There would be a Swiss wake at the house afterwards, the other refugees in southern California looking after each other. Mr. and Mrs. Stamm, Frau Luber, the Albrechts, and Hans Boller who lived down the street. He was Uncle Hans when I was very young, taking me on long walks, while we recited out loud the German days of the week, numbers to one hundred and the largest cities, starting with Zurich downwards. He was father's best friend, in the cool way that Swiss men were friends. They played chess together in the grapevine pergola behind the house, occasionally conversing in their Schweitzerdeutsch, softer and less guttural than the Hoch Deutsch from Berlin. When he came up in my mind now, I wondered about Uncle Hans's full intentions back then and his hot hand as we walked. A single man, he taught languages at the local preparatory school.

The Obermann family plot was in the cemetery behind the Episcopalian church in San Gabriel, an odd choice for us Lutherans. In the months when my mother knew she was going to die, she drove us around checking out the burying grounds in the towns surrounding Pasadena. The Lutheran ones were too severe she told her six-year-old son, too cold like Switzerland. The Methodists and Presbyterians were also found lacking for reasons I cannot remember. She told me that if one had to die, one ought to be laid to rest in a beautiful place, like a modern Garden of Eden.

San Gabriel's Church of Our Savior, at the end of a long drive lined with weeping pepper trees, pleased her right from the start. We walked around the adjoining cemetery, planted years before with old French shrub roses and the jacaranda trees which dropped their violet blossoms across the grass, a memorial tribute season after season. I waited in the car as she conferred in the dark-shingled sexton's cottage, emerging with ownership papers in an envelope and a smile. It reminds me of Andalucía here, she said, with a jacaranda blossom tucked into her buttonhole. A beautiful place to go to sleep.

I am in and out of the shower before Celia, our joint bathroom small by current standards. Maybe this is our next refurbishing project, to push out the wall and add the latest in bathroom technology. Celia will stand under the showerhead, washing her hair with no worry. Another of her Prosper family blessings, her hair is thick and full, easy to towel back into place. I cannot remember a time when she went into a beauty parlor or had someone else wash her hair. Her single vanity about hair was that it be cut right, a local woman keeping it sharp and angled at the bottom.

34

Pale Golden Brown

1994-1995

What awaited Karl at Paloma's house was his daughter—Dominique Linh Prosper, born after he left Vietnam. The papers announcing her existence had arrived before he and Graham left for Europe, but Karl had expected it would be late autumn before she herself came, using the open plane ticket and expense vouchers that he sent. The Catholic sisters took Dominique in after her mother died, the grandparents too frail for a five-year-old girl and never comfortable enough to write about her existence. Now she was a lithe young woman in her twenties.

"Why did you keep this to yourself?" Paloma asked at the door when Karl walked over to her house.

"I thought I would be back at El Molino in plenty of time."

"She has been quite worried when you had not come, after three weeks."

"I can imagine. Is she in here?" he asked, walking into Paloma's sitting room.

Dominique stood and turned his way as he came into the room. He could not see any Prosper family resemblances in her, only a thin, tall Vietnamese girl with larger eyes than usual. He reached out for her hands, which were cool, and they stood looking at each other. With a smile, he enclosed her in a tight hug and a kiss on the cheek.

"My very own," Karl said.

"You are my father," she said.

"I am so glad you are here. I had no idea that I had a daughter until this spring, when the state department sent the first papers. How was the trip across the Pacific?"

"Very long, but exciting."

"And you came by train from Los Angeles to Lamy. I thought it would be a good way to see your new country."

"Lamy is so small, so far away. I told the taxi driver to take me to this address as you wrote in your letter. There was no one at your house. Aunt Paloma heard me knocking at your door and came over."

"I'm sorry I was not here."

"But you are back now. Father."

"You may call me Karl if your prefer."

"I like the sound of Father."

"I have given Dominique one of the spare rooms in my house as her own," Paloma said. "I think it's more suitable for a young girl to be housed with her aunt than the irresponsible bachelor father who forgets important dates."

"What do you think, Dominique? Are you happy here with Aunt Paloma?"

"Yes. Now that I know you're just over there."

Dominique spoke very good English, with only a slight hint of Asia—hesitations and odd cadences rather than a true accent. The Catholic sisters had taught her French as well, she told them. She seemed very much the modern young woman. She wore slim orange pants and a long-sleeved blouse of a lighter shade, a batik scarf under the collar. Something in the way she moved reminded Karl of Celia—perhaps a Prosper bit of high style had come through with the genes. She was taller than other Vietnamese women, and definitely, now that he had time to observe, the eyes were western, a pale golden brown. If not beautiful, she was very delicate and feminine. He tried to picture her mother, without success, his mind erasing the unhappy year.

Karl held her hand as he walked her over to the log house, escorting her around the rooms. He called the extra bedroom *Your Uncle Mikal's Room*. Pointing out his writing table, he told the story of its monastic provenance. She sat in his writing chair while he stood beside her to turn over his manuscript pages, describing the story that they disclosed.

"Are you angry at me, Dominique? For not being in Saigon when you were young?"

"No, Father. I was angry with my grandparents, for telling so many bad stories about you. I knew they were not true."

"I'm glad you don't hate me. Maybe we can become what a father and daughter should be."

"I hope so too." She stood up and hugged Karl, then walked back to Paloma's house. Karl recognized that she was a self-possessed, full adult, that her years of growing up would always be lost to him. It would do no good to feel guilty about it. He wondered if they would continue to have this reserved, formal relationship. Did they resemble a stuffy monarch with his daughter newly home from a distant province—*Hello, king—Hello, daughter?*

Graham's book on the successful validation of the Modigliani portraits came out in the spring. It was the first of his biographies to cause what publishers love to describe as a sensation. Art critics came out of every piece of woodwork to lambaste or congratulate him. Several reviewers pointed out that it was common knowledge that, after O'Keeffe, Modigliani was one of the easiest painters to forge. Dozens of Modigliani fakes had been uncovered, several skillful forgers serving time in European prisons. What did an American writer know about such matters?

This, of course, only made readers more eager to read what Graham had written to validate them. Mallstone Books had paid for two separate authorities to authenticate the ten portraits, and a famed scientific lab in Brussels took X-rays and bits of paint to analyze the canvases, finding each one of them true and of the period, all of this technical data included in fine print at the back of the book. An august French historian still held out, claiming if the portraits were not bogus, then this book was merely a part of an American conspiracy to auction them for high prices in New York. Another clever rape of the French patrimony, he claimed.

The book only went higher on the best-seller lists, staying there for weeks. Representatives of both Sotheby's and Christie's made visits to the house in Old Nice, but no contracts for auction were forthcoming. Mr. Duvallier and Graham each turned down opportunities for television interviews, much to Mallstone Books' disappointment. By the first of June, when the uproar had settled down somewhat, Karl and Graham planned their summer at *Mas Moreau*.

After letters back and forth, Graham and Mr. Mallstone decided upon the interior paintings of Eduoard Vuillard as the next subject. Since the painter lived a quiet, very un-public life with his mother, and later his mistress, there would be few opportunities for interviews or anecdotes. Graham was now acknowledged as an expert writer on portraits of women and the techniques painters used to portray them; the subject was a natural choice. There were four dozen Vuillard paintings of interiors with women awaiting Graham's comment. Mr. Mallstone was assured it would be a popular book, sending to Santa Fe a parcel of high-quality photographs of the paintings. Graham now had a full summer to weave this straw into gold.

Karl's current project was a love story, an American Southwest family saga with many generations of assignations and denials, unexpected happiness at the end. He was nearly finished with the manuscript, a month more at the most. Karl never fully answered questions about how many of his own family entered into his novels, the reviewers eager to make connections. To one reporter's query about the true nature of his characters, he answered *Some are fictional, some are very real.* This only intensified the quest for an answer.

At *Mas Moreau* the two men gave in to the summer—mornings at their writing tables, afternoons around the pool and the occasional lovemaking. Graham was the one who most often instigated love, made it happen under the olive trees. They would be lying near each other by the pool and his hand went across to Karl's leg, slowly sliding above the knee. Graham knew that there must be a connection between the continued sexual activity with a lover and the continued ability to write well, but its workings remained unclear. When he introduced the subject of enduring love with friends at dinner parties, it was universally judged to be spurious and embarrassing.

Give it up, Graham, nothing of the sort exists beyond the two of you. But he knew something of the sort existed, many times over.

Marie Laure had a young assistant in the kitchen now, Nicole from a village family. The older woman did not want to relinquish her control over the men's meals, as it had become an important part of her life. Nicole could chop and grind, help with the stirring and lifting, but it was Marie Laure's kingdom at decision time. They shopped and arrived in the late afternoon, often eating together with Graham and Karl. Marie Laure always waited for the men to invite Francoise over, to not edge too strongly into their privacy.

Francoise was invited this night. Graham had questions about Vuillard and what she knew on the subject. What do you think of his work he asked.

"I love his paintings. The mysterious gray light of Paris coming in through the windows."

"Do you think his interiors with women were his best?"

"No. There are many interesting men."

"I'm just writing about the interiors with women."

"A mistake. You must include both men and women. Think of the beautiful reds in *Théodore Duret in his Study*."

So Graham expanded the scope of his book, a comment by Francoise more important than any suggestion from Mallstone Books. *Mysterious Light, The Vuillard Interiors* became the new title. Graham wrote Mr. Mallstone to send photographs of the interiors with men. The summer direction was set and the essays fell into place, Graham studying each photograph with his magnifying glass, something to write about in every corner. More than any earlier book, this was a subjective book, full of Graham's opinions and suppositions. He now felt fully capable of making those opinions.

In the first week of September, Karl asked Graham if he would accompany him on a trip to Asia, to establish his ideas of Saigon and Hanoi for a new novel. It was time to face the dragon again, he said.

"When should we go?" Graham asked.

"Soon. Maybe just after a few weeks back in El Molino."

"I will hunt up my notes on Victor Tardieu—he founded the Hanoi School of Modern Art and he was on my list of unknown French painters. There may be a book there."

"I hope that Dominique will want to go with us."
"Do you think she might be afraid to return so soon?"
"I'm hoping not."

35

Animal and Grass

24 July 2011, 6:00 PM

Celia will wear one of her Chinese dresses, a high-collared, modern *qipao* made of black silk with frog closures. I watch as she takes it off its hanger and pulls it over her head, smoothing out the black fabric over her body. It is a perfect fit for her shape, tailored into her waist and around her slim hips. The slits along the sides come up to just below her knees. She looks over at me as she pins on the baroque pearl brooch I gave her years ago, a single, large, oddly shaped pearl with a golden-pebble surround. When I saw it in a shop window in Rome, I thought it might be more suitable for some spinster aunt, but I remembered Celia's love for the strange, the out of the ordinary. I think it is now her favorite piece of jewelry. Without her asking, I fasten the closures on her back.

"It's still beautiful," she says, running her finger across the pearl.

"Karl and I had fun buying it, asking the old saleswoman to wear it for us to see."

"Let's all go to Rome again—perhaps this winter."

"Karl would love it, and I would too."

"I was thinking about our first night together. How blind love was. I must have got that from the novels we girls read in school—a brother bringing home the glamorous writer friend from the University at Heidelberg and the innocent sister overwhelmed."

"You know very well it was the other way around. Innocent sister, oh my."

"Was Karl taken up the same way, and David Lawston? Did you affect us all so we couldn't see?"

"I can't think I did any such thing, to any of you. What a foolish idea."

"Karl and I talked about this not so long ago."

"Maybe the two children were too sheltered here at El Molino. Aristocratic mother and willful, talented father. Nannies, tutors and boarding schools. European novels by flashlight under the bedcovers. None of these make for clear-eyed children."

"I'm not blind anymore. Karl and I are very lucky."

"We are all very lucky."

We seldom talk about such matters, but we seldom get dressed at the same time—I usually finish well before she even starts the process. The taking off of clothes must open other doors as well, the soul bared along with the body. Are there Lutheran vestiges in my persona, ones that walk away from personal disclosures? It is amusing that I am still uncomfortable with a close self-scrutiny.

Wearing a terry-cloth robe, I return to a chair on the far side of our room while she fine-tunes. I look at the seating plan for the dinner party and try to make any last-minute adjustments. Switching the Ludlows from chair to chair makes for a better conversation match. The niece and nephew will be happier to sit together, and I keep the chair unassigned on my left should David Lawston arrive. I think there is a good chance he will attend, coming in with the other guests as if he lived right here in Santa Fe, no advance warning that he is in town.

He had done that once before, a year or two after Marjorie's death. It was at an opening for Celia at the Ludlow Gallery, the first in her many series of rain paintings.

David stood off to the side, a wine-glass in his hand, and watched as we entered. I did not see him at first, shaking hands and introducing people to Celia. Then I glanced over and he did his quick raise of the eyebrows in greeting, and a big smile as he lifted his glass. I could see him continue to watch us as Celia and I drifted from group to group, well-wishers and arty types out for an evening on the town. Only after twenty minutes or so did I find an opening to leave the group and walk over to him.

"You look happy, Graham."

"I expect I am. You are always so tan and fit," I said.

"I spend a lot of time at Balboa. Remember?"

"I do. Some year I'll join you there, get some California sun again."

"I would like that. Celia looks well."

"Can you come by for lunch tomorrow? We've got a full schedule tonight."

"No. My flight leaves early. I just wanted to see Celia's exhibit. And you."

"What do you think of the paintings?"

"Impressive group. Are you proud of her?"

"I am," I said, putting my arms around him for a hug. He smelled the same, that mix of animal and, what was it, new mown-grass? Earthy, fresh, sexual. We looked at each other for a while, then I returned to Celia and the group. She did not say if she saw him, and as the evening events unfolded I forgot to tell her. But Celia knows things that have not been put into words, ideas in my head that transport to hers. She knows that a sector of my heart has not moved on to newer loves, my sibling loves, and she invariably appears amused on the subject.

"I'll go say hello to Lilli," Celia says, leaving the bedroom.

My clothes are simpler than hers, a loose, white Mexican cotton shirt over some black slacks, and the expensive Italian loafers that Karl gave me a few summers ago. Even though I prefer to wear socks with the loafers, Karl says that it is not the Italian way. They are smooth and cool as I slip my bare feet in. I open up the leather box on my dresser and put the gold drachma away in my trouser pocket, my amulet for high occasions. It is the signet that binds all my loves and lives together. Good things often happen with the drachma in my pocket—it must have the power to bring on a new act, to turn the page.

Few in Santa Fe dress up for parties anymore except for a fussy, clothes-proud group that spends many nights at opera benefit events, tuxedos for the men and sparkling dresses for women. They are a different people than tonight's guests, more working artist and free-thinking. I have tried to keep the entertainments at El Molino informal, comfortable attire for all.

36

Hooded Eyes

1996 and 1997

The trip to Asia was not to be until the following year, a late spring sojourn before the hot days of summer. The new Vietnamese constitution was in effect, relations with the United States had been "normalized" and Americans had begun to travel up and down the length of Vietnam again. Dominique, Karl and Graham spent the first day in Saigon unwinding from the trans-pacific flight, walking the French-built blocks around the old hotel. It was still Saigon to both men, not Ho Chi Minh City. Karl could see that his daughter was excited to be back, but anxious that they all be happy. She was a good person, it was now clear, wishing everybody around her to get along, no discord to mark the day. It was a trait that was bound to bring her grief, again, and again, but Karl admired it nonetheless.

Karl hired a car and driver to take them out to the suburbs, where Dominique's grandparents lived. These would be the dragons that needed facing, seeing once more the implacable faces and the hate behind them. Dominique could not lessen it, he knew, much as she wanted. They parked in front of the small, thin-walled house that he remembered when Dominique's mother took him out there, on a street filled with houses with no side-yards, only a plot of small vegetables to the side of the walkway. The entry door was closed, but the smell of the kitchen drifted through the open louvers, bringing up the unhappy times of a marriage going dead. The mixture of garlic, ginger and fish sauce was pungent, mnemonic of the dinners there, the hooded eyes looking over at the white invader who was clumsy with the chopsticks, the man who did not love their daughter enough. It was one meal of mistrust after another, from both sides.

Dominique hugged them, a small old man and woman, and spoke

quickly to them in the chopped syllables of their language. They looked without a change of expression first at Karl and then at Graham.

"I told them that since you are married to Karl's sister, you were my uncle." They nodded gravely and made a small bow to Graham. It was an awkward visit, Graham wanting it to be over as deeply as Karl. They did not look again at Karl as Dominique talked to the old people for twenty long minutes, then hugged them and got up to leave. Graham shook their hands and it was over. Karl might as well have been invisible.

"I am sorry, Father, that they cannot accept you," she said, sitting between the two men in the back seat of the taxi.

"You mustn't worry. We won't come again."

"I may have to come see them, in the future."

"You're a dutiful daughter, Dominique. A warm-hearted go-between."

"I believe that El Molino is my home now."

"Do you want to go visit the Catholic sisters tomorrow?"

"Maybe there are also too many memories there."

The hotel dining room, brown wooden fans turning in the high ceiling, was also redolent of the past. Dominique asked Karl about her mother, where and how they met, what she did for a living. Karl waited for a moment, then decided that a departure from the truth the best way forward.

"She was very pretty, Dominique. Shorter than you, but not as stylish as you."

"Did you not love her?"

"I must have loved her in the beginning, but it soon became obvious that we had made a mistake. We both knew it. We argued most of the time. You can make bad choices when you are young."

"I do not remember her at all."

"We will take some flowers for the grave tomorrow."

"I would like that, Father."

The train north to Hanoi did not leave until late afternoon, so Karl and Dominique took an early-morning taxi out to the burying grounds. The grave was in a concrete place to the side of the mossy gravestones of the wealthy. The rows and rows of gray stacked cubicles held the urns behind glass doors, small photographs of the dead fading in the sun, burned-out incense and joss sticks in the vases between the cubicles. There were long-wilted, dried flowers already at the cubicle on a small shelf in front of the space. Karl placed the new flowers on top of the old. There was no photograph of Dominique's mother, to Karl's relief. He placed his arm around his daughter's shoulder and they stood in silence for a few minutes.

The Transindochinois train left through the suburbs of the city just as the light was going. It was an old-fashioned double string of compartments for six people, glass doors to the passageway, toilets at the end of the car—perhaps a train built back in France decades ago. The other passengers peered into the compartment as they passed and left alone the two westerners and a young girl. The compartment was on the right side of the train, Dominique making sure they had a view as they went up along the coast.

Late in the evening, the train stopped for half an hour, soup vendors alongside selling the first meal of the trip. Other merchants crowded the station selling scarves and trinkets with great hullabaloo. The thousand-mile journey took two full days and a morning, with regular stops for the vendors' food. The high pass near Hue kept them all silent, looking out over the misty cliffs when they were not going through tunnels. The soups at the stations were getting spicier as they went north, more aromatic. Karl wrote with a steady pace in his notebook as the others looked out at the country. Only once did he offer to talk about the war.

"This is where I was for a while. Dang Hoi. See over there, the small town on the water?"

"Was the fighting bad out here?" Dominique asked.

"It was, but I was in a supply convoy. I was lucky. No actual gunfire."

"Did some soldiers die?"

"Many died at Dang Hoi, from both sides."

"Are you sad, Father?"

"This whole trip is sad for me. Do you mind my not talking about it now?"

Graham and Dominique did not bring up Karl's part in the war again, their conversation limited to what they saw passing by them. The center of the country near Vinh was dry and the bomb craters with ducks swimming circles in the brown water were visible from the train windows. As the train went farther north, the land grew greener and more lush on the approaches to the delta land of Hanoi. The soups became less spicy with more vegetables, fewer pieces of fish. The suburban outskirts of the old capital still had long stretches of rubble from the bombings, ruined bridges and jagged high walls in the distance.

They checked into the Metropole Hotel downtown, a restored world apart from the battered country of the last days. They could look out upon the manicured gardens with lily ponds and red bridges from their dining room windows that night, a blue willow plate tableau from lost times. It seemed disjointed, perhaps unfeeling, to have the elegant dishes of steamed delta fish with dill and sticky rice brought right to the table by stout waiters, the undernourished soup vendors at the train stations still on their minds.

Weeks ago Graham had arranged an appointment the next day with the director of the museum school of the arts to discuss Victor Tardieu, the Frenchman who championed modern art in the colonial Hanoi of the twenties. Dominique went with him to translate.

The director was a student there in the 1920s, just after the school was founded by Tardieu. Graham thought about the difficulties for a peace-loving art professor through the many war years, trying to keep alive an idea as fragile as painted modernism while the night rained bombs down upon the city. The director's staff and students had assembled a presentation for Graham, large flash cards depicting the founding by Tardieu onward. Each scene with costumed students changed with a high-pitched gong and the rustle of mallets on hardwood. It was painful to watch. They were all proud of their school and its founder. It was not Graham's role to tell them that Tardieu's paintings would never be revered in the West. They were uninspired genre scenes, peasants in sun hats leaning on their hoes, or overblown canvases with hundreds of citizens rejoicing the arrival of the goddess Art, rays of light breaking through the clouds. At the end of the presentation, Graham, the famous biographer from the west, gave a short speech of appreciation in French, turning to Dominique for words that would not materialize. To wrap it up, he ventured into the subjunctive future with *It might not be long before the word Hanoi is on the lips of the Western art world.* There was polite applause at the end. He knew there would not be a Tardieu book forthcoming, even though the world of art might have a shallow, guilty interest in Vietnam.

In the taxi back to the hotel, Dominique asked if Graham was disappointed.

"Maybe so. They seemed so earnest, so childlike."

"I could see that too."

"They have such a long way to go."

"Do you think Hanoi will be on the lips of the Western art world?" she asked, looking at him earnestly.

"I was foolish to say that, wasn't I?"

"No, Uncle Graham. They were happy to hear it."

"I could feel my nose growing."

"Will you write about the school?"

"Probably only a magazine article."

On the flight home, Karl told them that the trip was not a waste. He had outlined the story for a novel, a young girl coming west out of the broken country. There would be a poignancy, the girl losing the simple life for the rush of a city, the values learned in a village struggling to work well in another land.

Graham thought that Dominique's story would be very different from the story Karl outlined, many happy episodes to come, and told her so. Some people come into their own later in life, like me and you, on a different street from where they were born, or in an entirely different country. He knew as a boy that places other than Pasadena awaited him, places and people that would make him happy. Dominique smiled as he talked and put her hand over on his. Graham felt that he was the child and she the adult.

Returning to El Molino, they drove Dominique over to Paloma's and watched as she let herself into the darkened house. At the next house they were greeted by Celia; she had waited up to tell the news of the marriage of Paloma and Juan Carlos.

"They have gone off to Taos for a secret ceremony, knowing that Dolores might disapprove and object," she said. "I lent them the Mercedes for the trip and, Graham, we made them a wedding present of the bridal suite and a good dinner with French champagne at La Fonda."

"The Prospers seemed fated for odd pairings," Graham said.

"They were both so happy. Like kids, really."

"I can see why," Karl said. "They are the remainder children, the apparently least important of two clans. Looking after Dolores as she got older and crabbier was all Paloma could count on, and Juan Carlos was living by himself in the family house up the lane. Perhaps physical love was not important to either of them."

"You are too judgmental and harsh, Karl," Graham said. "Maybe Juan Carlos has other talents, ones we've never seen."

"Both of you are pussyfooting around Juan Carlos's being gay," Celia said. "Dolores would not be worried about that. She will be concerned about their being first cousins."

"But it's legal in New Mexico to marry your cousin, I'm sure."

"Dolores may have other rules."

◊◊◊

Morris and Margo were in their third year at Mills College, Aunt Artemis making sure that their education paralleled hers. Their schooling in Switzerland all but guaranteed that they would be accepted at Mills, but Artemis guided through their matriculation papers nonetheless. They were bright girls with good transcripts and would probably have been accepted anyway, but a high-ranking aunt on the faculty made it a surety.

Artemis had observed how Celia and Graham were not proving to be the parents the girls needed, many things left undone. Perhaps it was that the artist and the writer were so close, so involved with each other's thoughts and lives, that there was no extra room for the daughters. Artemis took the girls twice for a summer in the Alps, all three of them loving the outdoors. In California, they often spent holidays back packing up in the High Sierras, Artemis both a parent and a mentor.

Everybody at Mills knew that they were the daughters of Celia Prosper, and that their father and uncle were famous writers. An illustrious family had as many problems as advantages, but the girls were popular with other students and the circle of accomplished women their aunt, now the head of the philosophy department, had collected. They were regulars at Artemis's Saturday night dinners at her house in Maxwell Park, informal gatherings of students and professors, usually with only women in attendance. If there was a salon in Oakland where art, philosophy and music were discussed each week, this was it.

This night the gathering was small but there was animated talk about the ethics of women in wartime. Artemis started the talk after each dinner with a question, unknown to the guests until then. The questions always involved ethics, the hostess's specialty at the college, and this evening's was *What is wrong with a woman on the front lines, shooting the enemy?* No actual tempers had flared, but keen differences remained even as everybody was ready to go home. Artemis asked her nieces to stay behind as she talked to each of those departing. She strove to make her house a forum where divisive topics would not come between friends.

"That almost got heated," Morris said, after the others had left.

"Spirited exchange in the pursuit of truth, I would call it," Artemis said.

"You are so good at guiding the conversation, turning it away from trouble."

"Years at the seminar table, my dear. Not much different from being a referee in a game of field hockey. But I have something to tell you girls, something you might like. Let's go back and sit down."

"We're going back to Switzerland again?"

"No. It's about El Molino. I want to a have house built for you there, one that the two of you will call home."

"But we have a home with Paloma," Margo said.

"This will be truly yours, not a mere room in your aunt's house."

"Our own house..."

"Wingrave built all of us our own houses, perhaps more out of guilt than generosity. It kept us Prospers together in this new world where everything changes. We had a place to go back to, a place of our own. Even if we did not live there all the time, it was a center."

"Like Virginia Woolf's room of her own?" Morris asked.

"Very like it. Even if you should decide to marry, or move to Europe, it will be there. And you won't feel obliged to marry just to have your very own house. I will have a portion of my one acre deeded to you, and your cousin Juan Carlos has agreed to design it, see that it is built. He looks after all our houses when we're not there."

"Why are you doing this, Artemis?"

"Because I want to do it, and thanks to the Garcia family money, I can do it. It was done for me, and it is only fair that I pass it along. I trust that El Molino will continue to be one of the sure places in an unsure world, for all of us."

"Thank you so much. When will it be finished?" Morris asked.

"Juan Carlos says by next summer."

After more talk about the evening and El Molino, the aunt hugged both of her nieces and they headed back to their dormitory. While they walked away, she wondered what Celia and Graham would think, how they would react to her usurping the right to provide shelter for the girls. She supposed that Juan Carlos had already informed them of her plan and she had heard no objections.

Being childless, likely to stay childless, Artemis saw this house as a way to create a family within her family—a closer bonding than the extended clan. It was a sweet irony that she, the single daughter, best deserved to be a mother. She had not offered the real reason to Morris: the premonition that the girls would live together their whole lives, spinsters with no husbands. As Margo kept her girlish ways, Morris was striding ahead into womanhood. Celia and Graham had not perceived what was so evident to Artemis, that one daughter would have to take care of the other daughter. Artemis knew that Morris would do exactly that. Having their house might ease the pain.

37

A Gallic Myth

24 July 2011, 6:20 PM

Celia is in the kitchen as I come into the living room, and I can hear she is charming Lilli and the other helpers. There is a light, almost restrained laughter, the staff aware that they are in the presence of a great talent. Many people who know of her position in the gallery world are awed by Celia in person, the luminary who is now shaking their hand. She never takes advantage of her fame, often turning the conversation with shy admirers into questions about their hometown, school and occupations of their parents.

I had missed turning on the light over a painting, the only one in our house not by Celia. It is the portrait of a woman by Modigliani, a gift from Pierre Duvallier. His other nine paintings sold for nearly a hundred million dollars at an auction in New York two years ago, and he acknowledged my role in validating them by sending me the one I thought resembled Celia, the tenth one. It still does, in my mind, resemble her. I wonder sometimes if I should move it to a more important location, then I remember how much I enjoy the reaction of guests when they discover it, so off to the side. *Is this real*, they ask? It is fun to answer—*There was some controversy, but we think so.*

Every time I look at it I think about Duvallier's house in Old Nice and the summer air through the open slats of the window shutters. The Modigliani paintings were almost waiting for me, ten shy sisters in the dim light. It could have been a Gallic myth set up as an opera, the gentle old father waiting for so many years with his ten daughters, no words spoken in the occluded rooms, street noises changing over the years from calls of the fruit vendors to machine guns and mortar blasts to the sounds of radios carried on young shoulders. They waited for the foreigner to knock on the front door, release them into the light, restore the good family name. The grand finale with ten sopranos and a musky baritone would fade into a simple anthem, happiness regained. If I was ever a hero, an aging prince with the power to undo a wrong, that was it. The book about them and their provenance was my most successful, still in print and selling in unexpected peaks up and down on the publishers' charts.

I open the casement windows at the end of the living room to give a breeze through the house, the air still and dead. The clouds are overhead, but a low sun lights them from beneath as they move slowly away and off towards the mountains. There will be no rain showers this evening.

We have a long driveway beside the walled garden in front of the house with places for many cars to park. I think I hear the first car coming along the gravel and to a stop. Whoever they are, they are a few minutes early and will probably wait in the car until the exact six-thirty arrival time. People in Santa Fe are usually on time, but few come in early. Guests from New York are always late, fifteen to twenty minutes, and from Los Angeles a full half an hour. German collectors are prompt to the second, *Vee are right on time to visit with Fräulein Prosper, no?* English people are never the first to arrive. Soon I will hear the iron gate swing open, a soft echoing screech, and the first footsteps on the walk.

38

Sunny Side Up

2003

Graham was undecided about the wisdom of choosing his next subject, Henri Fantin-Latour. The editors at Mallstone Books were enthusiastic about the painter, despite his living a bit earlier than Graham's writing window. There were many reference sources in London, not direct ones for interviews, but citations in the numerous letters and diaries filed away in libraries and the archives of the British Museum. Whistler introduced the younger painter around smart London and many English houses ended up the owners of Fantin-Latour's pieces. There were at least a dozen journals to read.

It was hard for Graham to see what was modern about the painter, his many flower paintings resembling those of Manet and early Monet. But the more he delved into the painter's works, the more possibilities he saw. There was an agreeable flatness about his backgrounds, a contemporary way of organizing space, and a tilting forward of the tables, the Cezanne-like hithering spill. There were obvious comparisons to Chardin, but Fantin-Latour was clearly the newer eye with touches of the century to come.

This would be the first French summer for Graham and Karl after the events of September 11th, a year off at home while the world settled down a bit. Karl was eager to move along to Mougins, his novel about a single woman painter just begun, while Graham spent the museum-filled week in London. Since the old Brown's Hotel continued to bring up memories of Wingrave's death, perhaps they had made a mistake of booking there. London was in full season and a change from Brown's difficult, but they sought nearby restaurants rather than the hotel dining room.

At their breakfast place, a ten-table bistro called *Oeufs Au Plat*, they enjoyed the contact with a talkative young waiter, Derek Carpenter. They learned the first day that he had come to London from the West Country, working as a waiter until he could find a gallery for his artwork. He was fresh out of art school and he was going to have a brilliant career, painting every night after work at the bistro.

"So, Derek," Karl asked, "what is it like out in your Devon?"

"Boring, sir. Green and boring."

"Call me Karl, not sir. Do you really want to give up that lovely greenness for the dog-eat-dog life of London?"

"In a quick minute."

"Do you like to go to the art gallery openings?"

"They usually let us art students come in and mingle."

"Have you been to LaPlace Gallery, over on Dover Street?"

"The best of the lot."

"You might be interested to know that Graham, here, is married to Celia Prosper, my sister."

"There's a large canvas of hers in the window. Five hundred thousand flaming pounds they want for it."

Every morning Graham and Karl had breakfast at *Oeufs au Plat*, talking to Derek about his art, his possibilities. Graham told Karl that it might bring up trouble to tempt Derek with too many stories about a loftier world, their world. But Derek was resourceful, finding out for himself at an internet cafe the lofty reputations of the two men.

"Google says that Karl Prosper is a famous novelist," he said, reading from a spiral notepad in one hand while pouring their coffee with the other.

"Have you read any of his books?" Karl asked.

"Not yet. Here *New York Times Book Review* says—'forbidden love as no one else can describe it.'"

"Maybe a bit overblown."

Derek put the coffee pot down and turned the page in his notepad.

"And Graham Obermann, here, is an art historian, eight respected volumes in print."

"Guilty," Graham said.

"Google has a lot about both of you guys. Well-heeled, bohemian writers it says. Live in New Mexico, but often travel together." He flipped the notebook shut.

"We have been found out, it seems," Graham said.

"Where, then, is Ms. Obermann, the painter Celia Prosper?" he asked.

"Back home painting in New Mexico to pay for this breakfast," Graham answered.

"A summer free for the lads to play?"

"Celia is planning to join us later."

"London the whole summer, is it?"

"No," Karl said, "We take the train to Mougins tomorrow. You should visit us there, Derek. A young face would be welcome at the swimming pool."

"I just might do that."

After the last afternoon of Graham's reading journals at the British Museum, the men boarded the night train to Paris and south. Graham was positive that their new friend would show up for a swim. It was not a bad turn of events, since their sex life had grown more intense after the first plate of fried eggs, *Sunny side up, as you Yanks say.* A new face, an imagined new body between them, youthful vigor remembered.

They settled into their writing regimen at *Mas Moreau* as the weather each day grew hotter and hotter. Air-conditioning systems in French cities failed and old people were hospitalized. August became hotter than July, and the number of victims mounted. It was a national disaster, thousands dying. Celia called to tell them that she would not be coming to Mougins, maybe next year would be cooler. The men felt hunkered down, waiting for nature to relent, writing earlier in the morning when there was a semblance of cool. Fans at the windows kept the air moving and outdoors there was no hint of a breeze. By noon, they retreated to the waters of the pool, hiding in the shade of the olive trees between swims.

With a small bag, Derek knocked on the door as the men were in the water. Karl came across the house dripping and answered the door.

"Hello, Karl. I hope you were serious about that invitation," Derek said, placing his hand behind Karl's neck for a deep kiss.

39

Dragonflies and Water Lilies

24 July 2011, 6:30 PM

The guests start to arrive, the gate opening and closing, and then staying open for a steady stream. There are three steps up to the gate, then a thirty-foot walk across the walled garden and another two steps up to the house. In designing the front walk, I recalled a passage from Gertrude Jekyll's book about garden design, that gracious pathways must be wide enough for three people to walk abreast, arm in arm, laughing and talking. Single file, or Indian file as she calls it, is counterproductive for affable entertaining, where people plod one behind another in a single line without talking, like Chinese laborers carrying hods of bricks. Gertrude had her way in our front garden.

Her strict rule comes to life with the first three guests, Jullian Closson, her lover Carolyn Ward, and Johannes Adler between them, walking slowly up the path, talking back and forth. Johannes stops and takes his hands from the waists of the two women to make a gesture, a grand circular gesture as if describing a platter. They all laugh and start to walk forward again.

The only other pronouncement I remember from Jekyll's book was her insistence that garden ponds have wide steps going down into the water, so adventuresome dinner guests could stroll down amongst the goldfish, dragonflies and water lilies, their garments soaking up water as they stepped down, even if no guest ever took the opportunity to do so. Gardens were about opportunities, not boundaries. But we have no lily pond to test the fortitude of our guests, yet.

"Welcome, Jullian and Carolyn," I say. "You both look so beautiful tonight. And Johannes, you're beautiful too."

"What fun, Graham. Perfect weather, when we were terrified it would rain," Johannes says. He is wearing a checkered sand-colored suit with a yellow bow tie and orange Scottish oxfords. Even as early as our university days, he was a peacock.

"I think this is Celia's actual birthday, the twenty-fourth," Jullian says. "Please come in, the bar is right over there."

Walter Burley's staff have set up a long table with a white cloth folded just so at the corners, wineglasses and double old-fashioned glasses in solid battalions. One silver punch bowl is filled with ice cubes and another with bottles of white Côtes du Rhône cooling in shaved ice, bottles opened but lightly recorked. Liquor, red wine and aperitif bottles stand behind in a double rank, waiting to be poured and mixed, white napkins in tidy stacks. Vanessa, the bartender, awaits with a pleasant look of anticipation on her face.

More couples arrive, often walking arm-in-arm down the front path. Arlene and Thomas Ludlow. Quattro Latimer and his wife, Sybille, who is wearing a scarlet *qipao* very similar to Celia's black version. Hilliard Milano walks up with Carolyn Aarp on his arm. There is a large huddle around the front doors as I walk around to meet in person Hallston Wills and his lover, Blaine Warner, just coming through the gates. I know that Hallston is uneasy about arrivals, especially if there are new people to talk to. Guiding him into the middle of a crowd is always a good idea.

"You're a sweetheart to include us," Hallston says.

"I picked a Saturday night just for you."

"No weeknights, ever."

"Let me introduce you to Carolyn. You know Hilliard, I think?"

The huddle grows larger as I try to greet each one, if only patting them on the back as I walk by. The sound of people talking and laughing grows louder as I see the Prosper family members arriving by the garden doors—Karl, the young Parchment, Dominique and Paloma have walked over together from their houses.

After I greet them in turn, kissing each on the cheek, I turn around to see that David Lawston is already in and talking to Celia. She motions me over.

"Your David is here. All the way from Pasadena."

"Hello, Graham." We shake hands with an odd, manly reticence.

"David, we didn't know if you could come," I say.

"I should have called. Am I still welcome?"

"Graham has reserved a seat just to his left," Celia says.

"I want to hear about the newest bomb," I say.

"No more bombs. I'm just a Caltech physics professor now. Students want to go to Mars now rather than make explosives."

"Shucks. I wanted to show off the blue-eyed, killer scientist."

"It will have to be solely on my beauty now."

I know at least one who can still call him beautiful, his full head of hair all but white now and his pale eyes in a tanned, smooth face. An admiral's uniform would not be out of place—golden epaulets and stern rows of chest medals. How is it that he still has a hold on me? I see Karl watching us from across the room. I pat David on the shoulder and go over to Karl, standing alone by the piano.

"Hello, love. Everybody's here, it appears," he says.

"It's good to see David. Not since the last Pasadena funeral now."

"He's still quite handsome."

"Not so much as you."

"Just what I wanted to hear. You know how big parties make me nervous."

I do not look to see if the others watch me kissing him on the mouth, underscoring our love. Even after all these years there is that uncertainty deep down in Karl, perhaps only made stronger in the Vietnam years, lurking but alive to reappear in times of stress. He needs extra attention tonight.

I see Dolores arrive on Juan Carlos's arm, he bringing our mother-in-law by car around to the front. Although frail and slow, she can still walk in the grand manner, the *bella figura* never looking down. I presume that she is coming tonight as much to recognize me as the patriarch of the family as to celebrate Celia. I cannot forget that she for so many years questioned my motives in loving Karl and Celia. I could see that she wondered why does this man not live with his own family, why take up with the Prosper children? She often asked me to give a Lutheran prayer before her festive family meals, *It is good for us Prospers to allow foreign faiths at our family table.* Early on, Celia would say, *Mother, Graham is our family now.* Dolores would just smile, further underlining my status as the outsider. She was the last of the Prospers to accept my role as head of the family and I still wonder how happy she is about it.

Uncle Parchment was more understanding, more welcoming than his niece. I had wondered if this was because he, a life-long bachelor, was approving and somewhat envious of my life with Karl and amazed at how it extended to include Celia. His generation of men did not have the words to describe their own feelings and loves, ineffable thoughts that only on the rare occasion descended to the world of action. I was sure he wanted to have a man rather than a woman, and I wondered if there had ever been a man for him in those dark Galisteo nights. Monasteries, even secular monasteries like El Rancho Garcia, have a way of allowing love to happen.

"Thank you for coming, Dolores," I say.

"One hundred and three. Won't be many more."

"You could surprise us all."

"Aunt Efrimelda made it to a hundred and eight."

"There you are. May I get you some wine?"

"White, please. Just a little."

When I return with a half-portioned glass she is talking to others, so Juan Carlos takes the glass for her. Dolores stands iron-rod straight, like the stern English queen mother before the last sweet one—the one with the long neck circled in pearls and an egret-feathered and be-diamonded turban. I remember she also distrusted her American daughter-in-law.

"Juan Carlos, the flowers are perfect," I say.

"It was fun, Graham. We'll do it again next year, maybe all in yellows and purples."

"I see Paloma over there. How is she?"

"Fine. We've decided that next year we'll come to visit you and Karl in France. She's been reading about Matisse and his chapel."

"Vence is only twenty minutes away."

"Can you believe we have never been to Europe?"

"I'm glad you're coming. We have a perfectly adequate guest room and the South of France's best cook."

I think that Paloma may have at last settled her grief about Mikal and forgiven Karl and me for looking the other way at the wrong time. When Karl and I talk about Mikal, we have not entirely forgiven ourselves. Those dark days of twenty-some years ago have not lost their power, our failure to pull a brother out of the water and bring him back to life. Karl cannot let the feelings go. We know it is the easy, flippant way to blame the gods for our inaction.

40

A Murmuration of Starlings

2003

Derek Carpenter stayed on at *Mas Moreau* with the two men, moving into the room used by Mikal in the past. Both Karl and Graham understood his game, trying every chance to drive a wedge between them or flirt with one more than the other, to bring forth a season of jealousy. Derek knew that the men were attracted to him as he told them stories of the London art world. He had the skinny English build, tall and hard-muscled, what Johannes Adler called all bones and peter. Derek did not understand that neither of the men wanted to make love to him, that they only sought the catalyst of love his presence nearby brought. Karl and Graham's nights together grew more sensual and active, reminiscent of decades ago.

Marie Laure did not understand as well, thinking that they were replacing the memory of her Mikal with this crass young Englishman. While Karl and Derek were swimming one afternoon, she pulled aside Graham.

"He is an outrage. How long will he stay?"

"We don't know, dear. A few weeks perhaps."

"He is not near so handsome as our Mikal."

"Of course not. He's just a houseguest, Marie Laure. Nothing more."

"I see what he tries to do. First you and then Karl, smiling with a knife behind his teeth. Making eyes."

"He doesn't matter. Would you rather not cook for us for a while?"

"No, of course I will cook. It just pains me so."

"We'll go out tonight. Give you some time away from him."

The three men drove along the coast to Nice after it got dark and the windless, hot air had cooled down. Karl loved the dining terraces at the seaside hotels, white clothed tables on a level above the Promenade des Anglais, traffic between them and the pebbled beach. It was a world where Cole Porter and Fitzgerald still held sway, imagination seeing them at a far table. Dover sole in a pepper-strewn white sauce was the pride of the dining room. A gypsy orchestra played Hungarian melodies at the end of the terrace, alternating with a gypsy orchestra on the next hotel terrace.

Derek told them he had gone into the LaPlace Gallery on Dover Street, that attractive young men were always welcome there. It was a special Fourth of July night honoring the American painters that they represented.

"I saw the new Celia Prospers," he said.

"What did you think?" asked Graham.

"You are lucky to have such a woman in your life."

"I think so too. But sometimes she can also be a pain in the ass," he said, thinking it would be better to bring down the devotion level right off the bat.

"I would love to meet her."

"She would be charmed by you."

"Is she coming to London this year?" Graham could see Derek's mind working. If he could not make an entry into this threesome through the two men, surely his beauty would work on the woman. He did not understand the strength of a triangle, how impervious to attack it was. He was thinking more probably about the many uses for five hundred thousand flaming pounds.

"I don't think so, Derek. If the weather hadn't turned so hot here, we all might be having dinner tonight with Celia. She cancelled for the cool of New Mexico, our hot nights not to her liking."

"Graham, don't tease our guest," Karl said.

"The summer nights are cool in Santa Fe."

"You know what I mean."

The killing heat did not diminish as the days went on. This night Marie Laure cooked a summer dinner for them, a chilled soup, grilled fish and her cold rice and fava bean salad. Francoise was invited and it was getting dark as the meal got under way.

"Derek, what is it you do in London?" she asked.

"I'm an artist, but I have to wait on tables to pay the rent."

"A good tradition, to struggle at the beginning. It strengthens the backbone."

"Graham is going to buy one of my paintings, to help pay for this trip."

"Is that right?" she asked, leaning her elbows on the table. "Tell us all what it looks like."

"It's in patterns of black and white, a murmuration of starlings."

"That doesn't sound like a piece Graham would like," she said, looking with raised eyebrows over at Graham for a response.

"If I've learned one thing," Graham said, "it is that all artists need help at some time or other. Derek needs a bit of help right now. Besides, I saw a definite hint of Celia Prosper in those swirling black patterns."

"But I think of you as sunny and optimistic, not the one who would buy murmuring dark birds. So unlike the writer of the flower paintings of Fantin-Latour. Just to help out young talent."

"Francoise, you are trying to make trouble."

"*C'est vrai*, I am. Let's talk about your new book."

"Fantin-Latour is an odd choice, I'll admit. But I'm searching his paintings for signs of modernism, that he is a precursor. I think I've found some."

"Let me give you some better names for your new books. Villon, Vlaminck, Utrillo and his mother, Suzanne Valadon, Dufy, and Rouault. Forget Fantin-Latour.

"I've already signed the Mallstone contract. Besides, it's all but finished. I promise I will consult you on the next one."

"You have the keen mind and good eye. You proved me very wrong on a few of your other books. We should follow your lead and collect the work of Mr. Carpenter here. Black-and white-paintings for the next century."

Francoise, like Marie Laure, was not happy with the young man who was churning up unrest in their father's house. Graham found it all amusing. Derek thought that his ardor and beauty were notable enough to make a rift in the bond of the older men, like an open fault after an earthquake, and Francoise and Marie thought he was succeeding. When Graham looked over at Karl, he knew from his eyes that he found it amusing too. It would take more than this well-endowed interloper to make that rift.

Derek Carpenter on his own came to realize that his classic scheme of divide and conquer was not working. Although he had not announced it yet, he had decided to return to London at the end of the week, battle plans unfulfilled except for the sale of a painting. At the pool the next day, while the three men sat down in the shaded part of the shallow water, inert and cooling off, there was a knock at the far front door. It was Johannes Adler, driving through with a friend from Rome to Paris. Graham found swimming suits for the guests, and they all plunged into the pool, five heads bobbing in unison.

"I'm so glad you were at home—'to house' as the Germans say," Johannes said. "It must be every bit of a hundred and ten out there."

They made half-hearted attempts to swim, then returned to the listless circle of five heads facing each other. Graham and Karl had been close friends with Johannes in their graduate school days, when he was among those who drank into the night on the steps at their staircase apartment. Johannes often had three or four attractive undergraduates in attendance, keeping his glass full. He had a way of popping up in odd places as the years went on, bringing news from a randier part of the art world.

"If you stay on for a while, Johannes, we can all go over to the beach at Juans-les-Pins," Karl said. "And we have some great new restaurants here in Mougins—salmon sliced as thin as medieval parchment, with a topping of a perfect dill sauce."

"You remember how I love salmon, so costly back in our university days. I wish we could, sweetheart, but we're due in Paris for an illustrious reception at a noble house. Just these cooling waters are perfect. Who is this ravishing creature having a bathe with us?"

"Derek Carpenter, here, is our houseguest and a promising London painter," Graham said. "I've just agreed to buy one of his new pieces."

"What gallery shows your work, my boy?" Johannes asked. "We're heading on to your London, if we aren't too devastated by Paris."

"I don't have a gallery. I have stored the paintings with a friend."

"Johannes is a museum director," Graham said. "You should go out of your way to arrange for him to see your new paintings, Derek."

"Which museum?"

"On the West Coast, a small, but very tasty, city museum which will remain unnamed in my travels. Could your friend show us the paintings? My connections are impeccable."

"I could fly back and meet you in London."

"Better yet, you can pack up your smalls and drive away with us in about an hour," Johannes said. "Only if Karl and Graham can spare you, that is."

There was no impairment in Johannes's powers of perception. Thus the dilemma of Derek Carpenter was solved. Graham was positive that Johannes would not be at all reticent about finding a way that Derek could repay a gallery connection. The cheek offered, the cheek kissed.

◊◊◊

These were wet months back at El Molino. Artemis returned for the summer, as well as Morris and Margo in their own house nearby. The three women set up a schedule of hikes into the mountains, starting early in the morning and returning before sunset, earlier if storms threatened. As in their summers in the Alps, they walked briskly up to the higher altitude, through evergreens, then aspens and finally the high mountain meadows of grass. Tents and overnight camping had no appeal for them, like Wingrave and the boys, so they always arranged to be back at El Molino by dark, only a sandwich for lunch.

Celia offered to cook a dinner for them. It would have to be simple, she said, a pasta with meatballs and a salad from the vegetable garden. She was at the stove engulfed in Graham's white apron, the meatballs sautéing when the three arrived. The French doors to the vegetable garden stood open and the aroma of oregano and butter wafted out as the women walked in.

"Excuse our dust and mud," Artemis said, scraping her feet on the door mat.

"No matter, I'm still covered with paint."

"You must come along with us one day. It's not a difficult hike."

"Thanks, no. You and Mikal were the athletes of the family."

"I do love showing the girls the secrets of the mountains."

"We saw a deer family in the last meadow, under the aspens," Margo said. "A doe and her two fawns."

"I thought of you, Ceil. Mother and twins," Artemis said.

"After dinner, I want to show off my new painting. It's about just that matter, mother and twins."

"How can that be?" asked Morris. "You're a non-objective painter."

"Wait and see. Meanwhile, Morris, please set the table while I finish up here. And, Margo, you may open that bottle of Primitivo."

This summer Celia felt more like a mother than she ever had before. She wondered why at this late stage, when the girls had just turned twenty-eight, did this rush of maternalism spring forth? They were girls no more, she knew, but she viewed them as her fawns, spotted and fragile. Nannies, tutors, dance-instructors, headmistresses, teachers, tour-guides, professors and then Artemis had been responsible before—she, the mother, was a mere guest in the side seats at the drama. Perhaps they seemed like children because they were still unmarried.

Celia saw the trouble coming for the twins, despite Artemis's criticism. It was like watching a rock tumbling down the hill in slow motion, heading ever closer to another tragedy in her family. The Prosper family doctors could find no physical reasons after many tests and consultations. There were many unstudied but identified wasting diseases, they said, all without a cure.

Morris had accepted that she would be Margo's life-long caretaker, a strong sister giving up her own life to protect the lesser sister, who had stopped growing wings or even trying to fly. Artemis had seen the tableau unfolding, and made a place for her nieces at El Molino. This would be where the long performance would be played out. Was it a circle returning upon itself, adults turning back into children? Margo had never really attained adulthood before she began to slide back.

"It's so good to be with you, Mother," Margo said, as if hearing Celia's thoughts. "We never saw you before, always so far away in your studio."

"I should apologize, I know. For not tucking you in, for not visiting you at the academy, for not cooking every night."

"But you're cooking for us now."

"Maybe this will be the start of better days. I do think my oregano meatballs are first rate, right from the pages of Marcella Hazan. And the salad greens are from your father's garden, right out there. Also first rate."

The four of them moved on to less accusatory subjects during the dinner, if not binding up the wounds at least smoothing a salve across them. After washing up the dishes, they walked over to Celia's studio. The painting was on the easel, well lit in the bank of overhead spots focused down on the canvas. Her mother-and-twins story was all in the thickness of the lines, but still it was a painting of rain falling down at an angle. There was a new rhythm in the lines, going left to right, first a thick one, then two thin ones, then a space, then a thick one, two thin ones and so on. Graham had called it a syncopation, a tropical rhythm, when he first saw it in an earlier painting. One strong beat, a pause, then two soft beats.

She wished Graham were there to put the words to her art, to describe the painting to the others. He always knew where she was headed before she did. The colors grew paler and paler, then gradually picked up hue and became bolder across the middle, like a wide, colorful stream through a pastel valley. On the far right the lines were again paler and paler.

"It is beautiful, Mother," Morris said, "but for the life of me I can't see mother and twins. I, of course, saw a mournful Pieta with two fetching girls—same as us—splayed across the lap or a Picasso piece with overlapping circles and four small eyes and two big ones, or something like that."

"It's more of an idea than a reality, dear. If Graham were here, he would make it clear."

"I did not mean that I didn't like it."

"It's all right, Morris. In fact my paintings are not about anything."

"I see myself right there," Margo said, putting her finger on the second of the thin lines. Celia realized that being the child of the group did not mean that she was the least aware. It was exactly what Celia had wanted her to see.

"Thank you, Margo. You're quite right. I need to bring this evening to an end, dears. See you all tomorrow."

As she dressed for bed, she missed her Graham. Were he and Karl asleep now, seven hours later at night in the South of France? Were they making love at this hour, the hot air still lingering? Or sleeping back-to-back, like they did? What an odd life she had arranged for herself, an approximate but loving husband, a brother she loved and two distant, injured daughters. She did not feel sorry for herself, knowing most of it was of her own making, but she felt the strong apartness had grown stronger in the night, like the disturbing and unavoidable perfume of a night-blooming cereus. Graham always said she should call him anytime, so she opened the book of numbers on the bedside table and picked up the phone. It would be four in the morning there.

41

Library Frieze

24 July 2011, 7:00 PM

The cocktail portion of the party is going at full tilt now, conversations mingling with conversations, laughter in various registers. The young waiters pass around trays of canapés and refill empty glasses. Guests spill out onto the terrace to the south, sitting down in twos and threes at the tables there. Many are in the main room, standing in half a dozen small circles, the classic cocktail party arrangement.

Jullian takes my arm as she heads for the piano and says she has been practicing the songs for high voices by Fauré. They are ready to go and may she play some now?

"I would love to hear them. You mustn't worry if the others don't stop talking."

"Not a problem—I'll just play the music, not sing."

She cannot resist singing, though. Her soprano voice lofted above and over the guests, bringing only a slight diminishment in the chatter. I had earlier seen Celia talking to Jullian on the outside terrace and observed the fond way their bodies curved open towards each other. They are both slim and stylish, Jullian a more Nordic version of Celia. I see an attractive pair, the painter and the composer—perhaps from a portion of a painted frieze high in the library of a girls' college, illustrious alumnae of our very own, dancers with arms around novelists, scientists in a white-coated cluster and the poets in their own group farther along.

Jullian and Celia hold their wineglasses the same way, between their breasts, slightly tilted away from their bodies. I wonder if they have ever had the physical love that would be such a natural companion to their emotional love. Jullian has lived a lesbian life and it seems probable that she would have approached Celia about love. Would Celia have been happier as an open lesbian too? Jullian went on to live with her Carolyn Ward, but was that because I had taken away Celia? I knew that it was possible for all of us to live with many different loves at once, to not put them in descending order but side by side, all equal. I also knew that physical love was not the only important love to the women I knew.

I walk over to Karl, who is talking to David Lawston. Karl says they were talking about me.

"In good regard, I hope."

"David was talking about your time as boys."

"Graham was the dutiful son, always worried that we should tell his father where we had been, what we had been doing," David says.

"I don't remember any such thing," I say.

"He was, Karl, I assure you. And there was much to tell," David says.

"I've already told Karl about the exploits in Balboa," I admit.

"I wish the two of you had been my friends as a boy," Karl says.

"Maybe the three of us would be together today," David says, raising his eyebrows with a smile.

"David, why don't you come to us in Mougins later this summer?" I ask. "We are both at work during the mornings, but there's plenty to do in the afternoons and evenings. It would be fun to show you our Cote d'Azur. What do you think?"

"I would love to be part of your summer lives," he answers.

"Then it's settled. We leave next week for three months and you can come any time."

42

A Favorite Relic

2008

Dominique had accompanied Graham and Karl to France for the last several summers, her presence never an interrupt to their writing days. She listened to Graham reading a new chapter or to Karl thinking out loud a difficult page, her few comments always to the point. She had a light touch with her men. Marie Laure liked Dominique from the start, the young woman helping in the daily kitchen procedures, filling in when Nicole could not.

Jacques Villon was the subject of Graham's new book, thanks to Francoise's suggestion. Graham needed to decide between the landscapes or the portraits, winnowing down the voluminous output of a painter who worked right up to his death at the age of eighty-eight. The cubist landscapes were winning out. Graham had a stack of reproductions and decided to include just twenty of them in his analytical study. More closely focused projects were what his publisher wanted now, long discussions on fewer paintings.

Karl went back and forth between his two projects, a collection of stories about women painters, abstract like those early ones on Cezanne's trees, and a novel about an aging lesbian painter whose life is invigorated by a young woman who knocks on the studio door. His editor thought that the novel would be a blockbuster, many famous parallel stories in real life. The projects were not so different that he could not do a chapter on the latter and then a short story from beginning to finish.

With her new French driver's permit, Dominique took to driving the yellow Deux Chevaux with relish. Citizens waved or honked as she passed by in a cloud of fumes, the car a favorite relic of the quavering French automotive industry despite its noise and smell. She drove Marie Laure to the market shops each morning and the two of them went on sightseeing forays up and down the Côte d'Azur. Francoise hired Dominique to convert her handwritten manuscripts into the word processing files demanded even by French publishers now. Without fuss or trumpets, Dominique had become a necessary part of all their Mougins lives.

She had not returned to Vietnam for another visit with her grandparents, her life in the West filling her interest. El Molino accepted her in stages. First, she started looking after Celia's growing correspondence, making order in the files and other office matters. Her cousin Parchment bloomed from an anti-social orchardist and winemaker in her company and she took dinners with him almost every night at Paloma and Juan Carlos's house. Just a few years older than Morris and Margo, she treated them as an older sister, even taking over the mountain hikes when Artemis was busy at Mills College. They all missed her gentle presence when she went to France each summer, but they knew that she loved her father, Karl, most of all and needed those months to make up for the earlier empty years when she was very young.

While Graham and Dominique were swimming one afternoon, Francoise and Karl sat in the shade of the umbrella. Francoise asked him what were the plans for his daughter. Was it possible that she might be happier in France than back in New Mexico? Fashionable women had many possibilities for good positions in Paris and elsewhere. They were more respected, better paid in France than in the states.

"She seems more French than American," Francoise said. "There is a certain innate style about her."

"Dominique has already suggested that she might stay on for a while, after Graham and I go back," Karl said.

"My friends who own a perfumery in Grasse, where we sell the rose petals, have an opening. A sales assistant, and if it works out, although they did not say so, a manager."

"We'll have to ask Dominique."

"She will charm them, I know."

"If she does decide to stay on, would you look after her? I worry that she won't feel abandoned again."

"She will have dinner with us every night."

Dominique and Graham came up to the terrace to dry, sit in the sun.

Karl told his daughter about the opportunity in Grasse. What do you think, he asked her?

"I don't know anything about perfume."

"Francoise says that they will teach you," he said.

"Marie Laure and Francoise have asked me to stay with them, look after them for a while," Dominique said. "Don't you think they are as much our family now as everybody back at El Molino?"

"Maybe even more so," Karl said. "Since all of us made this Mougins family out of whole cloth, we may be more responsible for it."

"So it's all right for me to stay?"

"Only if you plan many weeks back in El Molino each year."

"We'll drive over to Grasse tomorrow," Francoise said. "I am sure it will work out. My perfumery friends have entry into the highest levels of France."

"May I use the car, Father? I know you're very fond of it."

"It is your car. And the house as well."

As Graham poured over the Villon reproductions, he found the absence of a long line in the man's work troubling. The artist dabbled in this idea and scurried on to another, one after the other. There were cubist arrangements in ovals, views of Mont St. Victoire, portraits, abstract landscapes, realist landscapes, etchings, drawings and on and on. There was even one lithograph with the almost exact view from Graham's own writing table, *Les Oliviers entre Mougins et Cannes.*

The essence of Villon was proving to be elusive. Could his being the brother of Marcel Duchamp have made a hurtful mark? Was there a family pecking order more divisive than ordinarily known? And why did Villon, the eldest of the brothers, change his name from Duchamp to distinguish his work from the other brothers? Wouldn't the eldest be the one who kept the family name? Perhaps an answer lay in this oddity. He would ask Francoise what she thought, since the subject was her idea. Francoise had some questions of her own, she said, as she opened a spiral-bound notebook.

"My new novel is about an artist who is also in love with his wife's brother," she said. "That might sound familiar."

"I've found it is a more widespread practice than you would expect."

"Would you mind if I asked you some things? About you, Celia and Karl?"

"After that, I have some questions about Jacques Villon."

"First off, is there no jealousy?"

Graham thought about that for a moment and said, "If there is, it is a very weak variety, alive for a short while only in the early morning hours. Then it dies as good sense takes over."

"You first came to love Karl, then Celia?"

"Karl and I met as students, Celia afterwards."

"Do you now view them almost as one person?"

"That's what Celia has said all along."

Francoise wanted to know about the nature of this curious arrangement, how Graham thought it came into being, did it make for happiness or the opposite, was it a hindrance to their work, their art, and was it hard to gain acceptance of family and those around them? She asked what would be the pattern of their graves: brother next to lover/husband next to sister, one-two-three, or something else? Graham thought about the other odd pairings at the camposanto, but he said that he hoped that theirs would be, left to right, Karl, Graham, Celia. But those who remain will decide the pattern.

He tried to explain to Francoise the difference between his double loves. Karl was where the sexual joy lived, the slow game of amorous tennis where one served and the other returned. He felt it was still a well-played game. Life with Celia nurtured in a different way, a constancy more than a fevered match. There was more unspoken between them, but perhaps more ineffable understanding as well.

"Would you do it all again?" she asked.

"It seems the only way now. I'm not sure I had a hand in doing it—it just happened."

"When you kiss Karl do you see Celia?"

"No. But I see him when I kiss her."

"What does that mean?"

"I don't know."

43

Apple-wood Smoke

24 July 2011, 7:15 PM

Lilli comes through the crowd to say that the first course, the lettuce and yellow tomato salad, is on the table. People may start to find their seats at any time. I know that converting a cocktail crowd to a seated dinner crowd will take some effort, so I walk among the conversation circles with the news. The guests on the terrace around the tables stand up as I tell them but do not move towards the table, and then I walk out to the front portal, where six or seven have stayed all evening near the bar. Traffic out to the dining table is glacial, conversations speeded up but not concluding. My guests are like a herd of willful llamas, resisting my gentle attempts to move them to another, better pasture.

I walk around them out to the portal, where the dining table is aglow with the votive lights and the dimmed overhead spotlights. I cannot help thinking of my father's table, a simple Swiss piece of polished wood, and our meals there. The principles of Luther stood strong in our Pasadena house, no Latinate ostentation and no unnecessary ornament. Certainly, there would be no twinkling tea-lights in special glass holders or bunched flowers cut willy-nilly from the outside perennial borders. Except for the Christian feast days, there would be no tablecloth, and wine would be poured into low tumblers, never stemmed goblets. Ella would come from the kitchen with a very small roast on a platter, potatoes and carrots huddled around, a gravy boat on a later trip. Pretentiousness and display were the enemy in Father's house, never welcome.

Before World War II, Father kept the car stocked for flight. A boyhood in the fractured Europe after the earlier war made him wary of sunny days. He was sure that the Japanese would invade California, but the Obermann family would have already departed in their heavily laden green Packard for Baja and points farther south to where it seemed safe. The trunk was kept filled with canned goods, bottled water, gasoline cans, a Spanish-English dictionary, blankets and large-scaled maps of all of Latin America. We could flee at a moment's notice.

As the threatening country switched to Soviet Russia, he maintained his readiness, updating the canned goods and maps. It was well into the 1960s before the Packard's trunk was at last thinned down to only a spare tire and changing tools.

If Father and Ella were still alive, I would of course have included them at this dinner. He would be sitting on my left, Ella across from him, both surveying this very un-Lutheran table. It was not from embarrassment that I had not folded them into my life with the Prospers, but probably fear of Ella's and Father's disapproval. It would have been so hard to meld the two families, but I was culpable for not even attempting it. I knew that I was a bad son, not the dutiful one David remembers.

Dolores, arriving on Juan Carlos's arm, is the first to be seated. She has seen many finer tables, but smiles up at me nevertheless. Juan goes back inside to find Paloma. Jullian Closson and Carolyn Ward are next and I point out their places. Then the full crush from cocktails comes to the table, circling and peering for their cursive names on the name cards. I guide the last ones to their seats before sitting down where David and Dolores are already talking across my empty chair.

"May I squeeze in between you?" I ask.

"Mrs. Prosper has just told me of a dinner party she went to in Italy as a girl," David says. "Only that, on an Umbrian terrace seventy years ago, was more beautiful than your table, Graham. Those are her words."

"I didn't know you had such a silver tongue, Dolores," I say.

"I never lie," she says.

Celia has already picked up her fork, signaling everybody else who cares for such niceties that they may start. There is a short silence as people adjust to being at table and then conversations grow with the metallic sound of knives and forks against the salad plates. Josh and Candy carry around the bottles of wine. I remind myself to go down later and talk to young

Parchment about his El Molino wine, to make up for my not choosing his bottles for tonight's fare. Making good wine is proving to be harder than he thought when Karl and I agreed to buy the vines. Parchment produces a very acceptable chardonnay in some years, but it is unreliable. I thought it only politic to choose a different variety, a white Côtes du Rhône instead of a white burgundy. I can see him and Dominique, first sniffing and then testing their glasses of the white, discussing it back and forth. Dominique has observed many aspects of winemaking in France, as well as perfume. It would be wonderful if Parchment had a breakout vintage, bringing the fussy world of wine to his two acres. Perhaps Dominique will be the one who helps, makes the difference. I must remember to suggest that they consider a new name for their project, Two Cousins Vineyard.

Celia says that she has a toast. She stands up, waits until the conversation has diminished and holds up her glass. "I thank all of you for coming for my birthday. July twenty-fourth is for the Leos of the world, bossy and forceful. My daughters are Libra, supposedly the darlings of the zodiac and nicer than the Leos. I don't give much faith to astrology, but it is my Graham who I want us all to toast for this evening. If there is a special sign, a thirteenth sign, for a prince of a man, a lover and a husband, that is his." Glasses go up and a ceremonial sip taken.

Despite this being a birthday celebration, I think it is better to limit the toasts to Celia's alone, too many speeches a clumsy barrier to a good meal. After she sits, we clink our glasses across the table. I remember her across the table from me before, at the Prosper family dinner when we looked at each other this way. We made first love that night, after all others were asleep in the Prosper bedrooms. That secret early morning love has stayed on the front my mind.

Karl is watching me and I reach out a glass for him, and we ring them together. Such an abundance of Prosper loves.

With difficulty, and Arlene Ludlow helping her from the other side, Dolores stands up, her hand on the table for steadiness. It is quiet as she reaches for her glass.

"In the beginning, Wingrave and I did not entirely trust Graham. Why was this handsome young man so eager to become attached to us Prospers?

Time passed and I still do not understand him. Perhaps I am a suspicious old lady and he wished merely to love our Celia and Karl, to make them happy. So let's all raise our glasses to that once untrusted man, Graham."

I have never heard a better example of damning with faint praise. What a mean one Dolores is after a hundred and three years. After I help her to sit down, I kiss her on the cheek. If she does not understand me, I in turn will never know what Dolores is about. As with England and its forever enemy France, the French president will continue to kiss with reluctance the powdered cheek of Queen Elizabeth II, eyes open sideways for oncoming danger.

"Celia, I saw a painting of yours at a house in Pasadena," David says. "It commands a whole wall in the house. It was one of your early ones, the bridge series I think they are called. A stunning work."

"Thank you, David. I wondered the other day if I should revisit and add to that series. My current work has become so light and linear."

"I would love to see more of that first series. So bold and strong."

"I think the Ludlows sold most of those," I say.

Arlene Ludlow has heard and raises her glass.

"I am sure I cannot afford a Celia Prosper," David says, "but I would love it if Graham would call me when the first ones are complete. Yes, Graham?"

"I will. When do you think that will be, sweetheart?"

"Next summer," Celia responds. "Put that on your calendar, David."

The servers take away the salad plates and return with the main course plate that I saw in the kitchen, plates now warm to the touch. The warmed plates recall a winter trip to Barbados—Celia, Karl, the girls and I in a rambling rented house on a bluff above the beach. The sea was a clear pale blue, fish swimming the other way beneath us. The staff served dinner every night, cooked by one of the island's best cooks. The plates were always warmed, Cissy, the cook, said. Unless it was salad—nobody wanted cold food, even in the tropics. I wonder why we have not gone back to Barbados, a lovely escape from the gloom of a Santa Fe January.

The talking slows down while the guests eat, the garden now in darkness beyond the lighted portal. We are like the upper deck on a small boat on a calm unlighted sea, moored for a while close to land so the rocking does not disturb the dinner. I can see across to the lights of Celia's studio, the new square canvas silhouetted against the far windows. I should be a happy man, surrounded by all that matters to me, celebrating the family I have interloped upon. Dolores will never fully accept me, but her skepticism gets lighter and somewhat more humorous. She had better hurry up if she wants to change her mind.

I watch Karl talking to Joseph McLarry on his left. I know that both men are still wounded, the war never very far away from their thoughts. They are the good friends that only ex-soldiers can be, enduring in their shelter of each other. Karl's nightmares have never left him and my hand on the forehead takes longer but still does its work. The two men meet with other veterans, gatherings that Karl never describes to me in much detail. I wonder if his dreams get better after talking to Joseph or worse.

Celia and Jullian lean towards each other as they talk. I know that it will do no good to eavesdrop, as they fall into that distinct way of talking, abbreviations and shortcuts not entirely understood by others. Theirs is a more rewarding friendship than Karl's and Joseph's. Perhaps only women can bond that way, their separate feelings open and fully lighted for each other. Jullian puts her hand over on Celia's arm to make a point and both women laugh.

Farther down the table, I can see Hallston Wills is charming Carolyn Aarp next to him. Her laughter reveals it was an off-color story that Hallston told. It was correct to keep him away from Quattro Lattimer, two over-bred dogs who can work up a growling storm about nothing. As if to underscore that, I can hear Hilliard's laughter, almost a deep-throated bark. At the other end, the younger people are leaning together almost in a huddle. There is a secret being disclosed there as I see two of them nodding to the talk of a third. I wonder if it is wine or sex they are talking about. Will they pass on the disclosure to the older guests or will the generations stay discrete and apart?

"Graham, do you believe we lived other lives in other times?" asks David while the others are talking.

"It's an appealing idea, but I don't think so."

"Marjorie believed strongly in other lives."

"Celia talks about them, too."

"And what about ghosts?"

"Definitely not."

"Then you won't come back to haunt me if I take your place when you're gone?"

"Is that your complicated way of saying you envy me?"

"You have such a lovely life. You must be happy."

"I still wonder what a happy life is, David. And by the way, I'm not planning to give it up soon."

"Then I must bide my time."

As David starts talking to Carolyn Ward on his left, Karl puts his hand across the table towards me, "Graham, I've forgotten the name of the painter whose uniform Picasso dressed up in."

"Georges Braque."

"Yes, of course." He is telling my concocted story of the two painters in bed, perhaps one still in military uniform. Love is where you find it, I can hear him saying, and there is laughter.

I look across the table at the guests in conversations with each other and have the strong feeling of becoming old, that this is one of the last dinner parties. Will Celia and Karl die before me, leaving me alone in this adopted family, the well-meaning interloper in a land not his own? I can imagine the other houses at El Molino staying empty most of the year, only the path back and forth to my writing studio cleared of the winter snow. The old bent writer, having outlived all his lovers, is slow to come in and take his seat, writing with a crabbed script in his journal and finishing one or two pages of a biography each day. In the midst of the dozens of conversing voices, I think that I smell the smoke of the apple-wood fires, sweeter and cleaner than piñon smoke, and I envision the early morning sun across the deep snow, nothing but the tracks of the fox circling from house to house and heading off towards the river.

44

Bombazine

A year later

It was not the Prosper brother or sister, but Graham who died the night of the birthday dinner, gasping and reaching out as he fell back in his chair, his head hitting the wall behind with a crack. Both Celia and Karl wondered silently in the days afterwards who or what he was reaching for, but it was a question without an answer. By the time the ambulance arrived, none of the other guests' amateur procedures had revived him. Being Prospers, they were able to sidestep the official autopsy, the death so clearly a matter of the heart.

The bricklayers Graham had hired earlier that week to repair the wall at the camposanto were let off for a few days, but their scaffoldings were still there during the ceremony. It was not very different from the burial rites that went before, Dolores's priest there to speak the words, but this time in English since Graham was a questioner. Karl directed that Graham, atheist or not, belonged in the Prosper camposanto, not out with the Obermanns in leafy San Gabriel. The mourners all knew the well-trod path back to Dolores's house, where the funeral supper had been laid out.

The months after the birthday party were grim, and the ambient loneliness that Celia had always felt in life now grew more acute with Graham's death. Like an unexpected gravity impinging the moons of Jupiter with their subtle, balanced circles and ellipses, this change brought lurching and spinning into the orbits at El Molino. Before she remembered not to, Celia turned to ask the empty chair in her studio, Graham's chair, about a matter on the canvas. Turning down family invitations, she preferred that there was no one across from her at dinners in their kitchen, where the perennial herbs and vegetables just outside the French doors grew tall and leggy. Work would be the solace that brought her around, she knew, so what had always been obsessive to her became pitched even higher. Paintings that took months before now were completed in several weeks.

She saw Karl every other day or so, he walking over to her studio, sitting in the other chair that Graham never sat in. Karl did not have Graham's supporting, all-abiding patience nor his keen eye for what was happening on the easel.

"How is the book coming?" she asked him.

"Almost done. I have a few pages left to rewrite, then I'll ship it off to New York."

"I have kept all the Monday letters from Graham. There must be several hundred. Do you want to edit them?"

"Why can't you publish them as they are?"

"I can, but I wanted to know if you should be involved."

"I am sure they are perfect as they are. Graham never wrote a bad sentence."

"We talked about the letters telling our story."

"What did he say to that?"

"I think he called it a splendid idea."

It had started as a rainy summer in Santa Fe, faraway El Niño currents bringing up a wet pattern of days without sun. It was almost the day of Celia's birthday again, but no party was planned this time. She told the others that she wanted to forget it entirely—now a death day as well as a birthday. The lights in her studio had been staying on late into the night, a new series calling to her at all hours. At first she was unsettled, unsure of the wisdom of going back to visit the earlier motifs as she painted, but the challenge of repeating their early strength kept her mind focused. The bridges and scaffolding were thicker and blacker this time, the canvases heavy with paint.

Karl had not left for the Mougins summer yet, matters with the lawyers and probate growing in complexity. The completed book was a project he had been so glad to have during the winter months at El Molino, the Prosper siblings turning inwards to their work. Time had promised to make things better, but it continued to shirk its duty. Karl knew that physical exercise would be even more necessary, the moving body a protection against the depression that lurked just down the road. Trips into the foothills on horseback each day took away the sting for an hour or two, but it all came back as he brushed down Homer III in the stables afterwards.

His log house became isolated in the deep snows of January and February. In the many years before, the house had served as a dark-walled sanctuary for him, a favored place away from the cold to write and think. He struggled to make it work this last winter, often just looking out the window at the white fields. Almost every afternoon the fox came near the house, leaving a three-toed track in the snow, unafraid of human movement. How many generations of vixens had he seen at El Molino?

Now the summer night rains brought up the vivid jungle and his sense of loss, never with the warm nurture of Graham against him or his hand to cool the brow. To be somewhere else on the night of Celia's birthday, he had decided to drive out to California for a week away from El Molino. Celia turned down his invitation to join him. He was already out the drive when he thought to go back for the gold coin, the one he retrieved from Graham's pocket on the last night. He still wondered about Graham's belief that it held great good fortune, considering where he found it. Maybe he misremembered.

He booked into the shuttered hotel facing the beach in Santa Monica and the next day, totally without fog, the beach was filled with sun worshippers. Was it coincidence or design that he saw a man on the beach who resembled David Lawston? Omens were there for a purpose, as he had written so many times in his novels. David had not been asked for the funeral, only a dark-edged card sent as an announcement, as to all the others who were not of the family. He looked up David's telephone number in Pasadena.

"It's Karl. I'm in Santa Monica. May I drive over?"

But the very real coincidence was that David had just that morning called Celia in her studio, to see how she was doing. Was the painting going well? How many times before had brother and sister opened the same door at the same time? David and Celia talked for a while, and she invited him out to New Mexico for a visit to see the new work.

"Figure out a time and we'll meet you at the airport," she said.

"I've been wanting to see you, to talk to you," he said.

"Do you remember at the party your talking about my bridge paintings, from so long ago?"

"The one I saw is still in my mind."

"I've been painting a new series of them. I thought I should move on, but maybe only so far as something familiar."

"I'm sure that is a good idea. Let me look at my calendar and I'll call you back."

Life had been troubled for David too. He had spent a restless week in Hawaii and a week in San Francisco, but neither was so rewarding as his last trips. Now that he was back in his Pasadena house, he would make a call to Santa Fe, see how things were going there. And here was Karl calling from just a few miles away.

"Great, Karl," he answered. "This afternoon late is good. Let me give you directions."

"My car has a new GPS. I'll just plug you in and you're mine."

"Sounds appealing."

"I'll be there soon."

The two men had an early dinner at the old ivy-covered hotel down the street from where David lived. Both of them were aware of the bittersweet duality of their dinner, a coming together in grief and a tacit awakening of their sexual attraction. It was both the end of a book and the first pages of another book. They talked about whether Graham would have been amused at this realignment of planets and stars. He seemed to suggest that very idea at the dinner party on the last night.

"Will you be going to Mougins this summer?" David asked.

"Next week, actually. Would you like to join me there?"

"Would I? I can't wait."

"Perhaps you know about it, David," Karl said. "After the Civil War, there was a certain number of months a widow had to wait before she changed out of black bombazine. To go on, make a new life and not feel guilty about it."

"It was a full twelve months, I'm absolutely positive. The bombazine can then be thrown away in the trash can," David said.

"It wouldn't do to go against long-held convention and make all the families in the neighborhood mad."

"I have an old book of etiquette in the bookcase back at the house, rarely even opened. We can look it up later while we're there, just to be sure."

"Despite his surface *joie-de-vivre*, Graham was always a stickler for correct form."

"Then, let's drink a toast to Graham and his correct form."

As Karl reached into his pocket for the car keys, the coin came out with keys and fell onto the ground with a golden ring, rolling only a few steps away. The coin was warm in his hand when he picked it up and pushed it down deep and safe in his pocket.

Books by Graham Obermann:

1964 **The Art of Wingrave Prosper**

1971 **Andre Derain Paintings**

1975 **Odilon Redon,** *The Library Decorations*

1978 **Pierre Bonnard,** *The Le Cannet Landscapes*

1980 **Sailboat to Byzantium,** *The Coastal Paintings of Paul Signac*

1988 **Chaim Soutine Paintings**

1990 **Juan Gris,** *The Best Cubist*

1991 **Kees Van Dongen,** *Portraits of Women*

1994 **Ten Women,** *Authenticating the Lost Modiglianis*

1995 **Mysterious Light,** *The Interiors of Eduoard Vuillard*

2004 **The Precursor,** *The Flowers of Fantin-Latour*

Books by Karl Prosper

1962 Cezanne's Trees *Twelve Stories*

1969 Living With the Monster

1971 Love on the Trail

1973 Rotten to the Core

1980 Curse of the Perfect Pitch

1983 Coffee and Cream

1988 My Sister, My Love

1990 Taken by the Gods

1991 Lost Melodies

1994 I Died for Beauty

2003 The Winsome Interloper

2007 Parting of the Ways

2010 Another Chance

2011 A Knock on the Door

www.ingramcontent.com/pod-product-compliance
Lightning Source LLC
Chambersburg PA
CBHW031951010726
47493CB00007B/2161
9781632931061